Every word I have written and published is from my noggin (brain, in case you don't know what noggin means). My fiction is all make-believe, from the deep dive into my wild imagination. All my nonfiction books have been researched until my brain has scrambled.

I0672199

Cozy Mysteries	
The Alcott Family Adventures	The Thol Series
Hot Chocolate	Prophecy of Thol
Bitter Chocolate	Gifts From Thol
Spicy Chocolate	Love of Thol
Nutty Chocolate	King of Thol
Katz' Cat Series	Earth Calling Thol
Katz' Cat	Sci-Fi Romance Adventure
Bill Hill's Pills	Forced Dreams
The Detectives	Dystopian
The Pact	The Last Dog
Discreet Conversations	Texmexzona

Books by my Alter Ego ~ DG Ireland	
Bonded Shapeshifter Billionaire Series	
Bonded	
Tothars	
Tilted	
Unforeseen	
Connected	

Need A Notebook?
See my 54 themed notebooks on my website
www.degreenfield.com/notebooks

Screenplays formatted as books	
Plan B (Dark Comedy)	Where's Ralphie? (Family Comedy)
The God Child (Action Adventure)	Standing Dead (Drama/Tragedy)
The Far Corner (Sci-Fi/Psychological/Creatures)	Block Captain (Action Comedy)

Screenplays as TV Episodes	
Hot Chocolate ~ Episode 1	Prophecy of Thol ~ Episode 1
Bonded ~ Episode 1	

See my screenplays and awards on my website: degreenfield.com
Filmfreeway, ISA Network

Texmexzona by Dawn Greenfield Ireland

Published by Artistic Origins

Copyright © 2021 Dawn Greenfield Ireland

Map: Peter de Jong (Maps_by_Peter on Fiverr.com)

Cover image and layout by Brandon White VictoryLaurel.com 11/10/2024

Interior layout by Yours Truly (me); Corrections 6/11/2026

ISBN 978-1-940385-42-6 (eBook)

ISBN 978-1-940385-43-3 (paperback)

Dawn Greenfield Ireland

Artistic Origins

http://degreenfield.com

or encourage electronic piracy of copyrighted materials. Your support of the author's rights is appreciated.

Please visit my website: http://degreenfield.com and sign up for my newsletter and get the latest news before the public.

❋ Formatted with Vellum

ACKNOWLEDGMENTS

The highly toxic curmontow plant mentioned in this book is compliments of Curtis and Monica Hightower, and my wild imagination.

Mapmaker Peter de Jong created the fantasy map. He was so easy to work with, and I love the map he created. You can contact him via his Fiverr.com account: Maps by Peter. Tell him I sent you!

The 2024 cover image was created by Brandon White of victorylaurel.com.

Editors and proofreaders find things by latching their laser eyes onto the page. I am so grateful for Jeff Gonyea, Richard (Grasshopper) Stone, Cicely Wynne and Amy Brantley. They all whacked me with wooden rulers dozens of times.

Actions Appreciated

Please leave a review on your favorite retailer and/or my website! Reviews help authors get recognized, get the word out, and sell more books. I will love you forever if you leave a review!

If you would like to join my **postcard brigade**, I'll mail you 4 postcards. One for you to keep, and three to hand out. Email me your address and I'll mail them. USA only. All others, I can email you the postcard for sharing with your world online.

TEXMEXZONA

BOOK 2 IN THE LAST DOG SERIES

D.E. GREENFIELD

ARTISTIC ORIGINS

CHAPTER ONE

Teresa Maxwell sat on the front porch of her and Bill's new house in Texmexzona, called TMZ for short. Abby, her dog-daughter, and Apollo, Abby's wolf-mate, sat with her, quietly watching human children playing in the street, with Abby's puppies romping after them.

Since the majority of men and women in 2087 were sterile because of decades of toxic forms of birth control, hormone therapies, and sperm inhibitors, watching these human children pulled at Teresa's heartstrings.

Back home in WestUS, Teresa was lucky if she saw a child once or twice a year. Then it was difficult not to have an internal rage about the disbanded FDA and pharmaceutical companies. She hoped those CEOs burned in Hell for eternity while choking on their bottom line.

Teresa and Bill had only been in TMZ for two months, having defected from their sector at Edge 10-SJ (formerly known as San Jose) in WestUS. That was the west coast of the United States, previously known as California.

In 2044, Texas, New Mexico, Arizona, and the country of

Mexico merged to form their own independent district. It was not a state or a country. The United States government declared that TMZ was an outlaw district, and anyone who moved there forfeited their US citizenship.

A family glider approached the house. Teresa watched as Bill parked the vehicle in the holding area, which used to be known as a garage. Bill and Rex, Bill's dog-bot creation, got out of the glider and walked to the front porch of their beautiful Southwest-styled house with the red-tiled roof.

"Rex!" Abby rushed down the four steps and greeted Rex. The dog-bot turned this way and that as Abby pranced around, happy to see her friend.

"Abby-dog!" Rex said.

They stood face-to-face, unlikely friends who had met in an illegal lab where Abby had been held captive as the last known dog in the world. Rex's role in the lab was to study Abby so he could become more dog-like and pass his findings along to the other dog-bots who were supposed to be the new dog-children. Unfortunately, Dr. Julian Roberts, who had illegally seized Abby in the first place, had made a deal with the Tranquility Force to use the dog-bots as a policing force. That single act of greed and power abandoned all the people who would have welcomed a dog-bot into the bosom of their families.

Rex's red LED eyes lit up as he stood facing his best friend. He glanced at the porch and saw Mommy Teresa and Daddy Bill cuddling. Rex put all his efforts into becoming more dog-like, but he had moments of misunderstanding human idioms.

Apollo stood on the porch watching his mate and the dog-bot. He was slowly coming around to accepting Rex at face value. With his new Dot, the wolf was learning about mankind and the way of the world. Most of the time he was quiet—observing everything that was going on around him, trying to understand how things fit into his new family structure.

After Abby escaped the facility where she had been held captive, she hopped on an old hauler and rode secreted away among the junk the glider carried. She ditched her free ride in Roads End and made her way through the forest to the foothills of the Sierra Nevada Mountains.

Her cave had been at an elevation where she could see across the treetops, down the mountainside and into the edge of the forest. It had been a perfect location, with a convenient trickling of water that bubbled up between boulders.

The day she heard Apollo's lonely howl had changed her life. She was now a mother with six rambunctious puppies who only wanted to play with their Uncle Rex. The dog-bot didn't know what to make of the horde of romping, ear-biting, tail-yanking puppies. His circuits came close to overloading as he tried to avoid the worst of their affectionate attacks.

Upon hearing Rex's name, the puppies charged toward the house and swarmed around the dog-bot, jumping and barking their glee upon seeing the stoic member of the family.

"Order!" Rex wailed in his serious robotic voice. "Down! Sit! Stop!" The rowdy pack of pups who didn't have their voices yet ignored his commands. Those would kick in when they reached four months old, when Grandpa Bill inserted their Dot.

Abby was mobbed by her puppies alongside Rex.

Apollo huffed out a snort, stood and descended the steps. "Lulah! Esme! Star! Puppy Rex! Wolf! Jim!"

The puppies stopped their wild rampage around their mother and Big Rex, and looked at their approaching father. When Apollo spoke, everyone listened.

"You are acting like crazy rabbits," Apollo said. "Go and play, or you will have to take a nap."

The N-word got their attention. They romped off toward

the human children and took up the chase after scooters and bicycles. Jim tried jumping rope, but became tangled.

Apollo looked from Abby to Rex, who was called Big Rex when in the company of his namesake, Puppy Rex. "You must be more forceful when trying to get their attention. If you don't speak with authority, they will be unmanageable. That is not good for the pack or the family."

Bill and Teresa watched the little powwow.

"Apollo speaks with inherited wisdom from his wolf roots," Teresa said.

"We should catalog his early life. He's adapting to the human world quite nicely," Bill said.

"I'll bet he spends a lot of his time perusing the contents of his Dot," Teresa said. "Thinking and talking like a human must be an unusual experience for him."

Bill Maxwell had invented the Dot in 2077, a year after the 9.2 earthquake that changed the world. The Dot became mandatory in humans in 2080, and in dogs and cats in 2084. It contained an IVT—the Implant Vocal Transmitter, which enabled dogs and cats to talk as humans did.

Abby, Rex, and Apollo climbed the steps and sat on the porch.

"Hi, Daddy," Abby said. "I didn't mean to ignore you."

"That's okay, honey." Bill turned to the wolf. "Apollo, what happened to your wolf family before you met Abby? How did you survive?"

The wolf's forehead scrunched in thought. "My wolf mother was in the open front of the cave with my littermates and our wolf pack. I heard loud noises that scared me, and I ran deep into the cave to hide. When I calmed down, I called out to my mother and pack mates, but no one answered my whines or howls."

Apollo searched Bill's face. "They were all dead. Bloody as

if skinned alive, like Starlight skinned marmots. I watched some of your files. Humans and dogs died this way also. What happened?"

"A deadly chemical was released into the air. No one knows if it was intentional to wipe out a portion of the population, or truly an accident," Bill said. "What did you do when you discovered your pack dead?"

"I was four big moons old," Apollo said. "If I hadn't been raised with a wild wolf pack, I most likely would not have survived. When I smelled the death scent and saw what was left of my pack, I retreated to the back of the cave. The next day I left the cave; I was very hungry. There was a dead bear and her cubs not far from the cave. I saw more dead animals out in the open, so I went deep into the forest. As young as I was, I had to learn how to be a hunter in order to survive."

"How did you find Abby?" Teresa asked.

"At first, I kept within my alpha wolf-father's territory, searching for other wolves, game, and places to sleep safely. Then I determined there weren't any other wolves, and there would not be any territorial restrictions as to where I roamed. The day Abby answered my howls was a happy day."

Abby bumped his shoulder. "I scared you with my human-like voice."

"I had never heard human speech before," Apollo said. He turned to Rex. "I will teach you to be more wolf-like."

Rex's LEDs lit up as he contemplated what *wolf-like* might gain him. "I would like that."

Bill nudged Teresa. "I have to figure out how to contact Toby. It's been just over two months since we left, and they all expect me to return to work."

"How do you expect getting around all the spyware?" Teresa asked. "You can't put them in danger. I'm sure they're all being watched every minute of the day."

"Remember my little super bees? I should be able to send one on a trip. It should be able to get into Toby's area without being discovered."

"What would you tell them? 'Sorry, we're not returning, we've defected? Carry on?'" Teresa asked. "I feel bad enough for slipping away without telling Percy and Becky."

"I know, believe me. I'd like to be able to bring them all over here," Bill said.

REX WAS DRILLING down into his file structures in the middle of the night while on his dog bed. He loved that his name was embroidered on the material in red. It suggested his status in the family structure—he was important enough to have his name on this piece of personal property.

As his colorful LEDs flashed like Christmas tree lights in his relaxed working state, he suddenly stopped all activity. A message lit up internally in his secret place where all dog-thought coded messages entered and exited. He stood and quietly made his way to the master bedroom, careful not to wake Abby, Apollo, or the puppies.

Rex programmed a hidden claw-like device to shoot out of his shoulder and attach to the door handle. His programming inched the claw clockwise until the door opened. The claw retracted back into his shoulder with a zip and disappeared under the superstructure of his dog body. He nudged the door open with his snout and made his way to Bill's side of the bed.

"Daddy," Rex whispered—as well as a dog-bot could whisper. When that didn't wake Bill, he increased the volume. "Daddy. Wake up." He gave Bill a poke in the arm with his snout.

"Huhhh?" Bill sputtered, sluggish with sleep. He opened

his eyes, saw Rex's LEDs, and sprang to a sitting position. "Rex. What's wrong? Is the house secure?"

Teresa turned over. "What's going on?" She wiped sleep from her eyes. "Rex? Is something wrong with Abby or the puppies?"

"I have received a secret message from Jerry. Grandma Becky and Grandpa Percy have been arrested as enemies of the World Guild," Rex said.

"Oh, my Great Earth!" Teresa said as she flung the bedcovers aside and sprang out of bed.

"The Tranquility Force discovered that we defected," Rex reported.

"Lights up," Bill said. The bedroom lights lit up. He got up and slipped into his robe and slippers. "I need to see what GNN is spinning. I'll have to contact Toby through Rex's program. He might be able to help us rescue Percy and Becky."

Teresa grabbed her robe, stabbed her feet into her slippers and followed Bill out of the bedroom with Rex between them. They went into Bill's home office where three large monitors covered the upper half of one wall.

"TMZ Connect on," Bill commanded.

The swirling mountain stream morphed into a logo of TMZ.

"Connect to GNN, full red-level security on," Bill stated. The Global News Network came online among a few squiggles until the connection was fully secured.

Abby wandered into the office, followed by Apollo. "What's wrong? Why are you watching TV?"

"Honey, Jerry contacted Rex about some bad news," Teresa said.

They all stood in front of the central monitor and watched the screen.

"Search GNN for William and Teresa Maxwell," Bill commanded.

The screen filled with Bill's inventions and his office compound.

"Focus on current news," Bill said.

They watched as a squadron of Tranquility Force stood at the front door of their house in WestUS. Becky and Percy were seen hurrying over from their house to see what was going on.

"What's wrong?" Becky asked one of the Enforcers. He ignored her.

Two Enforcers used electronics to override the security system; they never realized that Bill had left it disengaged. The door opened, and the Tranquility Force stormed into the house. Percy and Becky followed them. They looked around, shocked. Everything, with the exception of the kitchen counters, was gone. They discovered Bill and Teresa's Dots in plastic cases on the kitchen counter.

The lead Enforcer contacted the Tranquility Force headquarters. "The Maxwells have defected. They left their Dots on the kitchen counter. The entire house is an empty shell."

"Defected?" Percy wailed. "There's no way Bill Maxwell would have left all his wealth and his company behind. You've kidnapped them to make it look like this!"

The lead Tranquility Force Enforcer pocketed the Dots. They exited the house with Percy and Becky following them, then an Enforcer secured the house electronically so no one could enter.

Becky and Percy watched as the Enforcers entered their gliders, lifted off and flew away.

Next, GNN reported that Bill and Teresa were killed climbing a mountain in search of Abby. They flashed pictures of them, their businesses, and some of Bill's inventions.

"What!" Teresa shouted. "You'd better contact Toby immediately!"

"Why is GNN saying all those lies?" Abby asked.

"Because they are owned by the World Guild, and they are not to be trusted," Bill said.

The front door announced visitors. *Hello, we will be with you shortly. Please wait patiently.*

Rex went to the door. "It's Harold Injun Jim."

"Let him in, Rex," Teresa said.

Rex unsecured the front door and stood aside as Harold and several TMZ committee members entered. Rex silently scanned each one to make sure they were who they said they were.

Bill stuck his head out of his office. "Back here."

Harold Goanflower, a Native American with long, thick black hair, dark eyes and a six-foot-eight solid build, was dressed casually in thrown-together clothes. He led four people through the house to Bill's office.

Glacious Ersons, the chairman of the committee that oversaw TMZ, was in his white committee robe, followed by Pete Clearhanger, Baily Genderfer, and MaryEllen Smith.

They strode into the office and their eyes went directly to the monitors on the wall.

"What's going on?" Harold asked. "Rex pinged me about a situation."

They all watched as Becky and Percy Smythe, Abby's human grandparents, were arrested in the middle of the night and brought to the Tranquility Force headquarters in their pajamas and placed in separate glassed-in rooms. An Enforcer stood before the rooms and read a proclamation.

"Percy and Becky Smythe, you are hereby declared hostile enemies of the World Guild."

"What!" Teresa wailed.

"Who are they?" Apollo asked Abby.

"That's my grandma Becky and grandpa Percy," she said.

Apollo let the words spin through his head for a moment. "Those are your canine father's human family?"

"Yes," Abby said. "We have to rescue them!"

Jerry chose that moment to send Rex another report.

"Jerry sent me a transmission. He said the Smythes are going to have brain swipes."

"Oh, no!" Teresa gasped.

"They can't do that," Harold said.

"They're trying to lure you there," Glacious said.

"They haven't been able to beat me yet," Bill said. "They seem to forget that I'm the one who built their security system, and I monitor all the workings of the World Guild."

"Still, it's risky," Harold said.

Rex's system whirred and clicked. "There is a former Enforcer living in the tent city outside the TMZ gates." More sounds emitted from the dog-bot as Rex performed more scans through his database. "Rob Williams. He could be useful for gaining entry to the Tranquility Force headquarters."

"You're sure he isn't a plant?" MaryEllen asked.

"He is not a spy. My system uncovered his entire career path. He was written up for reporting undue force by his coworker on a civilian," Rex said.

"They wrote HIM up for reporting that?" Baily asked. "The system is worse than what I originally thought. Is there no decency left in the world?"

"We should go find this Rob Williams and see if he would help us," Bill said.

Teresa laid her hand on Bill's arm. "It would probably be best to do that in the daylight."

Harold nodded agreement. "There's too many trigger-happy people out there to be traipsing around in the dead of night."

CHAPTER TWO

S hortly after first light, Rex led Harold, Bill, and four guards through the tent and vehicle city outside the TMZ gates. People gawked at the dog-bot.

"Look, there's one of those dog robots!"

"What is that thing? Is it a machine?"

"That's one of Bill Maxwell's inventions!"

"What do you think they're looking for?"

Rex followed the map in his system to the big red X where Rob Williams was located. He led the group down one alley after another until he stopped before a lean-to that was semi-attached to a transporter.

"I have located Rob Williams," Rex said.

Harold took charge. He knocked on the plywood structure. "Rob? Rob Williams?"

A makeshift door opened, and a head popped out. "What's going on?"

"Are you Rob Williams?" Harold asked.

"I have identified and verified that this man is Rob Williams," Rex stated.

Rob stared at Rex. "You're that dog-bot! I thought you fell into the ocean."

"Jerry lied," Rex said.

"Jerry?"

"Rob, I hate to interrupt this reminiscing, but we need your help," Harold said.

A little kid popped out of the lean-to and squealed in delight upon seeing Rex.

Rex was even more worried about the actions of small children than he was about young puppies. He managed to avoid the tiny, grabbing, sticky hands and swiftly moved in between Bill and the guards.

"Who are you?" Rob asked as he warily eyed the guards.

"I'm Harold Goanflower with the TMZ committee."

"What do you want with me? We've been living out here for almost a year," Rob said. "Am I under arrest or something?"

"Rex informed us that you're a former Tranquility Force enforcer," Harold said.

"Yeah? So what? You going to kick me out of line to get into TMZ?" Rob asked. He shook his head, angry. "I knew when we defected I'd be damning my whole family from my awful career choice."

Bill stepped forward to talk to Rob. "Would you be able to help us break into Tranquility Force headquarters undetected so we can rescue someone?"

"Are you serious?" Rob asked. He stopped and thought long and hard. "People have tried to break OUT, but I've never heard about anyone trying to break IN."

"No one's ever tried to help someone escape?" Bill asked.

Rob's face showed he was thinking about that. "I don't recall anyone trying. The building itself and the logos are enough to put the fear of reprisal into anyone who even thinks of it."

Rob stared at Bill, then Harold. "But... it could be done. What's in it for me? My family and I have been sitting out here for months. No one seems to ever get inside."

"We are willing to admit you and your family into TMZ for the help you provide," Harold said. "You have a transporter to move your belongings once we sort things out."

"I'm not sure if the transporter will operate since it hasn't been charged in all these months," Rob said.

"Gather up what you have that can help us with our mission," Harold turned to the guards. "Help these people get packed up. If their transporter doesn't start, send for a charger, and get them inside the gate to be processed."

A woman with a huge belly popped out from behind the door. "Is there a hospital or doctor inside TMZ? I'm about ready to have my baby!"

ROB HANDED BUILDING PLANS, files, and other paperwork in file boxes to Harold and Bill. "I gathered these physical files in case my electronics were compromised when they discovered that we had defected." Rob grabbed another box.

The three of them marched back through the tent city with Rex leading the way to the gates. People gawked and whispered among themselves.

The committee was waiting for them as Harold ushered Bill and Rob through a door to a meeting room, followed by Rex. Rob set his heavy box on a table. He opened it and pulled out a complete Enforcer uniform. "I knew this would come in handy someday."

Bill and Harold emptied their hands onto the table. Rob dug through the box that Harold had carried. He found a plastic case with tiny discs. He handed it to Bill. "All the codes and files. They most likely have changed the codes since I left, but this will give you an idea of the coding."

Bill chuckled. "I'm the coder, Rob."

Rob stared at Bill. "Oh! You have to be Bill Maxwell! You defected?"

"Yes, I am, and I did," Bill said.

Rob rolled out the building plans. "Hmmm. This could be easier than I thought."

He anchored the unrolled plans with some of the clothes. He tapped an area to the left of the doors that was off to the side and out of the way of any comings and goings. "Here's the supply and tool crib where the uniforms are stored. I'll be able to get full sets without very much trouble. Badges might be a problem though."

He looked over to Harold. "How many people are going on this mission?"

"Don't you typically escort prisoners with four guards? One in front, back, and each side?" Harold asked. "If that's still the case, then four of us will require uniforms."

"There's two detainees," Bill said. "A man and a woman."

"In that case, you'll need a total of six, including one female. I'll count as one, so we'll need five of you," Rob said.

Harold looked over to MaryEllen with a questioning expression.

"Count me in," she said.

"We can enlist two of the TMZ guards to make up our team," Harold said.

Bill turned to Rex. "Buddy, we'll need to forge transfer documents."

Rex's LEDs lit up. "I'll contact Jerry. He should be able to provide those."

Bill clapped his hands together in front of him. "Okay. We have a plan. When can we head out?"

"We'll need to modify a glider with the correct colors and logos," Harold said. "We have the ability to do that. Every Enforcer glider that approaches TMZ is scanned so that we have the latest details. Our paint shop only has to press a button and we can replicate their color scheme."

THEY ARRIVED at the San Jose city boundary without any problem. Rob was dressed in full Enforcer gear. The first place they stopped was where all the Tranquility Force gliders were stored. Rob exited the glider, and it zoomed away. He presented a forged request to sign out a team-sized glider.

The employee didn't seem too concerned about anything, as he checked out the glider and pointed Rob in the direction where the vehicle was stored. Rob searched for unit TF-T871243. He entered the cab, started it up, and made it rise to the correct level for flight squad air space that was reserved for the military, Tranquility Force, Sky Angels and privateers.

Rob zipped through the sky to the Tranquility Force headquarters, which was a large fenced-in warehouse facility in the hub of the business district. Rob lowered the glider to align with the fence so that the glider ID could be scanned. Permissions were granted, the gate opened, and the vehicle sailed through the fenced courtyard. He settled the glider onto the ground.

"I'm inside the lot," Rob whispered. "Sit tight. Don't talk. Keep a low profile. I'll be back as soon as I can."

"Jerry will scramble electronics and weapons from the inside," Rex said.

"Roger that," Rob sent. He walked to the front doors,

gained entry and disappeared inside the Tranquility Force headquarters.

ROB WAS grateful for the helmet. It shielded most of his face, and there was no protocol about removing it indoors. He controlled his stride to not to appear to be in a hurry as he walked to the left, down a long corridor to the supply area. He approached the employee on duty in the tool crib and handed over a supply order for four male uniforms and one female uniform with specific sizing for all.

The man behind the grate looked over the order. "Should have everything in stock. You need the World Guild logo to slap on these?"

"Yeah. I'm the errand boy today," Rob said.

The man behind the grate nodded. "Had someone come in the other day with the same comment. Be just a minute."

Rob watched as the man stacked up separate sets of uniforms, down to the socks and boots, and stuffed them into separate gunny sacks. The guy returned to the counter.

"I don't have the right size for the woman's uniform. Should I go up a size or down?"

Rob held his hands out in front of him, indicating boob size. "Better go up a size." He winked at the guy. They shared a chuckle.

Moments later, the order was filled. Rob hauled five filled gunny sacks off the counter, thanked the guy, and retraced his path to the front of the building. As he was hauling the sacks, an office worker stopped him.

"You need help with those?"

"Nah, piece of cake," Rob said. He was sure his armpits were oozing sweat through his uniform. The worker went on his way, and Rob continued on. He reached the front doors and set two sacks on the floor so he could grab the door handle.

A squadron of Enforcers approached the doors from the outside. He grabbed his sacks and stood aside while they entered. The last one in held the door for him. "Here you go."

"Thanks," Rob said, then walked outside. He let out a quiet sigh of nervous breath as he controlled the pace of his strides to the glider.

Rob opened the rear hatch and deposited the sacks. He walked around to the door to the cab, got in and had the glider in the air in a heartbeat.

Once he maneuvered the ship through the gate and sped away, he exhaled loudly.

"Did anyone question you?" Bill asked via the communicator.

"No, everything went according to plan. MaryEllen, the lady's uniform is a size larger than desired, but they didn't have a set in your size on the shelf," he said.

"That's okay," MaryEllen said. "Larger is better than smaller."

"That's what I figured," Rob said.

"Jerry said the shift change is within one hour," Rex said.

Rob steered the glider over the downtown commercial area to a warehouse and set the glider down in front of an old docking bay.

Bill, Harold, MaryEllen, the two TMZ guards, and Rex stood in the warehouse's doorway.

"MaryEllen, you change in the warehouse," Bill said. "We'll change outside. Rex, scan for anything that might show an interest in us, or any beams coming at us, and nudge them away."

"Will do, Daddy," the dog-bot said.

The men stepped outside and changed their clothes.

"Daddy..." Harold said, as he chuckled and shook his head.

They stored their personal clothes in their gunny sacks. Rob stored the sacks in the rear hatch.

MaryEllen stepped out of the warehouse and joined the team. Rob adjusted her World Guild patch, looked everyone over and nodded that all was good.

Bill activated his communications system and brought up a holographic view of the plans Rob had provided. "The holding cells will be tough to get to with all the occupied areas up front. This will be a test of our acting abilities."

"Will Rex be able to come with us, or is that too risky?" Harold asked.

"Rex, ask Jerry about that," Bill directed.

Rex stood robot-still while he monitored the skies, the satellites, and contacted Jerry through his ingenious dog-thought technology.

"Jerry said that I could accompany you without any questions asked," Rex said.

"Okay. We have additional help navigating the headquarters building. Rex spent a lot of time there with the dog-bots, so he knows his way around," Bill said. "Rex, do you know of any shortcuts to get to those holding cells, other than what we have routed from Rob's plans?"

Rex beamed a red dot onto Bill's hologram. "Instead of going the long way around, we can cut through here. These offices will be empty if we wait another thirty-three minutes and twenty-two seconds. My systems do not show any exercises that would keep people from the current shift on duty. They will exit as if the building is on fire."

Bill stared at Rex. "Do you mean they won't hang around?"

"While I was at headquarters, my systems picked up employee correspondences with each other. Eighty-seven percent of personnel hate their jobs. They have fantasized about killing, or at least debilitating their supervisors and some of their coworkers who want to gain better positions within the force."

"Okay, that's helpful information—about them leaving on time," Bill said.

"I have scanned my databases, and according to statistics over a six-month period, employees end their shifts on time, or before the end of their shifts by five or more minutes, thereby stealing time from their employer," Rex added.

Rob, MaryEllen, Harold, Bill and the two TMZ guards stifled their laughter at Rex's observation from when he spent those months at the headquarters building.

"I sure would love to explore his databases," Harold said. "I'll bet he has all sorts of goodies stored that would entertain us for years to come."

"Everything is sorted and packeted away in a logical order for him to retrieve at a moment's notice," Bill explained. "Things that you wouldn't think were important end up being useful in making critical decisions, such as when people end their shifts."

Everyone checked the time on their communications units. They had twenty minutes to kill, and Bill had an idea.

"Rex, why don't you check this glider's trip records and see if there's anything useful we might need later on," Bill said.

"Sure thing," Rex said.

"You can't even tell that he's working," MaryEllen said.

They spent the next twenty minutes exchanging news bits among themselves, then they all boarded the glider and Rob steered them back to Tranquility Force headquarters.

High nervous energy permeated the inside of the glider. They were taking a huge risk. Anything could happen.

When they arrived at the gates, dozens of single and family gliders were exiting. Some gliders were more anxious than others, as they were on the tail ends of the gliders in front of them, wanting to get past the gate.

"This looks like an excellent time to carry out the mission. People seem to be on the edge of hostility to get out of here, so they might not pay a lot of attention to us," Harold said.

Rob settled the glider in the designated business parking area, and they all got out of the craft. He looked them over one last time and was satisfied with their appearance. He took a deep breath. "Showtime!"

MaryEllen's eyes widened.

They walked to the front doors with Rex between Bill and Harold. They gained entry without any problems and walked the route Rex suggested. At the midpoint, an Enforcer approaching them from the direction they were headed focused on Rob. He walked up to the group, making them stop.

"Rob?" the Enforcer asked, slightly shocked.

"Hi Corky, what's up?" Rob asked.

"I thought you had defected?" Corky asked.

Rob put on an air of superiority. He took one step forward and pointed to his World Guild patch. "Got a better job. Who told you I defected? I want their name!"

Everyone knew that the World Guild Enforcers were brutes. They made the Tranquility Force Enforcers look like kids playing at being tough.

"No, no... must have been a stupid mistake. No reason to get riled up," Corky said, as he backed away from Rob. Then he rushed away, worried that he might get written up for mentioning anything.

Everyone let out a sigh of relief. They continued on, letting Rex lead them through the maze of corridors. They finally approached the glass holding cells. Percy and Becky each held a hand against the glass in the only way they could stay connected. Bill immediately saw that Becky had dropped at least ten pounds. Percy didn't look so hot either.

"There they are," Bill whispered.

Rob approached the detaining module and held his forged transfer orders up to the scanner. Everyone waited in frozen anticipation. If anything could go wrong, it was with the transfer orders.

The green acceptance light lit. The transfer order showed the authorization codes. The two doors clicked open.

Becky and Percy looked frightened as their doors popped open. Becky started to cry, knowing they were supposed to get their brains swiped.

The group surrounded the criminals without any verbal communication. They retraced their path, while having to prod the man and woman to keep walking.

Bill silently prayed that neither Becky nor Percy would do anything to cause more attention to them than what might already be on them. They made it to the front doors without any problems, left the building and entered the glider.

Rob got them out of there posthaste. As soon as they were through the gate and a couple of miles away, Bill removed his helmet.

Becky fainted.

"Bill!" Percy yelled. He patted Becky's face to rouse her. "We thought for sure this was it... we were going to have our memories swiped. How did you manage to get through all the security?"

Becky came to. Percy hauled her into his arms. "Hon, It's Bill!" He looked to the others who were removing their helmets. "And Harold!"

"I know you have a lot of questions. I'm so sorry you got pulled into this nightmare, but there's a better life ahead," Bill said.

"Where have you been? Have you found Abby?" Becky asked.

"We defected, Becky. We live in TMZ, and Abby found us. She has a mate and six puppies," Bill said.

"A mate? I thought she was the last dog?" Percy asked. "Did the World Guild lie about that as well?"

"Not really. Abby is the last domestic dog that we know of. Her mate is a wolf—probably the last of his kind," Bill said.

"My data shows there may be wolves in the far reaches of Alaska or Siberia," Rex said.

"Oh, my Great Earth! Is this one of your creations, Bill?" Percy asked.

"This is Rex, one of my dog-bots. You probably saw the pack on the news when the trial against the doctors took place," Bill said.

Becky reached out and patted Rex's head.

"Abby-dog will be very happy to see grandma and grandpa," Rex said.

Rob landed the glider at the abandoned warehouse.

"Rex, did you capture all the trip files?" Bill asked.

"Yes, all files are in my database. We can exit and return to TMZ," he said.

Everyone departed the Enforcer glider. Rob opened the rear hatch, and they retrieved their civilian clothing and transferred it to the TMZ glider.

"Rex, run a cleaning and sanitizing program so all our prints and DNA are removed from the Enforcer glider," Bill said.

Rex stood outside on the ground and faced the opened Enforcer glider. "You must turn away from the glider so your eyes are not damaged while I perform this task."

Everyone entered the TMZ glider and turned their backs to the Enforcer glider.

Rex beamed a high-powered light into their illegal vehicle. The light turned from a bright sun yellow to blue, then white. Once he finished his program, he entered the TMZ glider. "Mission accomplished."

Rob lifted the TMZ glider off the ground, and they headed home.

CHAPTER THREE

To avoid a disturbance among the hopefuls outside the gates by seeing a Tranquility Force glider deep within protected territory, Rob avoided the TMZ tent city. He flew the glider around through the back gate where Abby and Apollo had entered the compound. He settled the glider with the fleet and everyone disembarked. The team members retrieved their gunny sacks of personal clothing.

"Harold, you might want to keep the Tranquility Force colors and logo on this glider in case we need it in the near future," Bill said.

"Good idea. I'll alert the troops," Harold said. "After you clean the clothing, return it to me so we can store the uniforms for future use."

Becky and Percy looked around at the gray and green barrack-type buildings. Becky clutched Percy's hand. She was thankful for being rescued from having her brain swiped, but all she could think about was everything she had left behind: Jimbo's drawings, his ashes.

Bill could practically read their minds. He would never

forget how he and Teresa had first stared at the tent city as they had approached the huge gate that kept the denizens outside the territory.

"Don't worry. The housing does not look like this," Bill said.

"All we have is the clothes on our backs," Becky wailed. "Everything else is back in our house."

"I know. That's the tough part, leaving everything behind," Bill said. "Teresa and I were very fortunate; we had the opportunity to take everything with us."

"We couldn't believe it when we saw your house back home. All that was left were the kitchen counters!" Percy said.

"That's because I had had the forethought to make sure everything was bolted in place instead of being more permanently installed," Bill said. "Abby and Teresa are going to be so excited to see you!"

Harold approached them. "You'll have to go before the committee to be approved, processed, and assigned to a house."

"Is that going to be difficult?" Becky asked. "Our Dots may have been deactivated."

"Bill, Teresa, Gayle and I can vouch for you," Harold said.

HAROLD LED Becky and Percy to the meeting room to stand before the committee. Bill, with Rex by his side, joined them to give testament to Abby's grandparents. He was followed by MaryEllen and Rob Williams.

Glacious and Baily Genderfer were joined by Pete, Mary-Ellen and Harold.

"Welcome to TMZ, Mr. and Mrs. Smythe," Glacious said. "I'm happy to see you both unharmed by your incarceration with the Tranquility Force."

"We Thank the Earth for being rescued from a fate worse than death," Becky said.

Pete took over the proceedings. "Entry into TMZ constitutes a strong emphasis on protecting our territory. A call to arms may become necessary at any point in our pursuit of independence against the World Guild. Do you have any qualms about fighting for your right to live here? To help your neighbors who may not be as knowledgeable as you? To lend a hand, even if it's ditch digging?"

"We would gladly step forward to defend our rights and the rights of TMZ," Percy declared.

"What is your profession?" Baily asked?

"I was the director of employees at the Planto Distribution Center," Percy said. "Becky stayed home with our dog-son Jimbo before he passed on. Prior to that, she was..."

Becky poked her husband. "I do still have my brains and can answer for myself, hon." She looked at Baily. "I developed and tested recipes for the food consoles."

"You both have desirable skills we could utilize here in TMZ," Glacious stated. The committee looked at each other, nodded approval. "We grant you access to TMZ. Since you don't have any of your possessions with you, we will find a furnished home for you. It may take a while."

"They can stay with us," Bill said.

The committee turned to Rob. "Your family has been situated in a house while you were on this mission. We'll have one of the guards escort you to the house. Your wife has been examined by the VHO, and is on the watch list for child delivery."

The meeting broke up, and Bill escorted Becky and Percy through the halls and corridors. When they passed through the last gate of the maze of barrack-like buildings, they gasped in awe at the beautiful scene before them.

"Are those streets?" Becky asked. She gasped again when she saw how many children there were outside playing.

"This isn't anything like I expected TMZ would be," Percy said.

"You didn't get to see the tent and transporter city outside the front gates," Bill said. "Teresa and I thought that was TMZ. We were shocked at how many families were sprawled across both sides of the road—it went on for miles up to the armored front gates. Rex estimated there are over a million people out there, waiting for entry."

Rex, who quietly walked beside them, piped up. "There were one million, four hundred thousand, three hundred eighty-three people congregated outside the gates of TMZ. Since our arrival, two hundred people have joined the ranks."

They walked over to where Bill's glider rested on the ground. "Let's get to the house. I'm sure you are exhausted from your ordeal."

Once they were all seated, Bill slowly drove the glider over the houses, giving Becky and Percy a full view of the area.

"This is so beautiful... and peaceful," Percy said.

"Hopefully, the committee will find you a place close by so you can be around your great-dog children," Bill said. "They're a handful. Abby and Apollo have their work cut out for them. The puppies don't have their voices yet."

"I can't wait to see them!" Becky said.

TOBY SAT in his office at Maxwell Industries, perusing a screen of scrolling code. His office communicator buzzed. He looked at the controls and saw that Angelica was calling.

"Hey, Ang. What's up?"

"Toby! Turn on GNN!" Angelica blasted out, alarmed.

Toby swiveled his chair and clacked on a different keyboard. GNN came to life. Pictures of Becky and Percy Smythe covered the big screen, and the screens in screens. He listened as a literalist emphasized that the Smythes, enemies of the World Guild, had escaped and were at large.

He turned back to the communicator. "I think I know where Bill and Teresa are."

There was quiet on the other end of the communicator. Then... "They would NEVER defect!"

"Listen, Ang, Harold and Gayle defected. I found Harold's moniker, *Injun Jim,* in a log from TMZ. It only stands to reason that Bill and Teresa have joined them. Do you remember his speech at the last meeting before they *took a sabbatical?* He said this was the reason the company was powered by employees."

Angelica sobbed on the other end of the communicator.

"I'll pull together the leadership team," Toby said.

THE REUNION WAS TEARFUL. Abby whined and cried in dog-voice and human emotions over seeing her grandparents after such a long time. Apollo stayed back, watching his mate interact with the new humans. For once, Rex was not mauled by six exuberant puppies.

Esme, Star, Puppy Rex, Wolf, Jim and Tallulah were happy to have two more people to fawn over them. Jim was favored by his grandparents, as he resembled his dog-grandfather, Jimbo. Becky sobbed upon seeing him and hearing his name when Abby introduced them.

Harold's wife, Gayle, manned the food console while the Maxwells and Smythes visited. They looked beat, barely sitting upright. Between Teresa and Gayle, they had found a change of clothes for the Smythes. The humans sat down at the table and ate.

Teresa put her arm across Becky's shoulders. "Why don't you and Percy go clean up and take a nap. You must be exhausted."

"We barely slept for fear of being separated, or anything else that might happen if we closed our eyes," Becky said. "They used that truffs on us twice!"

"Twice? That's uncalled for!" Bill said.

"I'm pretty sure we were overdosed," Percy said. "When they applied the second dose, Becky and I kept vomiting. They didn't get anything useful out of us, those fools."

Teresa showed the Smythes to a bedroom. "I hope the clothes fit. We'll get you sorted." She left them in the room and closed the door. Teresa returned to the living room and clapped her hands lightly. "Grandma and Grandpa are very tired, so you have to be quiet. Why don't you go outside and play with the human children?"

The pack of puppies didn't need to be told twice. They raced to the front door. Bill opened the door for them and laughed as they charged outside with Abby and Apollo on their heels.

"Hon, I'm going back over to headquarters for a bit. I want to discuss the external population with the committee. Rex will be able to help with the processing and validating. Percy would be very helpful with his background. I never realized what they did for a living," Bill said.

"I wasn't aware that Becky worked outside the home," Gayle said.

Bill told them what he had found out at the committee interview.

"Oh! She must have all sorts of secrets about the food

console. We would have starved if Ejonia hadn't left notes! It's a complicated machine," Teresa said.

"Come on, Rex, let's go talk to the committee." Bill smooched Teresa on the lips, then he left with Rex trailing behind.

BILL AND REX entered the TMZ offices, and sought out Harold to sound him out on his thoughts. He found him in the command center, standing in front of a bank of monitors.

"Hey, do you have a minute?" Bill asked. "There's something I want to run by you before I broach the committee."

"Sure," Harold said. He tapped a young worker on the shoulder. "Let me know if any abnormalities pop up." He turned to Bill and Rex. "Let's go into my office."

They sat down, with Rex standing beside Bill.

"Why are all those people outside the gates instead of in here where they could be productive workers?" Bill asked.

"We just don't have the ability to process all of them, and it would run our resources into the ground. We'd have to perform deep background checks to make sure we didn't let in spies. Then there's the housing issue. I don't know if we have sufficient housing," Harold said.

"That's all in the past now," Bill said. "Rex has already run comps on all of them. He could process them more efficiently than you could. And we can use Percy's experience. What do you think? Should I present this to the committee?"

Rex made a noise equivalent to someone clearing their throat to get attention. "When I arrived here, I discovered three hundred individuals who were former high-ranking government officials. I have broken down the entire population outside the gates into labor and educational groups. If someone could fly me over the entire TMZ area, I would assess the housing situation and determine whether there are enough vacant houses for the population. Since people came here in transporters and such, they would be able to live in those until a house could be built."

Harold stood. "Let's go before the committee. This is such helpful information. Rex, you're our shining star."

"Should I tone down my LEDs?" the dog-bot asked.

"That's an expression, Rex. It means you are valued highly for your skills," Bill said, as he and Harold shared a smirk.

"Oh," Rex said.

They walked through the maze of buildings and hallways until they found the committee members, their faces in front of their screens.

Harold and Bill took turns going over the suggestion of processing the denizens beyond the gate.

"How would we know where to start? First come, first served?" Pete asked.

"They should be processed according to their skills and usefulness," Bill said.

"There are currently one million four hundred thousand five hundred eighty-three people (1,400,583) outside your gates," Rex said. "If we processed one thousand per day, it would take 3.83721 years to admit them. That time would increase for others defecting and parking outside the gate."

Glacious, MaryEllen, Baily, and Pete stared at the dog-bot.

"Where would we put them all?" MaryEllen asked with wide-eyed concern.

Harold explained what Rex had suggested. "That should be our first priority. Determining the available housing. Next up, we should have Rex sort them by occupation. Bill suggested we have Percy work on this."

"This is an enormous undertaking, but in the long run, we

would benefit by using these people for their skills," Glacious said.

"One of the perimeter guards could fly Rex over the entire TMZ region," Baily said. "Would he have to fly low, slow—tell us how to go about this?"

"The glider can fly treetop level at a moderate speed," Rex informed them. "The total square miles of TMZ is 1,265,892. I will set my scans for a five-hundred-mile radius. It will take two thousand five hundred thirty-two scans, which could be accomplished within 3.437 weeks."

Glacious had to shut his mouth.

Pete was stunned beyond belief.

Baily shook his head. He could not believe their good fortune at having this resource at their beck and call.

MaryEllen realized what a gift Rex was.

Harold, upon seeing the stunned faces of his peers, rubbed his hands together in anticipation. "Okay. Now that we know how long that will take, why don't I round up a perimeter guard and explain the plan?"

HAROLD AND BILL stood beside the TMZ glider that would cart Rex around to determine what housing was available for the people outside the TMZ gates. They explained the details to Jonas Biggibottom.

"Your father saved my dog-bot patent. I'll be forever grateful to him," Bill said. "It must have been difficult leaving your family behind when you defected."

"Not really. My dad was so caught up in his work—having a first look at new inventions that would change the way we do things—that he practically forgot he had children or a wife. I don't know why Mom stays with him," Jonas said.

"I miss my younger brother the most, but those are the breaks."

"This assignment will be the most atypical task you will ever have," Harold said. "You can have regular conversations with Rex. He's quite insightful, but he takes everything at face value, so you have to be careful about what inane subjects you discuss. If you ask it of him, he will put it on his task list and it will get done."

"Remember, as a dog-bot, he does not require sleep or food. You take breaks when you need them. Find places to spend the night. Rex will keep busy with his data packeting and sending things back to me," Bill said. "Also, remember that he will keep you safe. If he detects something that he determines is a threat, let him handle it."

"Do you have adequate supplies in case of an emergency?" Harold asked.

Jonas nodded. "I'll restock every week, if necessary. I imagine I'll be able to find food and shelter along the way."

"This will be an expedition of discovery," Harold said. "Many of the places south of here, in the old country of Mexico, have not been explored in years. There are jungles with primitive people and wild animals. Do not take any chances, understand?"

Rex decided to include his dollar's-worth to the conversation. "I will protect Jonas and the property of TMZ. I will report to my father on an ongoing basis."

Jonas stared at Rex for a minute, then looked questioningly at Bill and Harold. "Who's his father?"

Both Harold and Bill chuckled.

"I am," Bill said. He reached out and ran his hand from Rex's head down his back. "He's the best son anyone could ask for."

"Well, we'd better get going," Jonas said as he and Rex

climbed into the glider. Jonas waved at them when the glider rose into the air and zoomed across the sky.

"This is going to be interesting. I wonder what data Rex will collect?" Harold asked.

"There's no telling. You remember how he collected every-thing we joked about when we first arrived? We'll have to wait and see what he picks up in his scans. I wouldn't be a bit surprised if he determined the age and materials used for all structures his scans pick up," Bill said.

CHAPTER FOUR

Jonas started the exploration at Blythe, on the California border where Abby, Apollo and two of their puppies entered TMZ after they left Starlight's cabin in search of Bill and Teresa.

They flew down through Mexicali where a few settlements remained, then continued to the tip of the Baja peninsula to Cabo San Lucas. The water was sparkling clean and clear, and the land was overtaken by nature.

"There are fewer than 400 people on this entire peninsula," Rex said. "We should request headquarters to contact these people to find out if they are harassed by anyone from the US, especially the communities near Tijuana."

"Go ahead and send them a message," Jonas said.

Jonas turned the glider back to Blythe. He and Rex decided to grid the trip from west to east over Arizona, New Mexico, and Texas. They would be on the lookout for Tranquility Force and World Guild Enforcers as they neared the Texas panhandle where Oklahoma jutted across. That was where the perimeter guards always had to watch carefully for sneak attacks.

With Rex on board, however, those pests didn't stand a chance of trying to get the drop on them. Since Rex planned to scan in five-hundred-mile chunks, they would fly down the Texas perimeter for that distance, then fly across from east to west.

Rex had a grid hologram so Jonas could keep an eye on their progress. It was a lot of territory to cover. They saw all manner of flying traffic along the route. Zoom Buses, commercial gliders, and family gliders. TMZ gliders hailed them in their friendly way as they patrolled their areas.

"Please hover," Rex said.

Jonas placed the glider in hover mode. "What did you find?"

"My sensors have discovered an underground structure that is multi-levels deep near Henderson, Nevada," Rex said.

"Should we report this back to headquarters?" Jonas asked.

"I have determined there is no activity, and I could not detect any life-force. It is an enormous structure. I will mark it on my hologram as something to discuss and possibly explore at a later date," Rex said.

"Okay," Jonas said. "Can we keep going?"

"Yes. We may resume."

"I'm going to have to get something to eat, Rex, and find a place to spend the night," Jonas said. It was just turning dusky. "Can you determine anywhere nearby?"

Rex's gears silently whirled. "There is an inn two miles straight ahead. Their menu offers hamburgers, fried fish, pork chops, and an assortment of vegetables."

"That sounds excellent." Jonas lowered to street glider level and slowed down. Sure enough, an old inn with four gliders parked in front came into view. Jonas settled the glider onto the ground.

"Do you want to come inside, or stay in the glider?" Jonas asked.

Rex was quiet for a moment. "I will stay with the glider and protect the TMZ property."

"Okay, buddy. I'll let you know what room they assign me." Jonas got out of the glider, walked around to the back hatch, and grabbed his travel bag. He gave a thumbs-up signal to the dog-bot and entered the inn.

The proprietor eyeballed him in his TMZ uniform. "Need a room?"

"Yes, just for tonight," Jonas said.

"Where are you from?" the heavyweight man asked.

"Headquarters," Jonas said.

The proprietor checked Jonas in, had him sign the electronic form, and then gave him a room key. "Top of the stairs, turn right. Second door on the left."

"Thanks. I'll drop off my bag, then grab a bite to eat," Jonas said.

AFTER A HEARTY MEAL of pork chops, potatoes in butter and parsley, and green beans, Jonas climbed the stairs to his room. He looked out the window. It was very dark outside with minimal light from the inn windows; their meager light all but completely swallowed by the pitch blackness of the area.

Jonas filled out his trip details and sent the report on to Harold, then he showered and went to bed.

Somewhere in the middle of the night, a loud commotion in the hallway jarred Jonas awake. At first, he thought maybe it was drunks stumbling around in the dark trying to get to their rooms. Then he heard Rex's voice calling out commands for someone to stop.

Jonas jumped out of bed, pulled on his uniform pants and yanked the door open. There were two husky men on the hallway floor, out cold, one of them being the heavy proprietor. Rex zapped a third man who had retreated down the stairs trying to escape.

"I have reported land pirates to the local TMZ office. They will be here momentarily," Rex stated. "I determined that the owner of the inn was being held in the basement. He and his family are not harmed, just frightened."

Jonas let out a heavy breath. "Thanks, Rex. You probably saved my life."

The front door of the inn burst open, and a TMZ patrol of four men ran inside.

"Hello? Who called about land pirates?"

"Up here," Jonas called out.

The patrol took the stairs two at a time. They stopped and secured the one pirate on the stairs, then continued up to the hallway.

"Jonas Biggibottom from headquarters," he reported.

The men stared in awe at Rex.

"This is Rex," Jonas said. "We'd better check on the innkeeper and his family. Rex said they were being held hostage in the basement."

"Is that a dog-bot? I didn't know headquarters had one," the leader said.

"Bill Maxwell defected. This is one of his creations he brought with him," Jonas explained.

Rex hurried down the stairs, stepping around the one pirate. He headed to a door, instructed his hidden claw to open the door, then he stopped at the top of the stairs to wait for Jonas and the others to catch up.

The patrol leader pointed to two of his people. "Go help the hostages. We'll gather the pirates down here."

After a few long moments, the innkeeper, his wife, two young daughters, and a boy climbed the stairs.

"Are you okay?" Jonas asked.

The innkeeper's wife burst into tears. The children joined in.

"We're so grateful you rescued us. I don't know what they planned to do to us," the innkeeper said.

"You can thank Rex, the dog-bot," Jonas said. "He is the one who discovered the plot."

The little boy stared at Rex, then approached the dog-bot and patted him. "Good boy!"

"Thank you. I have determined that you are eight years old and the middle child," Rex said.

The TMZ patrol hauled the pirates down the stairs.

"Are these the men who locked you downstairs?" Jonas asked.

The innkeeper and his wife nodded. "There's one missing."

"Rex, seek out the fourth pirate!" Jonas said.

Rex walked to the middle of the room and scanned the entire inn. "There are no other men or women in the inn. He is on the run."

"We'll keep an eye out for him," the TMZ patrol leader said. He indicated to his patrol to take the pirates outside and secure them in the glider. Then he turned to the innkeeper. "We will need you to fill out a report within twenty-four hours."

"We will. I want those pirates out of commission!" the innkeeper said.

The patrol leader shook Jonas' hand, nodded to Rex, then left the premises.

"Do you want me to help you secure the inn so you can go to bed?" Jonas asked.

"That's very kind of you."

"I will return to the glider and keep vigilant," Rex said. "Currently, all is well."

After Rex left the inn, the innkeeper secured the front door by sliding a six-foot 4x6 piece of lumber through two wooden brackets attached to the door.

"What if someone wants to book a room?" Jonas asked.

"There's a communication box at the side of the door," the innkeeper said.

Jonas and the innkeeper went around the inn and made sure the windows were secured.

"Everyone go to bed," Jonas said. "I'll see you in the morning for breakfast." He climbed the stairs to his room, undressed and fell asleep.

BREAKFAST WAS A SIMPLE, hearty fare with eggs over easy, a short stack of pancakes, four strips of bacon, two cups of coffee and toast. Jonas created another report and sent it to Harold, outlining what happened during the night. Headquarters would most likely send out a notice to all remote TMZ substation locations to alert them about this new threat.

He had been lucky. Without Rex's intervention, he might have been killed in his bed. Who knows what the land pirates would have done to the innkeeper and his family? They would have been able to identify them. As it was, one pirate was on the loose.

His communicator announced an incoming transmission. "Jonas," he announced. He saw that Harold was hailing him.

"How far have you gotten on Rex's scanning project?" Harold asked.

"We're on the first pass going from east to west," Jonas said.

"Have Rex make note of population density, commerce development, climate conditions, and whatnot. We should have instructed him about these things to begin with, but didn't think beyond housing for all these people outside the gate," Harold said.

"Are these far-reaching areas patrolled?" Jonas asked. "If we are populating these places, they need to have substations. We were lucky that there was a patrol nearby to assist with the land pirates."

"I'll take this up with the committee today. You're right. If those territories are going to add to their population, there needs to be policing in place to keep the peace when necessary, and to defend our territory from the World Guild trying to sneak in," Harold said. "How's it going with Rex? Are you communicating?"

Jonas belly laughed. "He's a conundrum. All facts and data, but every once in a while, he seems to try to tell a joke, but it falls flat."

"He jokes? That's interesting. I'll have to ask Bill and Teresa about that," Harold said. "The further south you go, the more treacherous the territory is going to become, so increase your security settings as appropriate. I'll let you go for now. Keep up the good work."

Jonas stood, grabbed his bag and waved goodbye to the innkeeper and his wife, and left the inn.

He found Rex standing in the driver's seat. "Move over, buddy. Time to get going." Jonas told Rex what Harold said about the data collection and the posing problems further south.

"I anticipated those things as we left headquarters. My data packets are broken down into multiple categories along with available housing," Rex stated.

"I knew you were on the job, Rex," Jonas said. "You're one dependable dog-bot."

"That is the whole purpose of our species," Rex said. "William Maxwell created super-brain chips."

"Let me know when you detect TMZ patrol substations. We need to keep track of how many miles they have to patrol and the population density of their areas. I think headquarters will have to train more people to protect the growing population," Jonas said.

"The units could be widespread if the gliders are upgraded for high speeds. Patrols can swiftly be on location from a call for help within a short time. The unit from last night arrived within six point four minutes. However, if I had not been in attendance, that would have been three minutes too late," Rex said.

"That's important information. Why don't you send that to Harold so he can take it up with the committee?" Jonas said.

They flew in silence for a while as Rex went about his business and Jonas kept his eyes peeled for anything out of the ordinary. As they made their next sweep, now heading west to east, the population became dense and the air traffic filled with different layers of flight space vehicles. Jonas enabled the collision evasion app to make sure they didn't get clobbered by nitwits too busy to pay attention to the airspace. While the gliders did not require hands-on input from the passengers, it was wise to go further beyond setting your destination.

Two groups of people caused the most accidents: the young and the old. Both had short attention spans. As Jonas thought about these things, a sports glider zoomed across the airwaves with two TMZ units on its tail, hailing the driver to land his glider immediately. Jonas steered his glider out of the way, but the sports glider made a huge arc in his hope of evading the patrols on his tail.

"This may get bumpy, Rex, so hold on," Jonas said. He tried to anticipate the sports glider's pathway, but it was all over the place. "They must be carrying contraband."

As the sports glider dipped down through several airspaces, it suddenly lost power.

"I have disabled the glider," Rex said.

"You can do that?" Jonas asked. He followed the gliders to the ground, keeping his distance. The patrols were on either side of the sports glider. Jonas landed in front of the disabled glider.

He and Rex got out of their glider and approached the two units who had weapons drawn as they approached the deactivated ship.

"Approaching to assist," Jonas announced.

The two units recognized the headquarters bar on Jonas' uniform. They were surprised to see a dog-bot.

"Glad to have you. We suspect Dot smugglers, but won't know until we get them out of that glider," the man said.

"Rex, get that ship open," Jonas said.

Rex shot a beam at the door of the sports glider. Within seconds, the driver-side door popped open.

"Hands on your heads," one of the TMZ guards called out to the two occupants of the glider.

Two expensively dressed men in their forties stepped out of the sports glider, their game up, hands on the tops of their heads. One of the guards entered the glider and searched, but didn't find any contraband.

Rex moved to the open door. "Allow me." He scanned the entire ship. "Contraband Dots are hidden between the upholstery of the seats on the underside."

A second guard joined the first. They ran their hands along

the underside of the seats. Each of them found a latch. One of the guards moved the latch on the seat he was checking, and a large handful of tiny Dot cases spilled out.

"Got 'em," he called out.

The two sportsters, thinking they were so smart, groaned that they had been caught.

After the TMZ guards secured the criminals and the contraband Dots, they called for a tow. The glider would be examined from front to back at its headquarters substation.

"Sure glad you crossed our path," one of the guards said. "These guys would have gotten away with selling these Dots on the black market. Wish we had a dog-bot to help out."

"Happy to help out," Jonas said. "Some people have no respect for hard work. Come on, Rex."

They returned to their glider and continued on with their grid work.

CHAPTER FIVE

Teresa and Gayle helped Becky pick out furnishings at the distribution center. Their new house was one street in back of Teresa and Bill's house, but didn't have a stitch of furnishings, except for kitchen appliances.

"Becky, this looks like your old sofa," Gayle said.

Becky made her way over to where Gayle stood in front of a beige corduroy-covered sofa. "Huh, it does look like my sofa." She sat on one of the cushions and rested her arm on the arm of the sofa. "Yes, and it's just as comfortable."

"Scan the tag," Teresa said.

By the time the women left the distribution center, the furniture had been chosen and scanned for delivery along with kitchen items, including an upgraded food console. Gayle flew them back to Teresa's in her family glider.

"I can't thank you and Bill enough for buying all of this for us," Becky said.

"If it weren't for our mess, you and Percy would not have been dragged into this," Teresa said. "We never thought you would be implicated in any way."

"Thank the Earth Bill and Harold showed up while we still had our brains! I can't believe how murky the government is now," Becky said. "Hopefully, we'll be able to pay you back. Any time you need a break, I'm available to babysit."

"Those puppies are a handful. Poor Abby and Apollo. When they hit their beds at night, they're exhausted," Teresa said.

"I thought maybe I could teach people how to use the food console to the best of their ability. Depending on the unit they have, it could be a challenge if they aren't technologically swift. Know what I mean?" Becky asked.

"I'm technologically savvy, but that machine is difficult to understand," Teresa said. "Ejonia left notes, so I knew how to do certain things, but I have not experimented beyond our basic needs."

"That's an excellent idea, Becky," Gayle said. "You'll have two attendees right here! I'll ask Harold how you could go about arranging a class."

They arrived back at Teresa's house, and the hoard of puppies charged over to the glider. They were jumping and somersaulting to get attention.

"DOWN!" Teresa commanded firmly.

Her determined voice shocked the puppies. They were not used to Grandma T yelling at them. Six confused faces stared up at her.

"You will behave like good puppy-children, do you understand? No more jumping on people! You could hurt someone," she said in her stern voice.

Abby and Apollo were stunned into silence when they realized their puppies listened and took the appropriate action, which was to sit and wait politely.

"Now, come greet Grandma Becky and Auntie Gayle like nice puppies," Teresa said.

The puppies stood, wagged their tails and went from Becky to Gayle, peacefully, giving the women little licks as their puppy butts wiggled happiness.

Apollo nudged Abby. "That is how it is done. You have to be forceful to get their attention."

"I'm so glad they are eating regular food," Abby said. "Daddy will be installing their Dots soon, which means they will all start to talk at the same time."

"I hadn't thought about that," Apollo said.

"Mommy will most likely have them attend school. She taught me and my canine mother, so she will most likely teach our puppies the ways of the human world," Abby said.

"I'm grateful that Bill installed my Dot. It was confusing at first, but then I started learning human talk and the ways of humanity. This human information has made it possible for me to surpass my wolf heritage intelligence," Apollo said.

"Daddy recognized your wolf intellect and said you would have a good advantage over your ancestors," Abby said.

"We need to go hunting in the wild, Abby," Apollo said. "We don't want to lose our wild skills—that would be a big mistake."

Abby thought about that for a minute. "You're right. We should keep those canine skills, and once the puppies are a little older, we should take them with us. It was very difficult for me to learn to be wild. When I escaped the lab, I had to call upon skills that I never possessed. I watched some documentaries about wild dogs over and over to learn how they survived. If I hadn't, I would have been dead within a few weeks."

"Our pups will know how to survive in case of an emergency," Apollo said, adamant. "They can't become slaves to the food console."

～

THE TMZ COMMITTEE welcomed Bill Maxwell into its fold. They now had two top-notch security people that would contribute heavily to keeping the World Guild out of TMZ. The problem was the manpower it took to patrol the entire area of the boundaries.

"It would be ideal if we had an entire pack of dog-bots," Glacious said.

"But then we'd need more gliders so the dog-bots could get around to patrol the district," Harold said.

Bill was quiet as he contemplated the issue. "I think I could solve that problem." He looked up at his waiting audience in the committee room. "If I upgraded the dog-bot plans to include a jet booster, we wouldn't need additional gliders."

There was nodding around the room.

"Would you experiment with Rex?" Pete asked.

"I'd rather build another dog-bot from scratch and experiment with it," Bill said. "Once that unit is perfected, then I can upgrade Rex. He's touchy about going offline."

"I swear, that machine is practically human," MaryEllen said.

"That was the whole point of developing the software to become self-aware," Bill said. "If you want a machine to be its very best to work with the human world, it has to think like a human."

"Don't you worry that these highly developed machines will want to take over the world?" Baily asked.

"I suppose that would worry some people, but all it would take for our preservation is one gigantic electronic pulse to wipe out their systems and take them permanently offline," Bill said. "If I could figure out how to convince my employees to defect, I'd move my entire company here. I'm concerned that the World Guild might attempt to take over my company and gain access to all my secret plans."

"Toby would come over, but I don't know about Angelica, or anyone else," Harold said.

"What about your entire complex?" Glacious asked. "You'd leave it all behind?"

"I'm here. It's there, and there's plenty of land here," Bill said. "I can rebuild. There's probably a lot of technical people here already that could help me move forward with some of the projects I want to get into place."

BILL RETURNED to his home office. He sat at the transfer surface and typed out a red-level encrypted message to Toby. He got up and walked to the cool cabinet and pulled out a tiny disc. He opened it and dumped a super bee onto the etched circle. Bill attached the message by drawing a line from the message area to the etched circle. Within moments, the super bee rose up and headed over to a wall socket and made its way through the structure of the house to the great outdoors.

Bill noted the date and time to track how long it would take the bee to get to WestUS and deliver the message. Knowing the bees, this one would probably hitch a ride or two.

ABBY AND APOLLO guided the puppies from the backyard of their house across lawns to Becky and Percy's house. It was a challenge keeping their young pups in a secure group between them. Apollo had to constantly round one of them up when they took off after a lizard or butterfly.

"Jim! Stay with the pack!" Apollo scolded. "Esme! Spit that out. It could hurt you! Wolf! Leave your brother alone!" Abby's mate looked at her. "I don't know how single canine mothers could handle their pups!"

"I'm sure if they were in the wild, the mother would be very strict with her pups. And she would have the entire wolf pack to help," Abby said. "If they were in a human house, there were humans to help."

"Just to herd them to their grandparents' house is a major challenge," Apollo said as he had to run after Lulah who galloped ahead of the group. "Lulah! Stay with the pack!"

They arrived at the house, none the worse for the trip, but Apollo was showing signs of being frazzled.

"Push the doorbell with one of your paws," Abby told Apollo.

The large wolf stood on his hind legs and bashed the doorbell with his front right paw. They heard the bell reverberate through the house. Percy opened the door and was happily surprised to see them.

"Come in! Come in!" he said. Percy looked Apollo over. "Did they run you ragged?" The puppies charged into the house, barking and romping. Percy closed the door.

Becky swooped into the room, excited to see Abby, Apollo, and the puppies. They surrounded her, jumping, whining and barking, happy to see their grandma Becky.

"Okay now, everyone needs to calm down," Becky said. When the puppies didn't respond, she put on her stern face and belted out an order. "DOWN! Right now!"

The puppies plunked their butts onto the floor, tails swishing across the wood.

"Now, one at a time, come see grandma, starting with Star," Becky said.

One by one, they received their hugs, pats, and kisses.

"Why don't we go into the other room so I can show you pictures of your canine grandfather and tell you stories?" Becky offered up. She led them into the other room where Bill had installed several floor-level monitors for when she had the pups over.

Percy grabbed the remote off the counter. In an instant, pictures of Jimbo in some of his escapades appeared on the screens. There was a picture of him climbing a chain-link fence.

Abby looked at her canine grandfather, then Percy. "Daddy Bill included many pictures and movies of Grandpa Jimbo doing all sorts of things. This is how I escaped from the lab enclosure. I watched Grandpa Jimbo climb a fence and fly over the top. The fence at the lab facility was very high—much higher than this fence."

"I don't know how he learned to do these things, but he was a natural at getting in and out of places," Percy said, a bit sadly.

Becky made the puppies settle down, then she told them stories about each of the pictures on the screens. They were excited to hear about their relative and see all his wild escapades. Then she became very serious.

"Your Grandpa Jimbo isn't with us anymore. Do you know why?" Becky asked.

Tongues lolled. Expressions were questioning.

"The reason he isn't here anymore is that while he was climbing over a fence, he wasn't paying attention. When he leaped off the fence, he crashed into a glider and was killed instantly." Her eyes misted, and she blinked rapidly, trying to avoid outright crying.

Apollo's forehead creased. "He jumped into the path of a glider?"

Percy nodded. "Yup. He didn't see it. Unfortunately, he was reckless. We couldn't keep him confined. All he wanted to do was explore. I hope his namesake is smarter."

They all looked over at Jim, who sat sweetly and watched the movies playing on the screens.

Apollo looked over his pups. "I want all of you to study how your canine grandfather scaled walls and fences. This is excellent training material if you ever have to escape from somewhere, like your mother did."

Abby licked his face. "You have to make sure you take in your environment to know you are safe every inch of your climb. It was very difficult. My toes and feet burned for many days, but I escaped Dr. Roberts and the lab."

Becky swooped down and hauled Abby into a hug. "We have your daddy Bill to thank for loading all of those movies into your secret Dot."

CHAPTER SIX

Toby entered the private lab on the fourth floor at Maxwell Industries. The windows between the lab and the work floor were in secret mode—occupants inside the room could see out, but no one could see in.

The immense room was stark white. Not a stitch of artwork or company posters adorned the walls. White counters with suspended monitors were positioned throughout the room, along with high-backed captain's chairs that sported side wings that completely enveloped their current occupants. Chairs contained what looked like vision-testing equipment suspended on a pole that rolled along the ceiling. Thick white gloves that seemed better fit for a spaceship than anything else were on either side of the equipment.

Toby slipped into one of the captain's chairs and eased the chair back into a slight reclining position. He grabbed hold of the Vision Core device when something buzzed by his ear. He swatted at the insect.

"Damn mosquitoes!" He squinted and tried to track the buzzing. Suddenly, he glimpsed the super bee.

"What the..."

Toby grabbed the lever and adjusted the chair to upright. He slid out of the captain's chair and held his hand out. The super bee landed in the palm of his hand.

His heart pounded. The only reason a super bee would be flying around was if Bill Maxwell sent one. Toby cupped his hands to keep the bee from drifting away. He rushed from the lab to his private office, closed and secured the door, and approached his transfer surface. He shook the bee into the etched circle on the transfer surface.

"Let's see what the boss sent," he muttered.

His fingers clacked on the virtual keyboard and the bee downloaded its contents. He saw a programming language that he didn't recognize. Then he discovered one file that was in a language he and Bill used to taunt each other with bad jokes. He clicked the file open and read the message. "Dog thought? Wow."

He studied Bill's instructions about the key components of Rex's language. "Brilliant!"

After a few quiet moments, he was able to access the files Bill sent. He read the first message, which also contained several images.

Toby, you most likely figured out that Teresa and I are not on a sabbatical that we swore to, but rather we left WestUS and defected to TMZ. Harold and Gayle are here. You can throw out every idea you ever had about this place. It's all a pack of lies. My dog-bot, Rex, also defected from his position with Tranquility Force. He and Jerry, his second in command of the bot-pack, devised a plan and carried it out.

Toby was astounded. "They carried out a plan and weren't detected? Holy shit!" He continued reading.

Abby found us. She has a wolf mate named Apollo—the last of his kind—and they have six puppies.

I'm sure you have figured out that a team of us from TMZ rescued Percy and Becky before the World Guild could have their minds swiped.

Toby, if there was a way to move my entire organization here, I would do it in a minute. Who would be willing to come over? It would mean giving up everything and everyone—a very tough choice to make, but people would experience complete freedom for the first time in their lives.

I feel sure that the World Guild is planning an attempt to take over Maxwell Industries. That can't happen. We must devise a plan to make sure they never gain access to any of the high-security projects and files the teams are working on.

I have all my files with me, but there may be sensitive files in storage. I have included instructions on how to send them to me. Once they are sent, you should destroy what you have on your end at Maxwell Industries.

Whoever decides to defect, you will find one of my messages that gives you access to a way to take your personal belongings as well as equipment from the office with you. This is how Teresa, Rex, and I escaped.

Only communicate with Rex's dog thought. Use encrypted red-level code with our destroying option in case of interception.

I look forward to hearing from you soon. Keep the bee for emergency communication.

Bill

Toby clicked on the images. He sank into his chair, completely floored and had to digest what he had read and seen. Then there were the other files to wade through. After at least six minutes of words buzzing through his head, he clicked on the next file. He found instructions for the safe-flying area of the grid, and the device Bill had built to stabilize the transporter at such a high level. The next file held the formulas for invisibility and uncloaking, and how to coat goggles to be able to see what was invisible. He included his contacts for supplies and unregistered transporters.

The last file contained the blueprints to create a dog-bot. The software was extensive. Bill noted that he would send any updates.

"Damn! This is possible. Who are the most valuable people who would be on board?" He realized this would take some thought. Once he had a team in place, the first thing they would do would be to build a dog-bot. Bill explained in detail the workings of Rex's brain and how the software was self-aware.

Not everyone would consider leaving WestUS, and he had to make sure there were no traitors among anyone he considered. It would only take one person who wholly believed in the World Guild, over all else, and thought it was their duty to stop anyone from defecting. Of course, Maxwell Industries employees mostly abhorred the global government, but who knew what was really in their heads?

If someone gave them up, the game would be over. Anyone turned in would be arrested as an enemy of the World Guild. All Bill's secrets would be exposed. Toby pulled up a blank document and started a list. Angelica, of course; Myra-June (Teresa's former assistant); Roland, the mechanical genius who helped Bill build many of his inventions; Sam, the head of the financial department. The list grew. He noted electrical engineers, coders, and researchers.

He thought perhaps the way to move forward would be to have a company-wide meeting to announce that their founder and leader had defected. Toby also thought that he could say that anyone who needed to talk could come and see him. That might lead the way to building the list.

Toby's head spun as he clicked the images open again. There was a picture of Bill, Teresa, Harold, and Gayle together, looking so happy. Bill sent pictures of the tent city outside the secured TMZ gates, then what the other side of those gates held. His and Teresa's house was beautiful. There was a family picture of Abby, Apollo and their pups, Becky and Percy, and Rex. Everyone appeared so happy and relaxed.

Toby wanted to experience that for himself. He wanted to not have to think twice about any message or communication, or what he did or said in his own home. The World Guild had cleverly stolen every single one of their rights. He itched to start on the dog-bot project. According to one of Bill's messages, Rex had routed Bill and Teresa's wealth in such a roundabout way that they hadn't lost anything when they left their Dots behind.

He thought about calling Angelica, but remembered her reaction when she had alerted him to the GNN piece. She was adamant that the Maxwells would never defect. Toby just didn't know where she stood, and he wrestled with discussing this with her.

He decided to approach Roland. If he was in agreement, they could begin on the dog-bot project, and between the two of them they could determine which software engineer and coder to approach.

ROLAND SAT, mute, with eyes wide as Toby finished showing the communication from Bill.

Toby waited patiently, but then freaked out a little. "Say something!"

"DAMN!" Roland belted out. Toby jumped in his chair at the loud response.

"Let's get to work on the dog-bot. I think Murray and Wynne would be good choices," Roland said.

Murray was a coder who could make anyone's head spin,

and Wynne was an electrical engineer who got a charge out of playing with wires and circuits.

"I think it would be wise to develop a couple of dog-bots," Roland said. "We could assembly-line the work and get them built in no time."

Toby nodded. "Good idea. Want to get Murray and Wynne over here to talk about this right now?"

"Time's a wastin'," Roland said as he rubbed his hands together. "Man, I can't wait to build these dogs!"

TOBY COMMANDEERED one of the large labs for the project and shuffled the people who had been using it to a different lab. He used Bill's highest security protocols for room entry to make sure no one could slip into the room while the team was not occupying it.

He, Roland, Murray, and Wynne put together a parts list so that the material they required for three dog-bots could be ordered. They also discussed the chemicals they would need to order in bulk when it came time to head out of WestUS. Since they were all bachelors, they determined they would only need a small transporter for their possessions, and anything they decided to bring with them from Maxwell Industries.

Toby pulled up Bill's message and used the dog-thought program to send him an update. He also asked him about Angelica—if he thought it would be safe to approach her to see if she would join them. She had been Bill's right-hand person in ordering all special project supplies, expensing them to the right accounts, and keeping tabs on every screw, bolt, and what-not, including tracking hours. They could really use her right about now.

He and the guys made a list of other things to discuss with

Bill. They asked if there was anything Bill needed them to bring from WestUS that they couldn't get in TMZ. Toby read it aloud for Roland, Murray, and Wynne to add their bits, if anything, then he sent it. Rex's program was an interesting creation and would mystify anyone if it were intercepted. Murray scratched his head every time he looked at the code.

∿

BILL RECEIVED a ping with a distinctive chime showing a response from Toby. He pulled himself away from the project he was working on. After he had read the message, Bill thought of his response. He rolled his chair over to the transfer surface and responded to the message.

Trust Angelica. She will have a moment of disbelief, then she'll hunker down and get to work. When you have a fully functional working dog-bot, do you think it would be possible to get into Becky and Percy's house and find their scrapbook of their dog-son and his ashes? That would ease their pain from leaving everything behind.

Bill typed two more pages, answering Toby and his team's specific questions about the projects they were undertaking. He wrapped up the message in Rex's proprietary program and sent it off.

∿

TOBY SAT in the secured room with Roland, Murray, and Wynne when Bill's answer zinged through. He clicked it open on the big screen, unraveled the dog-thought sequence, and Bill's message appeared. The three men read silently.

"You going to talk to her?" Roland asked, staring down Toby.

"Yeah. I'll get her over here and we can tell her. She'll be okay after she digests everything," Toby said.

"You sure?" Wynne asked. He looked skeptical while thinking of how his coworker was going to react to their plot.

Toby buzzed Angelica. "Hey, got a minute? There's something I want to show you."

"Yeah. Where are you?" she asked.

He gave her the room number.

"What are you doing there?"

"Ang, just get over here," he said, exasperated.

Ten minutes later, a tap on the door sounded. Wynne was closest, so he trotted to the door and opened it.

Angelica waltzed into the room and stopped in front of the guys. She folded her arms across her chest like a school teacher getting ready to ream her wayward students. "Okay, what's going on?"

Toby tapped the chair next to his. "Just sit down and stop being so dramatic."

She huffed out a little blast of air, but pulled out the chair and sank into the leather.

"We've heard from Bill," Toby said.

Angelica's head whipped around to face him. "Where is he? Is everything okay?"

"We need you to stay calm, to listen to what we have to say, and to act rationally," Toby said.

Roland pulled up Bill's original message to Toby. "Read this first, before we talk."

Angelica was wide-eyed as she read Bill's message. Twice. She clicked on the pictures multiple times, not believing what she saw. "Those lying bastards at the World Guild. How could they do this to us? Is everything in our lives a lie?" She stared at the four men around the table. "Are you going to build the dog-bots?"

Toby slid a piece of paper across the table to her. "We need you to order these supplies."

She snatched up the paper, glanced over the list, and nodded. "I'm on it. When do we leave?"

"There's more," Roland said. He queued up the other messages.

Angelica read Toby's and Bill's messages. "I attended Jimbo's memorial service, and I remember Becky showing me the album she put together with his coloring pages." She let her eyes wander from the monitor to the men and nodded confidently. "If I remember correctly, his urn is on the mantle. I can easily locate these in their house."

Four goofy smiles across the table met her serious face.

CHAPTER SEVEN

As Jonas and Rex flew over the lower border areas of Arizona, New Mexico, and Texas at the previously independent country of Mexico, they came across crumbling brick or concrete walls, and sometimes, chain-length fencing that at one time tried to keep people from crossing the border into the United States.

"I wonder why those walls and fences were built to begin with?" Jonas asked. "Everyone in the old United States had emigrated there from other countries."

"They soon learned walls would not stop anyone determined to enter the country," Rex said.

They were at the point in their journey where the landscape became tropical countryside with only scattered colonies of civilization.

Rex scanned in a wider swath, as there wasn't much to document due to the lush jungle-like area. Jonas had lowered the glider so they could get a visual of the ground and any activity thereabouts. He manually steered the vehicle around the trees. He and Rex took in the crumbling adobe houses that

had been abandoned decades ago. Now, those houses had vege-
tation growing out of them. The earth happily reclaimed all
that was dormant.

A ping sound from the bottom of the glider startled Jonas.
"What was that?"

"Ground fire! Raise the glider up while I scan the area,"
Rex said.

Jonas grabbed the controls, and the glider rose above
normal hand weapons' reach.

"I have detected natives on the ground. They do not have
gliders or other modes of mechanical transportation, so I do not
deem them a threat," Rex said. "I will send a report to the
closest substation warning them not to fly too low in this area."

"What type of people are they, do you know?" Jonas asked.

"They appear to be Mexican or indigenous natives. Their
weapons are old model handguns and rifles from the 1960s,"
Rex stated. "We could land and try to communicate with them.
I speak all early languages."

"Let me send an alert to our home base to let them know
where we are and what's happening," Jonas said. "Then you
can attempt to talk to them via the communications system.
Better to try from up here than on the ground where we could
be captured."

"Excellent plan. We would not be in any danger on the
ground, though. I am more than capable of protecting us," Rex
said.

Jonas sent the alert.

"Go ahead and give it a try," Jonas said.

"Greetings from TMZ headquarters," Rex sent via his
built-in megaphone-type system option. "We come in peace
and would like to talk to you on the ground."

He sent the message first in English, then Spanish, then
Tex-Mex, then an Aztec dialog. Rex and Jonas observed the

group on the ground who looked from one to another, then up at the ship.

"They are wondering what we want. The one who appears to be the leader fears we will take them away and make slaves of them," Rex said.

"How can you tell?" Jonas asked.

"I can read their lips. They are speaking Mexican Spanish, which is only slightly modified from Castilian Spanish," Rex said. "We need to find out if people are disappearing."

"Could the World Guild be rounding people up and taking them away?" Jonas asked.

"That is a possibility. We need to talk to them. I will record our interaction with these natives and send the communication to Harold," Rex said.

Jonas lowered the glider to the ground. The group of people skittered back toward the trees, but did not disappear. They talked excitedly among themselves as they watched Jonas and Rex exit the glider.

Rex and Jonas stopped at what they determined was a safe distance from the natives. They pointed at Rex excitedly.

"My name is Rex, and I am a dog-bot. Jonas and I are from TMZ headquarters. We are not the World Guild or the Tranquility Force. You are safe and will not be harmed. Please talk with us and explain about people disappearing," Rex said.

The group talked among themselves, then the man who appeared to be the leader stepped forward.

"We are searching for five people who disappeared from our village during the night," the leader said.

"Were they snatched from their beds, out walking about—where were they when they disappeared?" Jonas asked. Rex translated for him.

The natives talked among themselves, then the leader spoke up.

"We don't really know. It happened when everyone was asleep."

"Where is your village?" Rex asked.

"That way. It isn't far," the leader said as he pointed.

"Will you lead us there? We want to investigate the immediate area," Rex said.

The leader waved his arm forward. "Come. We will go there now." His group started through the trees with Rex and Jonas following.

They walked through the jungle for a good twenty minutes, dodging heavy, tripping ground foliage. When they arrived at the clearing at the edge of the village, Jonas noticed a group of people in the middle of the village crying.

"No one heard someone sneak inside your huts? It seems as if there would have been a struggle that would wake others," Jonas said.

"We didn't know anyone was missing until hours passed, then we discovered that no one had seen these five people," Manny said. "We tried to find them, but they just seemed to vanish."

"We will walk the perimeter and work our way into the village to see if we can detect any clues of strangers entering the village," Rex said.

"Tell your people who we are and what we're doing," Jonas said. He then talked to Rex. "You go that way and I'll go this way."

Rex started out, scanning the area as he went. Jonas studied the footprints on the ground. The natives all appeared to wear sandals, and children either wore them or went barefoot, but their feet were small in comparison to the adults.

After only approximately 100 feet, Jonas noticed footprints of barefoot adults that went in both directions—out of the forest and into the village, then returning to the forest with additional footprints. He pulled up his communication device. "Rex? I've come across what appears to be unshod adult footprints."

Rex was at his side within a few moments. He scanned the footprints. He quickly searched his database for a match. "They appear to be native footprints."

Jonas turned to the leader. "I'm sorry for not asking earlier, what is your name, sir?"

"Manuel Torres, but you can call me Manny," the leader said.

"Has anyone in your village seen any natives in your area?" Jonas asked.

A small crowd had gathered around them.

"Natives? We're natives," Manny said, confused.

Jonas thought about old-world natives. "Indigenous people."

"Oh!" Manny said. He turned to his people. "Has anyone seen any Nahua?"

"Nahua is another name for Aztec," Rex told Jonas.

Someone turned toward the village and hollered out the question, which brought more people to the circle. A young boy ran up to the group, waving his hand in the air.

"I saw some Nahua!" the boy said excitedly.

"Where did you see them?" Manny asked.

The boy showed a moment of guilt. "Over at the banana tree grove."

Manny gave him a stink-eye. "You know you're not supposed to go over there unescorted by adults! There's jaguars and other wild animals that could attack you! You're lucky the Nahua didn't take you away!"

The boy squirmed in place. "I was hiding in a tree. They didn't see me."

"When did you see these people?" Jonas asked. Rex interpreted.

"Two days ago," the boy said.

"It sounds as if they were scouting," Rex said.

Jonas turned his eyes to the ground. These adults all wore sandals. The footprints in question were adult-sized, and all were barefoot.

"Manny, does your village trade goods with the Nahua people, or have any interaction with them?" Rex asked.

"We rarely see them," the leader said. "They are very superstitious and mostly keep to themselves far away from here."

"Well, it appears they've been in your village." Jonas used his communicator to light up the footprints with an infrared-type light that distinctly showed the tracks coming into the village, then leaving with several additional footprints among them.

Manny and the villagers looked at the ground Jonas had lit up.

"If you study the pattern of the footprints, you will notice the footprints in the middle are surrounded by the larger group," Rex said.

"Why would they take our people?" Manny asked.

"There are a couple of reasons I can think of," Jonas said. "They might need women to breed with, and men for labor. They don't sacrifice humans to a god, do they?"

Manny looked horror-struck. "Sacrifice? I don't know. They wear all these feathers in their hair and paint their bodies."

There was a steady murmuring among the village people after Rex interpreted Jonas' mention of sacrifices. This brought on hysterical crying from the families of the missing people.

"Who exactly is missing?" Jonas asked.

"Three women and two men," Manny said.

"I would like to see where they were taken from," Jonas said. "We might be able to detect a clue."

Manny, Rex, Jonas, and a small group walked over to one of the huts. Rex and Jonas went inside. The hut was very modest. Four sleeping pallets were on the floor. A crude, low rack made from branches secured with vining, stood to the left of the doorway and held a pair of sandals. Odds and ends that Jonas did not recognize were strewn about.

Jonas drew in a breath. "Do you smell that, Rex? It's sweet in a strange way."

Rex's LEDs blinked while his olfactory sensors analyzed the pungent aroma that just barely clung to the hut's interior. "My analysis has determined that the odor is from the highly toxic curmontow plant. The toxicity has dissipated, but this tells me that from the faint leftover smell, the original dosage that was applied was enough to keep the sleepers knocked out. The Nahua grabbed their victims without any struggle whatsoever."

"Let's talk to the victims' families," Jonas said. They left the hut and walked to the center of the village, where the family members sat on the ground. Some rocked back and forth while wailing about their lost family members.

"Rex, have Manny ask them if anyone has a headache," Jonas said.

The dog-bot translated.

Manny turned to the group and asked.

"Ai yi yi!" an old woman said. "My head hurt very badly this morning."

Jonas nodded. "Tell them they need to air out the huts. Someone should fan air into the huts to clear out the curmontow."

Some people left the group and headed into the jungle. They returned with large, broad leaves on thick, long stems. The men handed out leaves to people, and they stood at the doorway of the five huts and fanned air into the huts.

"Why don't we go to the Nahua village and find out what's going on?" Jonas asked.

Manny and the villagers appeared frightened when Rex interpreted what Jonas said.

"What if they kill us? Or keep us there as slaves?" someone called out.

Rex translated for Jonas.

"You do not have to worry about that," Jonas said. "Rex is a formidable weapon. Who wants to go with us?"

There was a lot of shaking heads and backing away, but finally, two men stepped up to the task to go along with Manny, Jonas and Rex.

CHAPTER EIGHT

Even though the footprints were hours old, Rex had no problem tracking them through the jungle. His LED eye sensors easily detected the kidnappers' progress through the thick foliage.

After they had traveled approximately three miles, the dog-bot halted the group. "I detect a water source ahead. We will approach cautiously because there may be wild animals drinking," Rex said. "Walk softly."

They continued forward, trying to avoid snarled areas that would create more noise than progress. Up ahead they discovered a stream where a large jaguar drank as it walked along the edge of the water. The cat lifted its head and sniffed the air. It turned its head in their direction, then leaped over the stream and bolted through the jungle in the same direction they were headed.

"We will need to be cautious as we continue," Rex said.

Manny shook his head. "He won't bother us."

"How can you tell?" Jonas asked.

"There's too many of us and he won't take the chance," Manny said.

Rex walked to the edge of the stream. "The footprints stop here. I will scan the other side to see if they continue on the opposite bank of the stream. They may have walked downstream in the water to try to throw us off their direction. Stay here until I find their route."

The dog-bot walked through the water and stopped on the opposite bank. He scanned the shoreline but found no human footprints. He walked further down to the right and scanned the ground ahead for several hundred feet. Then he turned around and walked in the opposite direction, scanning as he went. He was out of sight of his group of people when he discovered the footprints leaving the water.

Jonas' communicator sounded an incoming message. "What did you find?"

"Cross the stream and walk to your left. I will wait for you at the point where they emerged from the water," Rex said.

Jonas waved the group forward, and they met up with Rex.

"The path veers off in this direction," Rex said. He commenced leading the group once again.

After they had walked for another half mile, a coconut landed close to Rex. Then another one. "We are under attack!"

They looked up into the trees and saw a couple of spider monkeys.

"Just spider monkeys being mischievous," Jonas said.

Rex sent a red laser beam toward the one who was ready to toss another coconut at the group. The monkey yelped as the beam stung him. He and his buddy took off through the trees.

"Pesky creatures," Rex grumbled. "Abby's puppies would like them."

Rex continued to follow the footprints that were invisible to the human eye. After trekking for another three-quarters of a mile, Rex slowed, then stopped.

"My sensors detect an encampment or village ahead with an abundance of activity. We should approach with caution," Rex said.

"Can you determine the number of people?" Jonas asked.

"Not at this time," Rex said.

Manny and the two men who accompanied him talked among themselves.

"We have never ventured to their village, so we don't know how many people live there," Manny said.

"We will announce our approach and hope for a peaceful meeting," Jonas said.

They moved forward cautiously. Rex used his megaphone to alert the Nahua of their approach in their language. "Hello, we come in peace and would like to meet with you."

Within moments, they were surrounded by eight Nahua pointing spears at them.

"You are on our side of the stream," one Nahua accused.

Manny raised his eyebrows. "Since when was there an "our" side and "your" side?"

"It has always been that way," the Nahua said.

"Rex, tell him we want to speak to their leader," Jonas said.

The dog-bot passed the message on.

The group of Nahua nudged Manny's group and Jonas forward. One of the Nahua rapped Rex with his spear.

Rex took offense and zinged the man's foot with a pinprick beam. The Nahua howled, grabbed his foot, and hopped.

"Why did you do that?" Jonas demanded.

"I simply put him in his place," Rex defended. "We will be okay."

The leader of the Nahua group stepped back from Rex. "Machine-dog is a weapon?"

Manny opened his mouth to reply, but Rex cut him off. "I mean you no harm, but when I am provoked, I retaliate. Shall we proceed to your village?"

The Nahua leader nodded, warily, and the entire group moved forward through the jungle. They broke through the trees into a tiny village. The Nahua villagers stayed their distance, talking loudly in the Aztec language upon seeing who their tribesmen escorted. Many fingers pointed at Rex.

A decorated Nahua man emerged from a hut and approached the group. He was a stately figure with a full head-dress of feathers, face paint, and wearing traditional decorated clothing (Click the link to see the pictures) which included a decorated wide band of colorful cloth over the shoulders and an elaborate loincloth.

The Nahua leader in charge of escorting the visitors stepped forward. "These people come from across the stream. They brought this stranger and his war machine." He pointed to the prospective people as he spoke. "War machine hurt Notty."

Everyone looked at the Nahua who limped away from the group. He showed the chief his wounded foot.

Jonas decided it was time to jump into the fray and get to the bottom of the village raid. "We have come to find out why your people have stolen villagers from across the stream."

At that moment, Manny and his friends pointed to two women across the expanse in the middle of the village. "There are two of our people! Where are the others?"

Their eyes searched the village to no avail.

The decorated Nahua stepped forward. He pointed to himself. "I Yaotl Chief Nahua."

"Chief Yaotl," Jonas said. He pointed to Manny and his friends. "Why do the Nahua steal villagers from across the stream?"

The chief took a few minutes. He spread one arm wide, toward his village. "Nahua people are small. Not many. Need to build tribe." He walked away toward an area where his people typically sat around a fire in the middle of an open area. "Come." He waved his arm for the others to follow. "Sit. We talk."

Rex, Jonas, Manny and his people walked to where the chief now sat. They chose their seats. Jonas sat opposite the chief, with Manny to his right, and Rex standing beside him to his left.

A woman brought a tray of reddish drinks served in coconut shells. She served the chief first, then handed out the rest of the drinks. She stared at Rex, then shifted her eyes to Jonas, questioning.

"I don't require a beverage," Rex chimed in, speaking in the Nahuatl language.

Jonas sipped his drink. "Very good. Thank you."

"The Nahua tribe would be better served if they moved across the stream and integrated with Manny's people," Rex said. "Both tribes would benefit by building a larger community." He translated into both of the native's languages.

At first, there was huffing and puffing between the two groups. Neither wanted the other. The Nahua didn't want to show weakness, but eventually, by the look on Yaotl's face, resigned to the fact that their way of life was changing.

CHAPTER NINE

S hortly after Angelica ordered the parts for the dog-bots, Maisey, Josh, and Timmy were being observed responding to commands. The three new dog-bots ran, jumped, hopped, zigzagged, and raced through a manmade course in the large lab area while Toby, Roland and Wynne watched closely looking for faults.

Murray noticed a slight tick when Josh hopped over the paper hats they strewed along the course. "Come here, Josh. I need to make an adjustment."

The tan and white dog-bot wagged his manmade tail and scampered over to Murray. The coder's fingers flew over the holographic keyboard in front of him and made a change in the coding sequence. He reached under the dog's belly and pressed the reset button. Josh's head crashed to his chest as his system went offline and he shut down. After a full minute, Murray pressed the bellybutton and the dog-bot lifted its head and became alert.

"What day is it?" Josh asked.

"You were offline for only one full minute, boy, check your internal clock," Murray said.

There was an almost silent moment of whirring and clicks as the manmade dog verified his system. "All systems are online."

"Okay, boy. Go hop over those paper hats."

The dog-bot raced over to the course and hopped like a bunny over the paper hats that hadn't been trampled by his mechanical brother and sister.

Toby's communication system received an alert from Bill. He brought up the message and unraveled the dog-thought. There were attachments. "Bill sent upgrades for the dogs, and a link for them to connect to Rex."

Murray and Wynne watched as Toby unpacked the files and transferred the coding to the software engineers.

"Okay, we're going to have to take them offline so we can upgrade their coding," Murray said.

Toby and Roland approached the three dogs.

"Everyone's going to take a nap for a few minutes," Roland said.

"I already took a nap," Josh said.

"Your grandfather sent better coding and we're going to implement it," Toby said.

"Our grandfather?" Maisey asked.

"Bill Maxwell. Look at the files where your creators provided you with the information, and you will see the plans and find his name," Toby said.

Almost silent whirring could be heard as the dogs searched their systems.

"Bill Maxwell created our alpha, Rex. We will nap," Timmy said.

Roland and Toby shut down the dogs. Their heads crashed to their chests.

Murray skimmed through the lines of coding. "I'm going to adjust this sequence to make their systems as quiet as they are now. Send this back to Bill with a note. He might want to quiet down Rex."

After Murray and Wynne finished going through the sequencing, they uploaded the new coding to the three dogs and brought them back online. Timmy stood quietly checking his system. His LEDs flashed, alerting the team that his systems were A-OK.

"I don't remember who I am," Josh said as he faced the guys.

Murray and Wynne harrumphed.

"Shut him down again and let's see what's wrong," Murray said.

"Joking!" Josh apparently was the joker of the three.

"You need to ask Bill about this upgrade and mention Josh's personality," Wynne said. He, Toby, Roland and Murray stared at the dog.

Maisey quietly waited her turn. When she realized that the focus was one hundred percent on her bot-brother, she sat. "I'm okay."

Toby looked at her. "Good girl." He walked over to the transfer surface and put together a message to Bill, wrapped it up tightly with Rex's dog thought program and sent it. Almost immediately, a response came through. The four men read the message from their company founder.

Sounds like Josh is a lot like Rex, but more advanced. Sometimes Rex tries to tell a joke, or be funny, and it falls flat. Explain to Josh that he will have to analyze his jokes so that he doesn't accidentally cause problems.

Thanks for sending the code string to soften Rex's system sounds. Volume control doesn't seem to help unless he mutes himself. Your dogs will have to mute themselves when you are in incognito mode.

Be sure to let me know your plans: how many will accompany you, the number of transporters, when you are leaving WestUS. We will have TMZ security waiting. Tranquility Force will try to stop you on your approach if you reveal your transporters too soon. Teresa and I didn't think we'd make it across the boundary because they were shooting at us, even beyond the TMZ line.

After they finished reading the note, they huddled.

"I propose we have a company-wide meeting," Roland said. "Need to find out who wants to continue on with Maxwell Industries in the new location."

"The people who stay behind will have to look for work, because we're going to strip the buildings of all Bill's technology," Toby said. "I want to take the communicator, all the cool storage cabinets where we keep the bees and backup files, Bills secret docs, unless he took all that with him, and the transfer surfaces—as much equipment as we can haul."

Wynne nodded. "Need to get the dimensions of everything so we can determine how many transporters we need to get our hands on. Maybe get a few ZoomBuses for people transporters. We'll have to make room for peoples' possessions."

"Maybe Bill can let us use his transporter," Murray said. "Depending on how many people are going to ditch the World Guild, we don't want to call attention to ourselves with buying a fleet. People would want to see permits and stuff."

"I'm only taking my clothes and some personal items I don't want to give up," Toby said. "Most of my furniture is second hand and I should be able to replace it there."

They talked for another forty-five minutes while making lists.

~

TOBY HAD Angelica organize a company meeting in the open area of the main building. They had thought about meeting outside, but there was no way of knowing whether Tranquility Force would be spying on them. Plus, there were the satellites that could invisibly spy so easily. They wanted to keep the dogs a secret from the outside world for as long as possible.

Timmy, Josh and Maisey scanned the Maxwell Industries property searching the airways for beams directed their way. So far, they hadn't discovered anything. Toby, Roland, Murray, and Wynne knew that would change as soon as the exodus happened.

Employees gathered in the open area on the first floor where tours typically took place, and the second-floor open area quietly talking among themselves. This was the first meeting since their founder had gone on sabbatical after Abby had been given up as lost in the wilderness.

Toby stood on the third-floor platform that overlooked the lobby, with Sam, who headed the financial group. Sam had been shocked when Toby approached him about the plan. He spoke to his wife, and they decided it was never too late to escape the World Guild.

Toby opened his communicator to address the throng of people. "Hello? May I have your attention, please? We'd like to get started."

The employees quieted down.

Murray sat on the sidelines on the third level, working at a transfer surface that had been moved to the open area.

Roland and Wynne were on hand in case of technical difficulties.

The huge screen over the receptionist communicator on the

ground floor came to life, and Bill Maxwell stood there looking over the crowd. Teresa and Abby stood on either side of him.

Cheers filled the area. The employees were so excited to see the Maxwells and Abby, the last dog.

Bill held out his hands, motioning for people to stop talking. "Settle down, we have a lot to talk about."

The area became quiet.

"It's been quite some time since we were all together in a room—even if I'm not there in person, I'm here talking to you. Teresa and I have made major changes in our lives that we wanted to share with you. As you can see, we have been reunited with Abby."

There was an uproar of clapping and cheering, then people settled down.

"First and foremost, we have defected to TMZ. If there is anyone there among you who feels completely loyal to the World Guild, you should leave this meeting immediately. We are not returning to WestUS, and you wouldn't either if you lived here. We've all been fed a pack of lies about TMZ. My goal is to move Maxwell Industries here so we can work on top-secret projects.

"Again, if there is anyone there among you who is a World Guild loyalist, if you breathe word of this meeting or the plans I am about to present, I will personally hunt you down and see to it that you have a brain swipe." Bill looked over the throng of people gauging what he saw on their faces.

"Tomorrow, I want a full count of who will accompany my team leads to TMZ. We have to make plans to accommodate you once you get here, but more importantly, how you get here. Toby and his team will discuss this with you once I turn the meeting over to him. He will show you authentic pictures of this area. It is nothing like the lies we have been fed for decades."

"You're going to abandon this complex?" someone called out.

"Yes. It's just a building. We will start fresh here in TMZ," Bill said. "No one will regret this decision, but I know how difficult it is to come to this point and choose what type of life you want.

"I know many of you are young people who may have just started out on your own, or recently married. It may be difficult for you to leave behind family and friends. I get it. You can choose to stay there in WestUS and seek other employment. It was a difficult decision for Teresa and me to leave all of you behind, but we had Abby to think about."

The meeting went on for another forty minutes with Bill finally taking his leave and turning it over to Toby and Sam. Toby queued up the pictures to show everyone what TMZ actually looked like. He showed the picture of Bill and Teresa with Harold and Gayle, their house, the whole neighborhood, and pictures of the vast TMZ area.

There was a rumble of discussion among the employees.

"It's up to them," Sam said. "Hopefully, there aren't any traitors here."

Angelica, Roland, Murray, and Wynne joined Toby and Sam.

"It would have been a lot easier if people had the time to find work out of WestUS and disappear like Harold and Gayle did," Angelica said. "That way they could easily take everything with them and would have the travel permits."

Toby and Roland raised their eyebrows in thought.

"We might be able to pull that off," Roland said. "Let's talk to Bill about this and see how we could come by air-tight forged documents. It would be easier to transport a lot of the equipment in the open instead of using the formula on a transporter."

"Hopefully, tomorrow we will have an idea as to how many

people will want to make the move," Angelica said. "Maxwell's currently has 463 people employed."

They all quietly thought about that number. Before the tragic event of the deadly XSKL435 that decimated the population of the entire world, there had been 500 Maxwell Industries employees. Over the past year, there had been many references denoting a skull and crossbones whenever the poison was mentioned. It wasn't hard to make the leap from the formula's name, X**SKL**435, to the image on social media. People in conspiracy theory groups attributed the chemical name as an indication that the wipeout of people, dogs, and other animals was not an accident.

TOBY HAD A RESTLESS NIGHT. He worried that his door would be kicked in and the Tranquility Force would drag him out in handcuffs. When he finally got through the night and daybreak broke, he didn't linger in bed. There wasn't any point. His mind was busy with plans for the exodus.

He showered, stood before his low-end food console and ordered a basic coffee and a hard-boiled egg, then left his apartment. He walked across the grounds to his glider, climbed inside, plunked down into the seat and pressed the pre-programmed button for Maxwell Industries.

Toby slurped coffee and chewed the egg as the glider made the brief trip. He looked to the blue skies around the Maxwell Industries complex as he left his glider to see if any governmental gliders were in the area. None were detected, so he approached the building and went inside. He was the first of his team to arrive, so he checked to see if there were any messages from Bill. He didn't find any, so he checked on the dogs.

"Maisey, Timmy, Josh—anything to report?" Toby asked.

"I detected Robert Brunwell working late in building three last night," Timmy said.

"Oh, what was he doing?" Toby asked. He wasn't too concerned because a lot of people worked into the wee hours when they were on a roll.

"He was downloading files to his personal communicator," Timmy said. "I determined these may have been company files that shouldn't have been released, so I invalidated them."

The door opened at the same time a tap sounded, and Roland entered.

"Hey," Roland said.

"Do you know Robert Brunwell?" Toby asked.

"Yeah, he's a design specs guy, why?" Roland asked.

"Timmy said he stayed very late last night and was downloading files," Toby said.

Roland was about to blow a gasket with the information when Angelica, Sam, Murray and Wynne came through the door.

"We've got a traitor!" Roland burst out.

"Let's get over to building three," Toby said. "Come on, Timmy. The rest of you bots stay here and monitor operations."

"What happened?" Angelica asked, her heart beating overtime.

Toby explained what the dog-bot discovered. "Could be nothing—maybe he's preparing files to take with him to TMZ. I don't know, but Timmy did something to the files so he won't be able to use them if he's thinking about going into business for himself."

They trooped down the stairs, out the side door and hurried along the winding path where, less than a year ago, thirty-seven of their coworkers fell over dead from the poison. Toby led the group into the building.

"Where's his area?" he asked.

"Third floor, northeast corner," Timmy provided.

"Lead the way," Roland said.

Timmy easily climbed the stairs to the third floor, waited on the landing for the group to catch up, then led them to Robert Brunwell's area. The design engineer was stuffing something into his backpack.

They all stared at the bulging backpack on the desk as they crowded the doorway.

"Going somewhere, Rob?" Toby asked as they came fully into the room.

"Oh, hey," Rob said, ending with a nervous chuckle as he took in the group. He tried hard not to show any fear on his face, but failed. "I'm going to meet Carlita for lunch."

Roland checked his communicator. "Uh, it's not even eight in the morning, Rob."

"Oh! Did I say lunch? I meant breakfast. We're going to grab some breakfast tacos," he said.

"Robert Brunwell has an appointment with Focus Enterprises at eight-thirty," Timmy said.

"What? Who said that?" Rob asked.

"Were you going to sell Maxwell Industries' secrets to a competitor?" Sam asked.

Brunwell was sweating. His eyes swept the group, then the dog-bot. "I'd never sell out Maxwell Industries!"

"Timmy, how many communications have there been between Robert Brunwell and Focus Enterprises?" Toby asked.

Without skipping a beat, Timmy presented a holographic timetable of Brunwell's communications to and from Focus.

"Want to explain that, Rob?" Roland asked. "These were retrieved from your communicator, so you can't say there's any mistake with what..." Roland counted, "...eight lengthy discussions with Focus."

Rob Brunwell stammered and stuttered, but couldn't come up with any explanation that could possibly refute the hard evidence before him.

"Timmy, terminate Robert Brunwell's account, swipe his communicator clean of any and all Maxwell information, and invalidate any Maxwell Industries information on his person. Monitor his communications so you can invalidate anything he tries to pass on that pertains to Maxwell Industries that he might have at his home environment," Toby said.

Angelica was busily working her communicator. When she was finished, she met Brunwell's eyes. "You have been terminated from Maxwell Industries. Your Dot has been credited with the remaining salary due to you."

"Should we have his brain swiped?" Murray asked.

"Oh! Please don't swipe my brain! I promise I will never mention the meeting with Bill Maxwell to anyone," Brunwell whined.

"You honestly think we would ever *trust* you or any promises you make?" Sam asked with a sneer.

"I made a mistake in judgment. Take me with you to TMZ!" Brunwell begged.

A beam shot out from Timmy's eyes. Rob Brunwell staggered back a full step and plopped into the office chair, his feet flopping to the floor.

"What are you doing, Timmy?" Angelica asked, freaking out.

The men started forward, then stopped.

"Rex determined I should delete the company meeting and this current problem," Timmy said.

"You talked to Rex about this?" Roland asked the dog-bot.

"Yes. My alpha suggested only a partial brain swipe. You should check his backpack and remove anything that shouldn't be in there," Timmy said.

The design engineer was splayed out in his chair, arms and legs dangling like a resting marionette puppet.

Wynne grabbed the backpack and dumped the contents onto the table that doubled as a desk. He dug through the pockets, sorted out the company items from personal items, and grabbed a sweater from the back of the chair and stuffed it into the backpack to fill it out. He distributed the company items among the group so it looked like they arrived with them in their hands or pockets.

A few minutes later, Timmy sent a short beam to the designer.

The man snorted and made a few more sleep noises before becoming fully cognizant. He spluttered for a moment, then gathered himself and sat up.

"You doing okay, Rob?" Murray asked.

Brunwell jumped to his feet. "I'm so sorry. I didn't sleep very well last night."

"We just got here," Angelica said. "I had to be firm with Roland so he wouldn't toss an eraser into your mouth."

Rob Brunwell turned beet red. "I'm sorry. Did you need something from me?"

"Nah, we just wanted to wish you well with your new employment," Sam said.

The engineer looked confused. "New employment? I don't have a new job."

"You came in to clear out your workstation," Toby said. "You're supposed to be starting with Focus."

"Focus?" Rob questioned. "They're our enemy!"

Toby shrugged. "You no longer work here, man."

Two security guards entered the room.

"Mr. Brunwell no longer works here. You may escort him to the door," Angelica said.

Brunwell looked at his former coworkers with that *deer in*

the headlights expression, picked up his backpack and walked with the guards out of the office, down the stairs and out of the building.

"Good job, Timmy," Toby said.

"Thank the Earth Timmy discovered this!" Sam said. "I wonder if there're any other employees that are going to try to sell us out?"

"I'm pretty sure the dog-bots will be on top of that," Wynne said.

"How do we know what was actually wiped from Rob's brain?" Angelica asked.

"He was fully functioning when he left here, and he couldn't recall any communications with Focus," Roland said. "That tells me Timmy did a good job."

"Let's get back to our day," Toby said as they left the room.

"I put together a form for people who are joining us in TMZ to fill out," Angelica said. "I figured we should collect data for Bill beyond just the numbers."

"What'd you put together?" Sam asked.

"Roles and responsibilities of all in their household who are coming with us, and the typical statistical information," Angelica said.

They all walked down the three flights of stairs and out the door.

"I'm heading back to my office," Angelica said. She strode off to Building Two. The men tromped over to the main building and went inside.

TOBY'S COMMUNICATOR buzzed an incoming from Angelica. "Hey, what's up?"

"Can I borrow one of the dogs? My communicator is filled

with forms, and I figured it would be quicker to have one of them chart all the data so we can get it to Bill as soon as possible," she said.

"Why don't you work with Maisey? I'll send her over," Toby said.

"Thanks, Toby. I'd typically do this myself, but we don't have a week for me to compile everything," Angelica said.

"She's on her way," Toby said.

Angelica ended the call and rushed downstairs through the two checkpoints. When she opened the door to the outside, she saw Maisey trotting along the path.

CHAPTER TEN

A pollo, Abby and the puppies stood at the back gate with Teresa and a guard.

"We are going on a hunting expedition for prey," Apollo told his youngsters, with a very stern look on his wolf-face. "You will be very quiet, stay with the pack, and watch what your mother and I do. Does everyone understand?"

Six sets of eyes were wide with excitement, and six pairs of ears were perked up.

Apollo turned to the guard. "We are ready to go."

"Message me if you need reinforcements," Teresa said.

"We will be back in three or four days," Abby said. "Don't worry, Mommy, it will be a very good lesson for the pups. Apollo and I will keep them safe."

Teresa squatted and hugged her dog-daughter. Abby was actually her dog-granddaughter, but since she raised her after Lilith passed away, she considered her a daughter.

The puppies surrounded Teresa, pawing and whining for attention.

"Everyone calm down and stop pawing your grandmother!" Apollo said.

The puppies complied for about thirty seconds, then resumed their love attack.

Teresa stood. "Okay, everyone. Have a good time. Learn a lot—pay attention to your parents."

The guard unlocked the gate with an electronic code from his communicator, and the gate slid silently to the side. "Contact headquarters when you return, and they'll open the gate for you."

"Thank you," Abby said.

The puppies rushed ahead of Apollo and were outside the gate, running wild.

"Esme, get back here! Puppy Rex, Wolf, Star, Jim—return here at once! Lulah—where do you think you're going?" Apollo was at his wits' end with his out-of-control pack.

He and Abby herded their puppies into a group.

"Sit!" Apollo barked out.

The six puppies sat, anxious to begin their adventure.

"We will be out in the wild for a week. There is no food console in the wild. Grandma and Grandpa will not bring you food if you are hungry. We will catch our own food, or go hungry. We will find safe water to drink, or go thirsty. Do you understand?" Apollo looked each puppy in the eye as he dished out the harsh reality of their little freedom.

Abby bumped her mate. "When we leave here, you will have to be very quiet. If prey hears you coming, they will run away or hide. When you make a lot of noise while hunting, you won't catch anything to eat. Your father and I spent time with grumbling stomachs in our cave. It is not easy to sleep when you don't have anything for supper."

"It is very important for you to pay attention to what

Mommy and Daddy tell you. You could die if a wild animal attacks if you don't do what we say," Apollo said.

He shook his head slightly, turned to Abby, and licked the side of her face. "We can only hope for the best."

"Follow Daddy," Apollo told the puppies. He started forward, and his six pups loped behind him. Abby brought up the rear behind her troop.

After approximately fifteen minutes of crossing the field, Esme whined. Then Lulah.

"What's the matter?" Abby asked. The puppies didn't have their Dots yet, so they could not talk in human speak. "There isn't a bathroom closet in the wild. Just squat and do your business."

Her puppies looked at her, dumbstruck. They were used to going to the bathroom closet where they did their potty, walked through the water, stepped on the mat to dry off their feet, then left the closet.

Abby huffed out a sigh. "Do you see a bathroom closet, Esme?"

The puppy looked all around, even turning in a circle.

Apollo and the others were several yards away. When he realized two of the girls were not following, and Abby wasn't behind them, he stopped and saw her talking to their daughters. He sent her a silent message through his Dot. *What happened?*

They have to go potty and I've explained there's no bathroom closet in the wild. They're having a difficult time realizing what this trip is all about. You'd better talk to the others and explain, Abby said.

Apollo sent an exasperated sigh to his mate. *They've become too domesticated for their own good.*

It will all turn out okay, Abby said.

Apollo turned to his pack. "What do you do when you have to go potty in the wild?"

The puppies looked at each other, then looked around. Apollo supposed they were looking for the bathroom closet.

"No one in the wild cares if you have dirty feet. When you have to go potty, you squat and go, or for the boys, you lift your leg and go. Right where you are. Do you understand?" Apollo looked them over for understanding.

Abby and the two girls rejoined the pack. "We're ready."

Apollo got their attention. "Rabbits and squirrels are very fast. If we work as a pack to cover all their escape routes, we will catch food."

Jim wagged his tail and made a little excited bark.

Apollo made eye contact with Abby. *I never thought I would say this, but it will be much easier when they can use human-speak. It will be noisy, but better.*

FOUR DAYS later the pack stood at the back gate while Abby contacted headquarters. The gate slid across the ground, and the bedraggled and exhausted puppies followed their parents inside the community. They didn't run wild. They didn't bark like crazy rabbits, as Apollo called them. They were too tired to misbehave.

They walked through the maze of buildings and houses until they reached their home. The front door opened, and Teresa stood there, her eyes wide with wonder at what went on during their four-day adventure. She looked them over. Apollo and Abby were the only ones who looked okay—tired, but fit.

The puppies, on the other hand, looked like they had not had steady meals. Their pelts were dirty, tongues hung out from thirst and exhaustion, and their eyes were dull from their trek.

"Oh, my... don't you look... tired!" Teresa said. She stood

aside. "Come in. Looks like you puppies could use a bath. I'll call Grandma Becky and Auntie Gayle and see if they can help." She looked at Abby and Apollo. "We'll talk when they nap."

The puppies made a beeline toward the kitchen. When they got there, they discovered there were no food or water dishes on the floor.

Teresa hurried after them. She filled the large water bowl with water. "Stand back so I can put your water bowl in the stand.

They seemed to move as a group as they backed up. When the bowl hit the elevated stand, they rushed in and formed a circle around the large stainless steel bowl. They lapped water until they refreshed themselves.

Teresa moved to the food console. "I'll give you a snack for now. We will have supper in an hour."

The kitchen door opened. Gayle and Becky stepped inside. "Oh, look at you!" Becky laughed at the sight of the scruffy puppies before her.

"We can divvy them up," Gayle said.

Becky headed down the hallway to the first bedroom. "Come on, Jim and Rex. Let's get you all cleaned up."

"Wolf, Star, come with Auntie. You'll like getting clean," Gayle said.

Teresa led the remaining two girls to the master bath. "Esme, Lulah—let's have a nice warm bath. You'll feel so much better, and you won't get your bed dirty." She put the stopper in the tub, then ran the water. She opened a cabinet and pulled out a large pump container with her homemade dog shampoo.

After experimenting with different ingredients, she settled on a formula that contained a quart of water, a cup of baby shampoo, a cup of apple cider vinegar, 1/3 cup of glycerin, and 2 tablespoons of aloe vera gel.

Once there was enough water to soak their feet, Teresa lifted each of the girls into the tub.

"You ready to get squirted?" she asked.

They were a sad sight. Esme and Lulah seemed too tuckered out to play in the water. Typically, they would be romping and splashing each other in the large tub.

Teresa used the sprayer hose to wet down Esme, then pumped shampoo onto her back, and began scrubbing her. She discovered burrs and bits of grass, and twigs in Esme's hair. She rinsed her thoroughly, lifted her out of the tub and wrapped her in a towel.

The puppy was so tired, she flopped on the floor in the towel.

Teresa washed Lulah. After everyone had dried off, they all left the bathroom and master bedroom like ducklings following their mother. They went to their bedroom and flopped on their doggy beds.

"Abby, would you and Apollo like a bath?" Teresa asked. They were joined by Becky and Gayle and four more clean doggies.

"Where's Esme and Lulah?" Becky asked.

"Napping," Teresa said.

Rex, Jim, Star, and Wolf joined their sisters on their beds.

"Yes, Mommy, we would enjoy a bath," Abby said.

"Okay, I'll wash you. Becky, would you be able to wash Apollo?" Teresa asked.

Becky looked over at Apollo. "Would that be okay with you, big guy?"

"Yes. My feet are sore from being lazy in the house. This trek was a challenge," the wolf said.

"Call me if you need me," Gayle said. She headed to the kitchen door and let herself out.

Becky and Apollo walked to the first bedroom and entered

the bathroom. She explained what she was doing so that he would be comfortable with the whole process. Becky didn't know if the wolf had ever had a bath before and didn't want to startle him.

"What I do is run warm water in the tub so there's enough to cover your feet. They'll get a nice soak and will feel good later. Then you'll hop into the tub." Becky showed Apollo the sprayer. "This will spray warm water on your body." She held up the pump bottle of shampoo and let him sniff it. "This is the dog shampoo Teresa made that will get you nice and clean. Ready to give it a try?"

Apollo hopped into the tub, and Becky began the process of cleaning him up. When he was thoroughly rinsed, she instructed him not to shake yet. He hopped out of the tub, and Becky dried him with a thick towel.

"Now you can go outside and shake off any excess water," Becky said. "Did you like your bath?"

"Yes, I feel clean, and my feet are not as sore," he said.

They left the bathroom and returned to the living room. Abby and Teresa joined him.

"Let's go out back and shake," Abby said. She and Apollo went through the kitchen dog door to the backyard.

"Everything go okay with Apollo?" Teresa asked.

"He really appreciated that someone would take the time to give him a bath," Becky said. "He seems like such an old soul in that wolf body."

The dog door flapped open, and Abby and Apollo came back inside. They joined the women in the living room.

"Tell us how your expedition went," Teresa said.

"We spent the first day laying down the ground rules of hunting in the wild," Apollo said with a huff.

"Mommy, Grandma, our puppies have no attention span

whatsoever," Abby said. "We had to tell them over and over they needed to be quiet and to stay together."

"Did the next day see progress?" Becky asked.

"We did not catch a lot of prey the first day, so they were hungry at bedtime," Apollo said. "I will thank Bill for not installing their Dots yet. It was bad enough that they whined pitifully until they fell asleep. If they had been talking—just think of how six hungry puppies would have complained."

"The second day, they seemed to understand that paying close attention to instructions would get their bellies full," Abby said. "There were only a couple of times when one of them would wander off and one of us would have to return them to the pack."

"Jim almost drank stagnant water from a pond," Apollo said. He shook himself. "We had to walk a long way before we found clean water. Then we had to find a place where we could sleep safely."

"All in all, it was a good experience for them," Abby said.

"Yes. Next time they will be better prepared to live in the wild," Apollo said.

BILL STOOD in his home office at the transfer surface with Abby and Apollo standing close by. "Apollo, you've had time to explore your Dot. Can you think of anything that would be useful for the puppies that isn't in the files?"

"No, but I'm still exploring," Apollo said.

"Daddy, can you find the movie about wild wolves that I found on GNN when I was in the lab?" Abby asked. "That's how I learned how to live in the wild, by watching my ancestors."

Bill nodded in thought. "Let me see what I can find, and I'll include those files. It's going to be a lot noisier pretty soon. Are you two up for that?"

Apollo seemed to shudder. "They will be chatterboxes. We will have to be stern and teach them when it is crucial to be quiet."

Abby bumped her mate with a shoulder. "When I was their age, I was a nincompoop. No one—human, dog or wolf—has a lot of common sense at that young age."

Bill discovered four videos through a search. These were from years in the past from organizations that documented animals in the wild. He uploaded all four to the Dot files. He also transferred the files to both Abby's and Apollo's Dots.

"I've shared four video files with you two. Apollo, you might like to watch these because they show how wolves lived in the wild," Bill said.

After a few more clacks on the virtual keyboard, the six Dots on the transfer surface blinked. They were ready to be inserted.

"Go get your puppies and I'll insert their Dots," Bill said.

Abby and Apollo left the room and walked through the house to the front door. The puppies were outside playing with the human children in the street. They gathered them up and herded them through the house to Bill's office.

"Grandpa is going to insert your Dots," Abby said, as they walked through the rooms.

"Pretty soon, you will be able to talk like we do," Apollo said. "Remember, if we need you to be quiet, you will stop talking."

They entered Bill's office as a large group.

"Who wants to go first?" Bill asked the excited puppies.

He soon discovered that was the wrong question, as six puppies bounced, yipped, barked, and shoved into each other trying to assert themselves to be first.

"Listen, you crazy rabbits," Apollo said. "Stop right now! You will go one at a time as Grandpa calls your name!"

The puppies eyed their wolf-father warily. They settled down and practiced patience.

"Star, you're first," Bill said. He loaded the Dot with her ID number into the Dot insertion tool. He looked over the group of puppies. "Your Dot will be inserted into your scruff." He used Star as an example, as he gently rolled her scruff to show them what he was talking about. "This may feel like a pinch. Ask your father. He had no understanding of the ways of man when I inserted his Dot. He didn't attack me, as his wild wolf might have done. This will not hurt you more than a sting."

Star trembled as Bill rolled her scruff for the process. He pressed the insertion tool against her scruff, pressed the trigger, and the Dot was inserted.

Star made a tiny yip sound, shook herself, and raised her tail high in the air. She had her Dot!

"You won't start talking immediately. It may take another day or two," Bill told them.

The other five puppies received their Dots and were rambunctious until their canine parents herded them out of the office.

"Grandma will begin teaching you in the schoolroom soon," Abby said.

Her six pups ignored her as they raced to the front door.

CHAPTER ELEVEN

A pollo opened his calendar app. He never thought he would ever have a use for a calendar—wild wolves didn't use anything other than the sun, moon and stars, or the seasonal changes for the advancement of time. But this was an event to document.

Tuesday at 2:00, three of his puppies, Wolf, Jim and Esme, started talking. It was chaos.

"Mommy! Wolf bit my butt!" Esme whined.

"Did not! Jim pushed me!" Wolf said.

"You stepped on my paw!" Jim said.

Wednesday, Puppy Rex found his voice. "Lulah farted!"

Lulah didn't have her voice yet. She took offense and bit his ear.

Thursday morning at breakfast, Star and Lulah joined in the racket with their tattletale chatter.

Teresa and Bill took control of the situation, much to Abby and Apollo's relief.

Teresa clapped her hands. When that didn't do any good to quiet the puppies, she opened a drawer and pulled out a whistle. All it took was one shrill whistle blow for the puppies to stop talking and focus on her. "After breakfast, you will join your mother and me in the schoolroom so you can learn how to be nice, polite puppies."

Puppy Rex jumped. "We're going to school!"

"You're too dumb to learn anything," Star said as she bit his tail.

Wolf growled at Lulah as she swiped some of his food.

Esme bonked Jim on her way to the water bowl.

"You did that on purpose!" Jim wailed.

Abby and Apollo had no idea how to control their rambunctious progeny.

"Apollo, why don't you come with me to work?" Bill asked the wolf.

"Yes! I would like to find out what you do during your stay away from the house," Apollo said. "It's a good thing Big Rex is not here right now. He would not like all this chatter."

Bill kissed Teresa on the cheek. "We're going to the office. Why don't you call Becky and Gayle for reinforcements?"

Teresa looked at the puppies and shook her head. "This will be quite a challenge. I'll see you later." Teresa focused on the puppies. "Everyone follow me to the classroom!"

There were six mats on the floor of the schoolroom in a variety of colors: red, yellow, blue, green, orange, and purple.

"Everyone choose a mat. That is where you will sit every day when we are at school. Do you understand?" Teresa asked.

The puppies charged forward. It reminded Abby of a human game she watched on the Universal Connection Platform (UCP) called Musical Chairs, but without the music. There were some scuffles when two or three puppies wanted the same square. Eventually, they each planted their butts on individual mats.

"Where is everyone?" Becky called from the kitchen.

"In here," Teresa hollered.

"I'll bring Grandma back here," Abby said. She trotted out of the room to the kitchen, "Hi Grandma. Mommy needs all the help she can get. The puppies have started talking and they're going to school now."

Becky walked beside Abby. "Oh, my. Your mom has more courage than I do!"

They entered the classroom, and the puppies swarmed Becky.

The front door announced visitors. Abby hurried from the schoolroom to the door and let Gayle into the house.

"What's that racket?" Gayle asked.

"My puppies have started talking," Abby announced.

"Oh boy," Gayle said as they walked through the house to the schoolroom. She stood in the doorway and took in the chaos.

"Return to your mats immediately!" Teresa said, using the sternest voice she could without actually screaming.

Six startled young pups ran back to their mats. Jim forgot which mat was his and tried to challenge Wolf. His brother was not willing to share, and bit Jim on the butt, sending Jim howling over to the vacant mat.

Teresa made eye contact with Becky, then Abby, then Gayle. She let out a sigh. "What was I thinking?"

REX LED the larger group back through the jungle, across the stream to Manny's village. Chief Yaotl resisted the change at first, no matter how Rex ran scenarios for him. Finally, after his people had gathered to join in the discussion, Yaotl relented to the pressure. Their numbers had dwindled to the point where they could barely support their village.

A delegation of the Nahua made the trip to Manny's village. When they emerged from the jungle, there was a riot of concerned voices from Manny's people before he sternly took control and quieted them down.

"Our neighbors, the Nahua, are here to meet you and to assess the village. We have spoken to Chief Yaotl's village about them joining us—living here among our people to strengthen both of our tribes," Manny said.

"Who will lead us?" a woman called out.

"There will be fights between factions over leadership," a man said.

"We will lose our heritage!" another woman said.

Jonas held up a hand. "There is no pure race anymore. All peoples the world over have had their family lines watered down by conquerors, migratory patterns, and most recently, the XSKL435 that killed off millions of people and animals that were outside when it was released.

"I realize you might not want to integrate with the Nahua, but you both have small villages with dwindling populations. Why not come together and share skills, duties, and learn from each other?"

There was some nodding, some heads shaking to the negative, some people clearly thinking before reacting.

"Come, meet our neighbors," Manny said.

Refreshments were offered. Women spoke with each other and discovered things they would like very much to learn from each other. The men were a little more into posturing until a conversation started about crops, hunting, trading with other distant villages, hut building and the like.

After nearly three hours of socialization and discovering the benefits of this union, the decision was made. The Nahua would move their village to Manny's village. It took careful consideration to plan where the new housing would be built.

Presently, there were only fifteen huts being utilized by the Nahua in their village. Both village delegates discussed the clearing of more land and other resources that were required prior to the move.

A small group from both parties crossed the stream and entered Yaotl's village to make a better assessment. Yaotl's people were informed of the decision and the plans being made. There were things to consider, such as the moving of looms.

The next morning, Jonas and Rex said goodbye to new friends and returned to the glider. When Jonas hovered the glider in the air, they saw a large group of people carrying housewares and whatnot to Manny's village.

"That turned out well," Jonas said. "We should have a scheduled wellness check in a year to make sure they haven't killed each other."

"I have determined that they will be happier as a new tribe. They will have more manpower to get things done, the two chiefs will balance out the leadership, and the women will have more choices of husbands," Rex said.

"Let's check in with the home base and let Harold know what we accomplished, and give him an update on the scanning," Jonas said.

BILL AND APOLLO flew over to the committee headquarters. Bill parked the glider and he and the wolf walked through the gate, then the maze of buildings until they arrived where the committee offices, and his own were located.

"This is my office where I work on special projects, Apollo," Bill said, as they walked through the dark doorway. "Lights up," Bill commanded, turning the lights on. "You can lie on Abby's cushion if you want."

Apollo walked over to the purple cushion, sniffed it and flopped down. She was much smaller than he was, but it was comfortable. "What type of work do you do here?"

Bill swung his chair to face the wolf. "Before we moved here, which was just two months ago, I ran a company with 500 employees. Then that virus killed all humans and animals that were outside, and the World Guild government discovered Abby was the last dog. She was a little puppy, younger than your pups.

He shuddered slightly with the memory of what he and Teresa had endured. "I have invented many things for the betterment of mankind, or so I thought. Now, however, some of those inventions have turned against society and have practically enslaved them. I'm trying to make amends. It will take a while before people will be able to see their freedom."

Apollo was a thoughtful listener. "All species make mistakes. Sometimes out of ignorance, sometimes forgetting the lesson they should have learned. It is good that you want to turn things around. My species would not understand the ways of mankind unless they had Dots. While it is good to have wild instincts, it is beneficial to have the know-how of the modern world."

Bill nodded. It was strange to be having this conversation with an animal. Apollo seemed to carry the intelligence of his whole decimated species.

"Why don't you and Teresa have children?" the wolf asked.

Bill let out a huge sigh. His entire demeanor changed, and Apollo sensed the deep sadness.

"A long time ago, scientists discovered they could help women to stop having babies until they wanted one," Bill said. "They took what was called birth control pills. There were also sperm inhibitors, and surgeries that helped to prevent unwanted pregnancies, such as vasectomies for men, and having a woman's fallopian tubes tied so that male sperm could not reach the eggs."

The wolf's furrowed brows made Bill pause.

"Why wouldn't you want to have babies?" Apollo asked, more than a little confused.

"There's more than one reason. Women wanted careers. It was difficult balancing careers when you had children to raise," Bill said. "Then there was the world population. Starving people. A disproportionate gap between the wealthy and the poor. The middle-class people who worked, had good incomes, owned houses, had families—they were disappearing. There was a tilt in that portion of the population leaning towards the underprivileged. It was costly to have children. People had big dreams and overspent.

"But what happened over time was that the population began to dwindle. Scientists discovered that from decades of taking various forms of birth control, many people were sterile. Teresa is one of them. Her ovaries are severely damaged, as are those of so many women today, and no one has come up with a solution. In another few hundred years, man might become extinct, which might not be a bad thing." Bill shook his head sadly. "I'm working on a solution, but you can never, ever mention this to Abby or to Teresa, Apollo. No one needs to know, because I don't know if I will be successful or not. I'd rather not have my wife get her hopes up, then be severely disappointed."

"I hope you are successful so you can experience being a father," the wolf said. "Abby and I are fortunate to have had Starlight's help, then yours. It really does take an entire pack to raise young ones."

There was a tap on the doorframe. Bill swung around to see

Harold and Percy holding back. "Come in! What are you two up to?" he asked.

"Hi, Apollo. Escaping the many voices back at the house?" Harold joked.

"This was a welcome break," the wolf said. "Teresa and Becky are going to teach them in the schoolroom. Gayle will help keep them under control."

Percy shook his head. "That's going to take some doing. Wait until Rex returns. He'll have to tune them out."

"Speaking of Rex, he sent a mind-boggling report of the entire population outside of our gates," Harold said. "I've enlisted Percy to help sort the report by occupations so we can determine the best possible way to bring people on board."

"Rex should be sending statistics from his first scans pretty soon," Bill said.

"They're down in the jungles of old Mexico right now. I think they'll be returning home soon because they said the population was very thin in those parts," Harold said.

Bill's communicator buzzed twice. He found a communication from Toby. "Hold on a minute, this is an audio file and an attachment from Toby." Bill quickly unwrapped the dog-thought program. He clicked the file.

Hey, Bill. Thought I'd give you an update on our progress. I'm sitting here with Angelica, Wynne, Roland, and Murray. <They all chirped in with: Hi Bill>. Our three dog-bots have been in touch with their alpha dog-bot, Rex. He's guiding them behind the scenes, it appears. We discovered one potential traitor who was going to sell you out to Focus, but Timmy discovered him. Rex implemented a spot brains swipe through Timmy, and we let the bastard loose. You should have seen it. The guy didn't know what happened when he left here.

Maisey helped Angelica with a spreadsheet of who's coming your way. You'll find the attachment in this correspondence. The dog-bots have received instructions from Rex on how to forge and authenticate travel documents for a company move at the request of the World Guild. This will be very helpful because we plan to strip the buildings of everything we can transport to your location. This also makes it easy for the commercial move. It will be a huge convoy, but we may break it up into having X many vehicles over X amount of days. We're still working on that, and I'll let you know as soon as we have things worked out.

Three hundred twenty people are on board. One hundred forty-three are looking for work to stay behind.

We have told everyone that they may have to share housing at first until adequate housing can be found for everyone. They're all okay with that—they just want to get the hell out of WestUS. Oh, we're going to stop by Percy and Becky's place and grab Jimbo's ashes, coloring book, and other things. A discussion was in the background, then Angelica spoke. Hi Bill, tell Becky I'll grab all their clothes. I remember her showing me her recipe binders. I'll get those as well. If you could let us know if there's anything else we should grab. The dogs will help with security issues.

Toby came back into the recording. I think that's all we have to report on. Murray spoke up. Bill, tell us what to do about our Dots. People are nervous about their money, since most of us are working people. There were some background conversations, then it seemed like an agreement about ending the audio.

We'll see you soon.

Toby signed off.

Bill, Harold and Percy stared at each other for a moment, digesting all that had been said in the audio.

"How does Rex do these things?" Harold asked, mystified. "It's inconceivable how he can forge these documents right under the World Guild's nose."

"What will they do about their Dots?" Percy asked.

"When Teresa and I defected, I literally cut ours out of our wrists," Bill said. "What I'll do for my employees is turn them off after Rex, or one of the other dogs, has rerouted their income and investments to where Rex parked mine."

"There's so much involved when someone defects," Percy said. "I'm truly grateful that Angelica and Toby are going to grab some of our things."

Bill appeared thoughtful. "If the employees who are staying behind all started looking for jobs at the same time, that would alert all sorts of agencies who would report their findings to the World Guild."

"That won't work," Harold said.

"Why don't you pay them a bonus and ask them to postpone looking for new work until all the others are here in TMZ?" Percy asked. "You might also ask them to stagger their work search so all 143 aren't searching for jobs at the same time."

Bill nodded. "That's a good idea, Percy. The severance pay and bonus would tide them over for several months. They might even consider creating their own company. I'll send a message to Toby about this."

CHAPTER TWELVE

"Rex, what are you supposed to do when company comes to visit?" Teresa asked. She looked expectantly at Puppy Rex, but he didn't respond. "Rex?"

"Do you mean me?" he asked, bewildered.

"That's your name, isn't it?" Teresa asked.

"I'm Puppy Rex," he said, clearly confused.

"You're only called Puppy Rex when Big Rex is in the room. You're not a dog-bot, so you should know who you are," Becky chimed in.

"What was the question? I forgot," Puppy Rex said.

"What are you supposed to do when company comes to visit?"

"Behave," Puppy Rex said.

"That's correct, but what does behave mean?" Teresa asked.

The rest of the puppies brows were scrunched up thinking about the right answer.

"Don't bark?" Puppy Rex put out there.

"Barking is acceptable when a stranger comes to the door, or steps on our property," Teresa said. "But you're right; it isn't acceptable after the stranger is invited into the house and introductions are made."

"Oh! Oh! What if we don't like the stranger?" Star asked, squirming on her mat. "What if the stranger smells bad?"

"That's a good point, Star. Dogs have a lot more senses than people, and your species can detect things that are not obvious to us humans. You could detect, for instance, if the stranger seems evil and is going to harm us," Teresa said.

Becky jumped the subject back to the original question. "What OTHER behaviors are expected when we have company?" She looked the group over, and called on Jim.

Jim perked up. "Don't jump on the company!"

"Very good!" Becky said. "No one wants to be mauled by a bunch of excited puppies."

"Don't steal their cookies or toys!" Esme said with her tongue lolling out of her mouth, and her tail wagging furiously.

"Esme, unless a human child is visiting, an adult will most likely not have cookies or toys. But you're on the right track. If we sit down and someone serves snacks and drinks, it isn't polite to beg for a treat," Teresa said.

"Wolf, did you want to say something?" Becky asked. The puppy looked about to speak, but shied away.

Wolf looked over his littermates. "We probably shouldn't monopolize the conversation."

Becky and Teresa stared at each other for a long blink. Finally, Teresa shook herself out of her dancing brain thoughts and focused on Wolf.

What did he say? Gayle mouthed to Teresa. She was clearly surprised.

"That's a big word, Wolf. You are correct. If someone asks you a question, you should have a two-way conversation, or more if others are involved. It is very boring being stuck in a conversation when someone talks constantly and doesn't let others share their part of the discussion." She turned to the last pup. "What about you, Lulah? Do you have anything to share about how to behave if company comes over?"

Lulah jumped to her feet. "Don't slobber on their clothes!"

Becky's face contorted. She tried hard not to laugh. "That's a good one, Lulah! Someone could have on special clothes—special to them, and it would not be polite to plop your muzzle on their lap and get it all gooey wet."

Teresa glanced at the clock. They had been at it for over an hour. She clapped her hands together. "This was a very good learning session. We will have school every day, unless there is something your grandmothers and your Auntie Gayle have to do with other human grownups."

The puppies were on their feet with tails wagging.

"Can we go outside and play with the children?" Jim asked.

Abby entered the schoolroom. "All finished for today?"

A chorus of *yesses* sounded from her litter. They thundered out of the room to the front door with Gayle bringing up the rear.

"That went well, Abby," Teresa said. "I think Wolf is more advanced than the others. He used a big word for such a young puppy."

"What did he say?" Abby asked. She hoped he hadn't said anything that was inappropriate.

"Monopolize," Teresa said.

"Huh. I wonder where he heard that?" Abby asked, just as Gayle returned to the room.

"Are you talking about Wolf?" Gayle asked. "They just got their Dots, so I'm not sure how he could have learned that word so fast. Maybe he's smart like his wolf father."

"I noticed that he's quiet and thoughtful in the school-room," Teresa said.

JONAS LANDED the glider among the TMZ patrol vehicles, and he and Rex stepped out and headed to the main buildings.

"Sure is good to be back home," Jonas said.

"Now the real work can begin with moving people inside to permanent locations," Rex said. He used his code to unsecure the door of the building, and they went inside.

They went in search of Harold, and found he and Percy in Bill's office, along with Apollo.

"Well, hello... the travelers have returned," Harold greeted.

"I have forwarded my detailed assessment of the entirety of TMZ," Rex said. He turned to Bill. " There is available housing nearby for your workforce, and I found an office building that would be appropriate for temporary use."

Rex swung around to face Harold. "There is more than sufficient housing to begin moving people into TMZ. People will be able to move into their new locations in Texas, New Mexico, Arizona, or old Mexico, start a business or find employment. With gliders, a commute to and from a work situation should not be a burden. The most difficult aspect of this process would be to determine those outside the gates who would be an asset you would want close by."

"Way down in old Mexico there isn't a whole lot of population anymore. Those places could be repopulated with new villages. There are literally thousands of acres where houses could be built," Jonas said.

"Excellent!" Harold boomed. "Let's contact the committee and set up a meeting to discuss this in depth."

Bill's communicator made an unusual sound—three short

spurts. He discovered a weak incoming transmission. "Huh, what's this about?" He opened the message and did a double-take. "Rex! Jerry's in trouble! See if you can locate his signal and find out where he is."

"Jerry is at the Southwest Recycling Center and is scheduled to be crushed and recycled!" Rex announced. "We have to rescue him!"

"Would Toby, Roland, Murray and Wynne be able to rescue him?" Bill asked. "They have the three dog-bots who could protect them and keep any satellite beams from detecting them."

"Call them," Harold said.

Bill pulled up Toby's profile and buzzed him through a secure transmission. "Toby, I need your help."

TOBY, Wynne, Roland, and Murray blended into the black of night outside the rear of the Southwest Recycling Center. Josh kept his LEDs on low light so as not to give away their presence. The men, dressed in black with black head and face coverings, crept around heaps of aluminum, glass, cardboard, and all manner of recyclables.

"I have latched onto Jerry's signal," Josh said. "It is very weak, but I can lead you to him."

"Do a perimeter scan for traps, alarms and satellite protection," Murray whispered.

"There is low-to-no security at this plant," Josh informed them. He headed around and between mountains of recycled materials and refuse waiting to be crushed and sorted.

There were no junkyard dogs because of the deadly event of 2086. Prior to that, the recycling centers typically had large dog breeds that were mean and well-trained to discourage anyone from stealing valuable junk. Laborers sorted the trash during the day. Anything that could be recycled into new products, or repaired and returned to the selling warehouses, was placed into appropriate bins.

A whole slew of people with mechanical and electrical skills worked in the big warehouse at the front of the center during daylight business hours, alongside people who shined or repainted products that were repaired. It was a good system. Anything that could not be repaired was tossed into the area where the big crane grabbed a huge mouthful and dumped it into the monstrous pit where the crusher plunged down, creating a huge pancake.

Trash that could not be reused in any way was eliminated by drones that mapped the trash heap and zapped it into oblivion. No offensive burning or fumes, just a blank space where the junk used to sit.

Josh stopped a few feet away from a huge pile of trash. "I have determined that Jerry is buried deep within this heap. It will be impossible for us to dig him out without making tremendous noise that would attract the Tranquility Force to our location."

"What are we going to do then?" Toby whispered, agitated.

"I will enlist the help of an eliminator drone," Josh said, as if the humans should have thought of it first.

The panicked, suppressed squeals from the men informed the dog-bot that they were not on board with his plan.

"There is no need for worry. I have reprogrammed a drone to help us," Josh said.

Within moments, a shiny black drone hovered in front of Josh. A silent communication took place with the LEDs on the drone flickering, then the drone went to work. It began at a shelf in the mountain of trash where some large items jutted out from the heap.

Josh monitored the drone's actions and effectively had the drone make a vertical slice through the trash on the shelf as if it were a birthday cake waiting to be served up. Then the drone mapped the pile and eliminated it. Josh checked for Jerry's signal and discovered him about a foot deep into the gigantic pile and approximately four feet off the ground.

The drone made another slice, this time horizontal, then vertical on three sides. When that area was eliminated, they saw the dog-bot.

Toby and Murray grabbed Jerry's legs and pulled him out of the compacted trash. Wynne and Roland grabbed onto the other two legs, helping them settle the practically dead dog-bot onto the ground.

Suddenly, a Tranquility Force glider swooped into the area and shone a beam of light onto them. "Raise your hands onto your heads," their PA system blared.

"We are totally screwed!" Wynne moaned as he raised his hands.

In the next instant, the glider was eliminated. One minute it was hovering thirty feet overhead, the next, a void of space.

"What just happened?" Toby asked as he searched the sky. Then his eyes flicked between the eliminator drone and Josh.

"I determined that the threat was severe enough to hamper our exit from this facility, and probably the exodus of Maxwell employees to TMZ, so I made the drone eliminate the threat," Josh said.

The drone flew off and headed back to the building where it came from.

The men shook off their fright, then shock, and focused on the task at hand.

"Stand back and I'll use forced air to clean him off," Josh said. "It would be best for you to turn your backs to avoid having debris fly into your eyes."

Within a few short bursts, the men turned back to Jerry. He was free of the encrusted bits and pieces of trash. They flipped him over for Josh to finish the job. Murray grabbed hold of Jerry.

"Let's get out of here," Roland said.

"Josh, any beams heading our way? Check for more Tranquility Force gliders," Toby said. "They might have called in for reinforcements."

"We are free to leave this place," Josh said.

They headed back to their glider and loaded Jerry inside, then Toby had the glider in the air.

"Murray, contact Bill and let him know Jerry is secured and we'll bring him with us," Toby said.

BILL'S COMMUNICATOR sounded at three in the morning.

"Who's that?" Teresa croaked out, barely awake.

Bill grabbed his communication device off the bedside table and checked the incoming message. "Toby and his team rescued Jerry. I'll contact him when we get up."

Teresa turned into her pillow. "That's good. Rex will be happy that his friend is safe."

Bill settled back onto his pillow, but his mind was too active to allow him to drift off to sleep. He listened to Teresa's sleep breaths for a minute, determined she had actually fallen back to sleep, and quietly got out of bed. He slipped into his robe and house shoes and quietly left the room.

He wandered over to the living room windows and looked up at the heavens. It was a moonless night, but the stars were brilliant across the sky. After a few minutes, Bill headed down the hall and entered his home office and lab. He slid into his chair at the transfer surface and pulled up his directory of files.

As his eyes wandered down the list of folders and files, his mind drifted to the secret project he was working on. He was sure Apollo would keep his confidence and not tell Abby. Bill worked on the problem of how to administer the formula to Teresa without her knowing about it. If she knew, her stress would ramp up, and stress contributed to infertility.

He knew her thinking process, and he didn't want her to be on high alert about every bodily twinge that typically occurs over the course of a day. She would overthink or overcompensate, adding a stress level that might be counteractive to the natural process. Bill didn't even know if he was on the right track.

His experiments included as many items found in nature as possible. He had secretly been communicating with Starlight, the Timbisha Shoshone woman who had helped Abby through the birthing process, to be on hand to deliver the litter. The Native American also watched over four pups, while Abby and Apollo made their long journey to TMZ with Star and Wolf in a saddlebag that Apollo carried across his back.

Starlight and her clan gathered the plants Bill required for his experiment, and he secretly visited her to collect them. Bill found the purest of the other items on the list and stocked those. The most difficult problem was the balancing of the amounts of each ingredient. He was going on two processes. Bill figured he was trying to reboot Teresa's ovaries from the massive destruction of birth control in her earlier years, along with the premature menopause. It was a juggling act.

Thirteen items (red raspberry leaf, stinging nettles, alfalfa, fish oil, phytoestrogens [red clover extracts], black cohosh, dong quai, evening primrose oil, kava, DHEA-Sulfate, folate, vitamin D, and calcium) were produced into small batches while he tried to figure out which ingredient required more or less. It was mind-boggling, but he was determined to solve the mystery and restore Teresa's childbearing system.

Bill and Starlight discussed the process. Should he create two separate formulas? One for the ovaries, and one for the menopause? They decided to combine the ingredients into one formula. Then there was another long discussion about the method of delivery. Should this be a liquid? Could it be slipped into Teresa's coffee or tea? Would it lose its potency in anything hot? Would it be better to deliver this in a food product?

It boggled Bill's mind trying to come up with the optimal solution. Yesterday, Starlight suggested that he turn the project over to Rex. He didn't know why he hadn't acted on that before. The dog-bot was amazing with his analytical abilities and the vast databases he had collected. Rex sucked in data from a variety of sources. Then he packeted the information, filed it according to how he might want to access it down the road, and structured it for cross-referencing.

Bill didn't know how Rex did a lot of the things he did. But because the dog-bot was self-aware and learning as he went along, which Rex referred to as *growing up*, his ability to analyze any problem down to the microns and cells was absolute. The dog-bot was like a dog with a bone. He just wouldn't let go unless he had the perfect solution.

As Bill thought about all of this, Rex entered the office and stood by his creator's chair. Bill knew that Rex would basically suck in what was on the transfer surface and begin to work on the problem. Still, he needed to set some parameters for the project.

"Rex, this is a top-secret project that we must hide from Teresa and Abby," he said.

"I understand, Daddy," Rex said.

"I have medical data from when Teresa and I found out she couldn't have children. There is a folder that contains unpub-

lished data from the disbanded CDC, the FDA, and pharmaceutical companies, which was never released to the public. It
contains reports that spanned several decades regarding how
those companies allowed toxic forms of birth control, hormone
therapies and sperm inhibitors that they promoted heavily,
which poisoned male and female reproductive systems."

Bill could sense Rex's system whirling data. "I'd like to be
able to have a child with Teresa, maybe more than one. And
think of the people we could help with this formula. They
wouldn't have to stand in line for a dog or dog-bot. They could
have a child of their own."

CHAPTER THIRTEEN

The massive caravan of commercial transporters, family transporters, ZoomBuses, and gliders was flanked by what looked like World Guild gliders. The TMZ paint shop painted eight gliders. While they only had six uniforms, they made do with World Guild patches for the two men who would wear regular clothing.

Harold, Bill, and Glacious seriously doubted that the regular Tranquility Force would dare to question a World Guild convoy. The forged permits were Rex's doing so that they would pass any inspection and verification process. When Toby, Wynne, Roland, and Murray arranged for commercial transporters and ZoomBuses, no one challenged the permits. Twenty-two commercial transporters showed up the next day at Maxwell Industries, along with six ZoomBuses.

A few families owned their own family transporters, so it was agreed those would haul anything that might not fit in the last of the commercial transporters. They had planned to section off a transporter for family possessions. Some commercial transporters had personal gliders strapped to the roofs.

Maisey, Timmy, and Josh had calculated the required number of commercial transporters for the Maxwell Industries equipment. Toby didn't know why his team was stressing out about things. They knew the dog-bots were precise, down to the number of inches left over.

It took every available employee to pack up equipment, dismantle everything that was movable and load up the transporters. The grueling preparation took five days with a workforce of more than four hundred people. While that sounded like an inflated number, the Maxwell campus consisted of four large office buildings that contained top of the line equipment and furnishings.

Toby, Roland, Wynne, Murray, Angelica, and Sam had decided they would take anything that was transportable. They well remembered the GCAUGHT and GNN news flashes that showed Bill's house literally stripped of everything. The only thing that was not completely dismantled in Bill and Teresa's house was the kitchen counters.

Angelica had Maisey create an inventory for each transporter. It was a per-building, per-floor equipment list that also included the number of boxes.

Toby, Roland, Wynne and Murray had restored Jerry. He joined the dog-bot force and was positioned outside the main Maxwell building, taking inventory. The other three dogs were stationed in front of the other buildings, all adding their inventory to Maisey's database.

Toby placed a secure transmission to Bill, letting him know they would be ready to depart within the hour.

"Make sure everyone understands there's no need to panic when they see the World Guild fleet approach. We have eight gliders to escort you," Bill said.

At the last minute, ten employees and their families changed their minds about staying behind, so they joined the massive exodus. They feared being rounded up by the Tranquility Force, or worse yet, the World Guild. If TRFS were involved, all their secrets would be opened wide and dumped into the wrong hands, then they'd most likely have brain swipes.

After every remaining piece of equipment was tucked into the commercial transporters, family furnishings loaded and separated by the dividers, there were three transporters left. People entered the ZoomBuses and settled in.

Toby, Angelica, Sam, Roland, Murray, and Wynne stood in front of the Maxwell Industries main building, mentally saying goodbye to their former lives. They saw the fleet of replicated World Guild gliders approach. The team walked back to the transporters they were assigned to guide; they boarded then the entire caravan lifted into the air and began their journey.

JONAS, in the lead World Guild glider, communicated with the Maxwell fleet drivers to arrange a safe flying block: four commercial transporters side by side flanked by personal gliders two deep, followed by personal transporters and ZoomBuses. Jonas estimated this would be sufficient for the eight fake World Guild gliders to protect.

Back at TMZ, Rex was working on his own coordination plan. He zeroed in on dog-bot Number Eight at Tranquility Force headquarters. All those dog-bots had been dead since Jerry had been decommissioned before a new lead could be brought online. Rex wasn't too worried about that because he was the only evolved dog-bot. He busied himself on this project and tweaked a few circuits, upgraded Number Eight's permissions, and brought him online as the new pack leader. The now-awake new leader's LEDs shone bright in the dark room, eliciting a nice glow.

Sixteen dog-bots waited in a dark room for Tranquility Force or World Guild to decide as to how to move forward. Since they had not thought things through before they decommissioned Jerry and threw him on the trash heap, there was no dog-bot leader.

Tranquility Force headquarters directors didn't know how to change an existing dog-bot. Plenty of people at headquarters silently cursed Bill Maxwell for making them look like buffoons over this latest shaft, but the fingers pointing back to them suggested they definitely were the idiots.

Number Eight's upgrade caused his head to crash to his chest as his system restarted to accept Rex's new commands. A few little bee-bops, twirps, and chirps sounded softly in the quiet room, then the dog-bot's head lifted. His LEDs blinked, then he turned to his new pack and woke them. After ensuring they were all fully online and functioning, Number Eight commanded his shoulder claw to open the tomb door. He led the pack out of the room, down back hallways to a fire exit door where he overrode the security settings and opened the door.

His mapping system determined their location, the distance from the front gate to the dog-bot dog door, and pinpointed where all the main exits were. He concluded it would not be safe to exit through the dog door at the gate.

He led his pack out of the building, down the steps and over to the chain length fence where he used his laser app to cut a portion of the fence away. Number Eight communicated with his pack to take precautions for their escape. They would monitor the skies for satellite beams, gliders, news Literalists, cameras—anything that would jeopardize their getaway.

Rex sent communications to Number Eight, Jerry, Maisey, Josh, and Timmy to coordinate the pickup point. Number

Eight led his pack, two abreast, keeping to the shadows where possible.

Timmy informed Toby to stop at a specific location and to await instructions from TMZ, and Rex in particular. The engineer was concerned that this was not part of the plan and could put their escape in danger. Timmy explained that there was no danger, that they had a pickup.

No amount of cajoling, arguing, or cussing provided any answers. Toby asked Jonas if he was aware of a change in plans. He wasn't. Just as Toby was getting ready to call Bill, Number Eight, and the pack appeared.

"Holy shit!" Toby shouted. He landed his transporter, exited at a run, and was joined by Roland and Wynne. "Open that last transporter and let's get them out of sight!"

Toby turned to Number Eight. "What's your name?"

"Number Eight," the dog-bot said.

"Run! We have to hurry before we're caught!" Toby said, panicking.

"There is no need to panic," Number Eight reassured him. "We will run, as you wish."

They all took off across the ground to the last commercial transporter and climbed aboard.

"You'll have to be in here for several hours until we reach TMZ," Roland said.

"Understood," Number Eight said. "We will see you again soon."

Wynne closed and secured the door.

"How...?" Wynne asked.

"I'll bet Rex did something," Toby said. "Won't Bill be surprised?"

∾

EVERY TIME TOBY saw Tranquility Force gliders, he broke out in a sweat. None of them paid any attention to the convoy since fake World Guild gliders surrounded it.

His communicator twerped an incoming message.

Murray's voice boomed. "One personal glider has failed and landed roughly. I don't think it will be airborne anytime soon."

"Okay, let me send a message and we'll deal with it," Toby said. He settled his transporter on the ground. "Attention everyone. We have a slight delay because of a glider malfunction."

He stepped out of his transporter, followed by Timmy, and walked back to where the glider had crashed softly. It was cockeyed, with one door bashed open onto the ground, and the other door in the air.

Murray, Roland, and Wynne joined Toby and Timmy. They watched a guy in his thirties crawl out of the glider.

"Hold up. We can turn it upright," Wynne called out.

"Allow me," Timmy said. His claw shot out of his shoulder and latched onto the right side of the glider that was up in the air. With a gentle tug, the glider was righted with a little thump.

Two more people, who looked to be his parents, exited the glider with travel bags in hand. The man Toby assumed was the father handed off a bag to the first guy out the door.

"Any other personal possessions or documentation in the glider?" Murray asked.

The driver ducked back inside his glider, took a few minutes to do a thorough search, then came back outside. "I'm pretty sure there's nothing left behind."

Toby turned to the dog-bot. "Timmy, eliminate any identification codes on the glider, then wipe out any traceable communications from the system."

"Will do, boss," Timmy said. The dog-bot walked around the glider and zapped surfaces with distinguishing marks. Then he stopped at the front of the craft and let loose a blast that fried the entire communication system.

Timmy returned to Toby's side. "All finished. All identifiers have been obliterated."

"Good job, Timmy," Toby said. He turned to Murray. "Which ZoomBus has room for them?"

Timmy jumped in. "If the people on ZoomBus number three would rearrange their seating, there are three available seats."

They walked down the caravan to the third bus, and Toby stepped inside. "People, we have a family of three coming on board. Can you rearrange yourselves so that they can ride together?"

There were comments of *sure thing* as people moved into different seats. The family boarded, took their seats, saying their thanks, and the caravan was airborne again.

WHAT WOULD NORMALLY TAKE nine hours to reach Blythe, California if the convoy were rolling on the ground like in the old days only took six hours. As they flew over Joshua Tree National Park, they spotted a few Tranquility Force gliders.

"Listen up, I'm pretty sure the Tranqs are going to guess where we are headed and that the World Guild gliders are fakes," Toby said, as he alerted all flyers.

Number Eight piped up. "Please release us so we can protect the convoy. We can ride with your World Guild gliders and wherever you need protection."

"Good plan," Wynne said. "Let's land."

Number Eight's pack was distributed among the gliders and transporters where they were needed, then the defectors resumed their forward movement with nerves ratcheted. They watched as the three distant Tranquility Force gliders were joined by several others.

"Yup, they've called for reinforcements!" Murray blasted out. "All passengers hold on. It may get a little bumpy!"

Toby increased his speed. He didn't dare push the glutted transporter into top speed for fear it would shift the load and cause a crash. He saw Murray's transporter out of the side of his right eye, and Roland's flanked his left.

The police force struck and blasted the caravan.

Toby engaged his communications. "Bill! We're being attacked at Joshua Tree Park!"

"We're sending our fleet. Don't stop for anything!" Bill yelled.

The dog-bots retaliated with force. A Tranquility Force glider swooped to the front of the convoy.

"You are under arrest! Stop before any lives are lost!" the Enforcer called out through his communication system.

A laser beam shot out from Timmy. The Enforcer glider crashed to the ground, spewing a ball of flames that most likely scorched the underside of Toby's glider.

"Do not slow down!" Timmy directed.

Their group zoomed through the air as the fake World Guild gliders made war on the Enforcers. The dog-bots took no pity on their former taskmasters. When the sky was clear of threats and all that remained were clumps of flames on the ground behind them, the TMZ fleet arrived. They escorted Bill's people the rest of the way to Blythe. Once they were over the boundary line of TMZ and far enough away from the US border, the commander requested them to stop. TMZ guards directed the huge procession to spread out on both sides of the old road, then park.

Toby and those up front saw the tail end of the tent and transporter city.

"Is THIS the TMZ?" Wynne squawked out, shocked. "Don't tell me we gave up our citizenship for THIS!"

"No! It can't be!" Toby said. "We saw the pictures that Bill sent, remember?"

They were out of the gliders and were joined by a couple of TMZ guards.

"Welcome to TMZ," the guard said. "It's going to take a little while for the front to process you and get you through the gate."

A TMZ glider approached quickly, landed, then Bill, Harold, Glacious, and Rex exited and walked toward the caravan.

"Toby! Wynne! Roland! Murray!" Bill and the men man-hugged and thumped each other's backs.

Rex stood several feet away from the reunion and silently called out to all dog-bots. Jerry galloped up to his old pal.

"Rex!" Jerry said, bouncing all over around Rex.

"Stop, Jerry, stop!" Rex said, turning this way and that as his best dog-bot friend celebrated their reunion.

Jerry calmed down. "What's the plan?"

They were joined by Number Eight and the fifteen dogs, and Maisey, Timmy, and Josh.

People stared at the huge pack of robotic dogs in a variety of sizes and colors.

"How'd you get the pack out of headquarters?" Bill asked, shocked, as he walked over to Rex's meeting.

"Rex was responsible for their escape," Toby said. "We picked them up on the way out of WestUS."

"Daddy, my team will speed up the validation and sorting

to get everyone situated," Rex said. He turned to Glacious. "Now that we know where everyone can be housed from my database, along with their occupations, we can scan and sort them and empty out this backlog."

"Has Percy shared his database with you? We determined the top skills that were needed and who out here has those," Glacious said.

"Yes, after we get Maxwell Industries employees sorted, we will begin with Percy's list. The bottleneck of people will be accompanied to their new lodgings as quickly as possible," Rex said.

Toby stepped closer. "So," he pointed to the end of the hopefuls wanting to get inside TMZ. "This glut of whatever—this is the waiting list? How long have these people been out here?"

Glacious and Harold appeared embarrassed.

"About four years," Glacious said.

"When I arrived, over a year ago, the end of the line was more than a mile closer to the gates," Harold said.

Bill turned to his friend and the committee leader. "We have to tackle the problem of the World Guild and take those bastards down. All these people want is to be able to live their lives in peace."

"We'll work on that, Daddy... After we get everyone settled," Rex said.

Jerry started hopping around, happy to be with his human family once again. "Where is Abby-dog?"

"She's at home with her puppies and her mate," Bill said. "I'm happy to see that you are back together again, Jerry."

CHAPTER FOURTEEN

"Here's what we'll do," Harold said, as he stood in front of the Maxwell Industries caravan. "The commercial transporters will proceed to the office building Rex found. I don't know if there will be room for everything you've brought, but that's where we'll begin."

Harold looked over the rest of the convoy. "All able-bodied men in the personal gliders and ZoomBuses will help unload and set up the building. Family members who are not employed with Maxwell will remain with the ZoomBuses or gliders until we can work out where you are to go."

Rex made a sound of clearing his throat—he deemed that since humans did that to bring attention to themselves, and to interrupt a speaker, he adopted it to fit in.

Harold looked over to the dog-bot. "You have something to add, Rex?"

"We already know where the Maxwell residents will be located. It will be best to bring them in and settle them. GPS is 100% functional in TMZ, so all that the people will require is the location of their housing, and if they require keys to open the doors."

Harold, Glacious, and Bill smirked. There was nothing like being bested by Rex, a true Mr. Know It All.

"I stand corrected," Harold said, with mirth.

"Jerry, Maisey, Josh, and Timmy will scan, sort, and provide addresses for the residents outside the gates," Rex said. "Number Eight and the pack will work from Percy's list. I suggest Number Eight communicate with the people who will be scanned, sorted, and housed. The people on the list will require time to pack their provisions. We will have to determine whether they require a transporter or other help to bring them through the gate.

"I will make an announcement to all these people outside of the gates that the process to move them into TMZ will begin in the morning," Rex said.

Glacious nodded in agreement. "Bill, your dog-bots will save hundreds, if not thousands of hours to complete this process that we were too overwhelmed to even begin to sort out. In a matter of days, Percy broke down Rex's list so the leadership could find people we needed for important jobs. We are in your debt."

"Let's get the procession rolling," Harold said.

"Would someone fly me to the gates so I can make an announcement? Otherwise, you may have a riot on your hands," Rex said.

THE ENORMOUS MAXWELL convoy moved forward, surrounded by TMZ guards in gliders. Dwellers from the tent city were irate to see the huge procession of gigantic transporters, family transporters, ZoomBuses, and family gliders slowly approaching the gates.

"We were here first!" an angry man screamed out. He threw a shoe at one of the transporters.

Rex ramped up his PA system. "May I have your attention, please?" The message was relayed via the dog-bot pack strategically located down the entire length of the tent and transporter city so everyone would hear the announcement. "Tomorrow we will begin admitting you to TMZ. You will be allowed sufficient time to load your possessions. If your transporter requires a charge, it will be provided. If you require a transporter to move your possessions, one will be provided.

"We will begin tomorrow morning at 8:00. Please listen carefully for your name to be called. This process will continue each day until the entire external community has been processed." When he was finished, Rex called the dog-bots to join him. They proceeded to the gate and entered TMZ amid the Maxwell procession.

ANGELICA, Toby, Sam, Wynne, Roland, and Murray stood in front of the office building.

"Let's go in and get the lay of the land," Toby said. "We might have to remove walls, but let's face it, this facility is way too small. I don't even know how we'd sort through everything we brought to furnish it."

Other area buildings included high-rises, short-rises, strip-centers, and everything in between.

Harold, Bill, and Rex joined them.

"This isn't going to work," Bill said, as he stared at the building.

"I have searched my database and found a better solution," Rex said. "There is an older business complex that consists of six five-story buildings. It is further away, but we should go and see it."

"Let's do that," Harold said, as he took in all the people waiting to unload the commercial transporters. "I'll go get a glider and we can see if the complex will work." He jogged toward the small glider, hopped in and took off.

Five minutes later, Harold settled a larger glider by the office building. Everyone boarded. "Where to, Rex?"

"Fly east for two miles, and we should see it," the dog-bot said.

They saw it as they approached. Sandstone-type buildings that looked in pretty good shape.

"Fly around the complex, Harold. Let's see if there are any visible problems," Bill said.

They discovered two eight-story buildings. The remaining four were five-stories in large configurations.

"This should do quite well. Let's hope the interiors are in good shape," Bill said.

Harold landed the glider, and they all exited and headed to the first five-story building. Rex triggered the electronic lock, and the door slid open. The reception area appeared to be in perfect condition.

"We're probably going to have to upgrade the electrical systems," Wynne said.

They stomped through the ground floor, climbed the stairs and explored each floor. Every building was checked out, ending with a high-rise.

"Executive offices in this high-rise," Bill said as he looked around the eighth floor.

"Let's make this the main building then," Angelica said. "We can have the communicator and the virtual storyboards on the ground floor. We'll need signage for each building, along with the security we had back in WestUS."

"Okay. Let's number the buildings and assign the departments so everyone will know where each transporter load needs to be unloaded," Wynne said.

"Better get all of our electrical engineers working on the elevators to bring them back online," Roland said. "Someone needs to see if there's a freight elevator in each building."

"I need my tools," Wynne said.

THE LAST OF the commercial transporters were unloaded. Inside the buildings, teams of employees were putting their domains back together again. While the complex was nowhere near as glamorous as the campus left behind in WestUS, there was more square footage.

Harold and Bill stood in the executive suite.

"Are you going to return the commercial transporters to WestUS?" Harold asked.

"We could. They're only leased for this move," Bill said. "Does TMZ have any use for them?"

"We should hold on to them until the people outside the gate are situated. We may need some to get everyone moved. Seems like a huge risk flying them back to WestUS," Harold said.

"You know, we could fly them to outside Blythe and leave them there. Tranquility Force will arrange for them to be returned to the lease company," Bill said.

"That'll work. You going to miss those secret mode windows in your labs?" Harold asked.

Bill's eyes twinkled. "You can never tell how this place will evolve." He started walking toward the elevator. "I'll leave them to it. My people know how to put the place together. We should focus on the big chore facing us tomorrow."

Harold pushed the ground floor button. "With Rex and Jerry taking the lead, everything will go smoothly."

They stepped off the elevator on the ground floor. Wynne and another electrical engineer were installing the Communicator. Bill recalled how a distrustful baby Abby used to avoid the electronic receptionist.

The storyboards had been installed. Mayvena, the woman who organized the tours, stood in front of the wall with a remote in hand. She clicked through the entire program to make sure every slide was accounted for. Mayvena wasn't sure how many people in TMZ would be interested in the tour of Maxwell Industries, but she would be ready. She spotted Bill and rushed over to him and Harold.

"Mr. Maxwell, how do you want to update the tour? Since we've moved to TMZ, it seems we need to rework the intro to include the company move," she said.

"Mayvena, that's a good idea. Why don't you get with Angelica? The two of you will be able to edit the slideshow to update all areas," Bill said.

"Okay. I'll contact her. Thanks, Mr. Maxwell," Mayvena said.

After the woman went back to her storyboards, Harold whispered to Bill. "Why does she call you Mr. Maxwell?"

"I gave up five years ago trying to get her to call me Bill," he said.

GLACIOUS, Pete Clearhanger, Baily Genderfer and MaryEllen Smith, along with Harold and Bill, stood on the sidelines watching the dog-bots, led by Rex and Jerry, organize the influx of people from the tent city.

"They're like drill sergeants," Glacious said, as he watched transporters fall into place in line before the huge TMZ gates.

Jerry barked out orders to the ruffians on both sides of the road.

"How am I going to get in line? That transporter is blocking my way," a man argued back.

If Bill's dog-bots were simple robots, there wouldn't be any snarky come-backs in this type of situation. But these dog-bots were developed with self-evolving intelligence. And evolve they did, with personalities that ranged from sweet to authoritarian, and everything in between.

You could practically see the growly expression on Jerry's face, who tended to be happy-go-lucky, as he turned to the man. "Back your transporter into the slot you came out of. Then turn in the opposite direction, go to the end of the lane, turn to the right and fly to the midpoint and join the lineup."

The man fumed and stomped back to his transporter.

Even Jerry had his limits when it came to dealing with those who could not think for themselves.

Rex monitored all dog-bot systems to make sure everyone did their tasks. He received an alert from Number Eight.

"I have detected and verified that one of the people on the list for skills is, in fact, a spy. How should we proceed?"

Rex approached Bill and the TMZ committee members. "Number Eight has detected a spy."

"We need to verify that," Bailey said.

"How did Number Eight validate that?" Harold asked.

"Rex, what were the protocols Number Eight used to determine this person was a spy?" Bill asked.

"The name and credentials of the man on Percy's list belong to someone who died in the pandemic," Rex said. "I will have Number Eight dig deeper to discover the actual name and credentials of this spy."

"Okay, good deal," Harold said.

"I find it interesting that the World Guild planted someone to live out here for the past four years to gather information," Pete said. "Other than spying on the surrounding people, they couldn't possibly gain information on TMZ operations."

MaryEllen contemplated. "There're most likely more spies among the population out here. Lucky for us, the dog-bots will root them out. What are we going to do with this current spy?"

"We should escort him to the boundary and kick him to the curb," Glacious said with a sneer.

Rex's system made bee-bop sounds. "Number Eight found the person of interest's salary information. His real name is Franko Schmidt, and his title is information gatherer for the World Guild, with a classification of G10."

"A G10 is of significant position within the Guild," Glacious said. He should know, as he defected from the World Guild in 2065 with a status of G18, taking many secrets with him.

"Do you have any TRFS here?" Bill asked. "It could be helpful to find out what his exact assignment was."

Harold nodded. "Sounds like a worthwhile plan." He looked to the committee to gauge their commitment or interest in Bill's plan.

"Let's invite Mr. Schmidt in for a cup of coffee," Baily said.

"His phony name is Herman Hooey," Rex said. "Mr. Hooey died while walking his dog. He had a celebrated career as a city planner."

"Who wants to go find Mr. Hooey?" Bill asked. "You can tell him his services would help move people inside the gates."

Everyone nodded yes to Bill's plan.

"Have Number Eight guide me," Harold said. "I can be very convincing when I want to be."

Bill soft-slugged him in the arm. "Sure can. Convinced Gayle to marry you, Injun Jim."

FRANKO SCHMIDT, aka Herman Hooey, sat in a comfortable small conference room with the committee members and Bill Maxwell drinking coffee. Number Eight sat over by the door, silently scanning the spy.

"So, you can see how we could use your services," Glacious said.

"I'm honored that you sought me out for my skills," the fake Herman Hooey said.

"Why don't we give you a tour of the facilities," Pete said.

They stood and made their way to the door. Number Eight joined the procession out the door and down hallways, as Glacious yapped about any number of things. They wove through the place to a section of mostly unused space and entered a room. A glass booth stood in the middle of the room. Harold shut and locked the door to make sure there was no escape route.

"What the...!" Franko/Herman squealed out as he turned to leave.

No one was getting through Harold Goanflower. At six foot eight, he was an imposing figure of solid muscle. The door would not be opened until Harold saw fit to unlock it.

"Mr. Schmidt, it looks like your game is up," Bailey said. "We'd like to invite you to spill your guts worth of information about your spying mission."

Bailey and Pete grabbed the spy by the arms and dragged him to the TRFS isolation box. Franko struggled, yelling and screaming the closer they got to the glass cage. He grabbed hold of the doorframe. Number Eight zinged his fingers with a jolt of electricity to release his grip.

They shoved him inside, closed the door and activated the TRFS mechanism.

"You'll pay for this! I'll make sure TMZ comes crumbling down!" Franko swore.

The committee waited a full five minutes for the TRFS to take effect. Then they started the inquisition.

"Name, rank and title," Harold barked out.

"Frrraaannnkkkooo Shhhmmidddttt. Geee Ssssss tennnn. Innnn forrrr maaayy shunnn gaaa therrrr eerrrr," Franko managed to get out.

"Oh, boy, this is going to take a while," Glacious said.

"Why don't we have the bots go through his transporter while we have Mr. Schmidt entertained here?" Bill suggested.

Everyone nodded.

Bill engaged his communicator. "Rex, have a couple of dog-bots and one or two guards search the spy's transporter. Let's see what they can find. Tell them to get back to me as soon as possible."

"I will put together a team and they will make discoveries," Rex said.

CHAPTER FIFTEEN

Timmy, Number 12, and two TMZ guards (Edward and Bob) entered Franko Schmidt's transporter. They found the normal household contents of someone who had pulled up roots and moved rather quickly. Stacked boxes, a basic food console on a bureau, furniture arranged to accommodate sleeping, lounging or sitting.

Edward headed toward the boxes where paper was sticking out.

Bob turned to an overly neat area in the midst of the chaos. It was a wall of small tables and other flat surfaces with other things stacked on top. He stared at the wall.

"This looks a little odd," Bob said. He left the transporter with Timmy following him. "What do you think, Timmy? That wall seems to be about here." Bob pointed to a spot that left at least six feet unaccounted for behind it.

Timmy scanned the area. "There are electronics behind that false wall."

They went back inside and approached the fake wall.

"There must be a way to access that," Bob said.

Edward stopped what he was doing and looked over to Bob and Timmy. "What'd you find?"

"There's something in back of this wall. Timmy scanned it from outside and said there were electronics back there," Bob said.

Number 12 and Edward joined them in front of the wall of furniture, then Number 12 assessed the area.

"I have determined that this wall must swing out this way due to how the empty floor space is over here," Number 12 said.

They all studied the floor space.

"Yeah, that makes sense. Let's see if it swings open, or if there's a switch," Bob said. He walked to the edge of the wall and felt along the furniture, but didn't find anything. Then he grabbed hold of a chest of drawers and gave it a little tug. The wall moved slightly.

"Here it is!" he said. "Give me a hand."

Edward was taller than Bob, so he reached over Bob's head and grabbed a small table stacked on top of the pile. They pulled at the same time, and the wall swung out. They stood, shocked at what they saw. It looked as if it would rival the control center where TMZ kept the World Guild at arm's length through their careful scanning.

"Harold's not going to believe this!" Edward said.

Timmy and Number 12 took over. They scanned and inventoried everything. Timmy sent pictures to Rex.

Rex used his control system to display holographic pictures of what was found in the spy's transporter.

"How do we want to handle this?" Glacious asked the committee.

"First, we're going to find out what data was captured and what was done with it," Bill said. "You don't want to be hasty.

Throw that guy in lockup and have one of the dog-bots keep an eye on him."

"Now that we know about this secretive area, every transporter will be scanned to detect any others," Harold said.

"Rex, send this new criteria out to the pack," Bill said.

APOLLO WAS outside the gates wandering around where he and his family had spent their four days in the wild. He wasn't hunting for game; he just wanted to feel less hemmed in by humanity. Living in a house with humans was totally new to him, and he was still learning the ways of mankind. He was grateful for the files Bill had loaded into his Dot. There was a lot to learn.

The wolf wondered what his wild pack family would have thought of this way of life, if they had survived. They avoided people as much as possible. He was raised to believe that humans were dangerous predators and that they destroyed the wild and wildlife every chance they got.

He was conflicted. When he met Abby, they were both relatively young with very little life experience. She taught him to trust Starlight—he had to fetch the female human in the middle of the night when Abby was birthing their pups. Starlight had been kind to them, bringing them food, fetching water in the bowl from the spring that ran down the mountain. She was a gentle human being.

Apollo was lost in his thoughts as he walked across the field of scattered wildflowers. He tripped over something, recovered and looked to the ground. Something in the ground was blinking. He stared at the device and wondered what it was. A thought occurred to him: maybe it was spyware from the World Guild? He had listened to many conversations of Bill, Harold, and Abby's grandparents about the way the global government enslaved people. He didn't understand some of the terminology, such as global or government, but he had a lot of files to sort through in his Dot. Right now, he felt it was his responsibility to alert Bill about this discovery.

He found Bill's name and picture in his head within the contact directory. This type of action was unfamiliar to him. He had never called anyone with this electronic equipment, not even Abby. He and his mate used silent dog language.

His mind nudged Bill's picture. Immediately, Bill spoke to him from wherever he was. Apollo looked around to discern that Bill was not outside near him, so he assumed he was in the communication thing in his head.

"Apollo? Is that you?" Bill asked, somewhat surprised.

"Bill, I am out in the wild and I found this thing in the ground," Apollo said.

"Look at it, then inside your communicator in your head, you will see this square with an X inside it. Blink on that, and it will take a picture," Bill said.

The wolf thought about a square and an X. He went into the dictionary app and read what a square was and saw an example. He repeated that for the X. Apollo was glad that Abby told him about the dictionary so he could look up words he didn't understand. Apollo found the symbol in the Dot structure and blinked hard at it. He heard a snick.

"That's it," Bill said. He was quiet for a minute, then he yelled across to someone, wherever he was. "Harold! Apollo found some spyware outside the gates!" Then, to the wolf. "Apollo, stay where you are. We're on our way. I have your signal. We'll find you!"

"Okay," Apollo said. He gazed down at the blinking thing, wondering what it was actually doing. He figured blinking meant something was happening inside it, but he knew so little about gadgets and other things. Apollo didn't understand how the food console worked, only that it delivered prepared food. Abby said it was like magic. He had to look up that word and read the definition ten times before he understood what magic meant.

As he pondered all these things, a glider approached and landed nearby. Bill, Rex, Harold, and Pete hurried over to him.

"Let's get a good look at this," Bill said.

Bill and Harold squatted and looked the device over. Pete looked over their shoulders.

Rex scanned the device. "It's collecting our beams to determine how the World Guild security can weaken them and get through our defenses."

Apollo overheard some words from Harold that he had never heard before. He thought they were bad words, what Abby called cuss words, but he wasn't sure. He'd ask her when he returned home.

"Rex, you'd better scan the entire field and see if there are any more out here," Harold said. The big man turned to Apollo. "You did good, Apollo. We're grateful you caught this."

The wolf's brows scrunched, thinking about what Harold said. "I didn't catch it. No one threw it at me. It was buried in the ground."

Bill ran his fingers through the wolf's thick coat. "It's just an expression, Apollo. It means you found it."

"Oh," the wolf said. He was learning that the human language had so many twists and turns.

"I have determined that these devices are spread out every 400 yards," Rex said.

Bill and Harold share a glance.

"What should we do about this? Want to leave them and reconfigure them?" Bill asked.

"Why don't we ask the spy if he planted them and what his goal was," Pete said.

Harold nodded. "Good idea. Let's return to the complex and see what we can pull out of Schmidt."

"Should I stay here?" Apollo asked.

"No, that isn't necessary. Rex has plotted the entire field to show the devices," Bill said. "Are you going to keep exploring, or do you want a ride back?"

"I'll return with you," Apollo said. He liked gliders. It gave him a bird's-eye view of the ground. None of his wild kin had ever experienced this, as far as he knew. He wanted his pups to be much more worldly than he was and thought they were already off to a good start.

Ever since Teresa started teaching them in the schoolroom, they were learning about time. Both types—the time of day that a clock or their communication devices showed, and the time passing as in days, weeks, months, and years. In his wild life, the only passing of time that was important was sunrise, sunset, and the placement of the moon and stars in the sky for navigation. Only, he didn't know what navigation was back then.

Apollo stayed quiet while the glider flew over the field. When it stopped at the back gate, Pete entered a code into his communicator that was sent to an electronic device. He didn't understand why they didn't just fly over the gate, but Bill had explained there was some kind of barrier. The wolf squinted his eyes, but he didn't see anything.

The glider flew through the opening and Pete parked it among the other gliders. They all got out and walked through the maze to a secured door. Bill rested a hand on Pete's arm to stop him from opening the door.

"Let's have Apollo try to open the door," Bill said. He turned to the wolf. "Think you can open this door?"

Apollo gave the door a hard look. He had watched Abby

open secured doors, so he figured there was something in his communicator that would trigger the door open. He approached the door to see if there were any identifying words or numbers. He saw a faint B5 etched on the panel, then looked through the place where he found Door Codes. He blinked hard on B5, and the door popped open.

Bill thumped his back. "That's great, Apollo! Now you won't have to worry about being locked out or having to wait for someone to come open the door for you."

The wolf looked at Bill. "There's a lot to learn."

They all marched through the open door. After Harold cleared the threshold, the door closed and the electronic locks engaged.

"I'm going home," Apollo announced. He turned to the right, as the men turned to the left.

"Thanks again, Apollo. You did good work today," Harold said.

AFTER INTERVIEWING THEIR CAPTIVE, they discovered he had planted fourteen devices in a semicircle three deep. Schmidt hadn't gotten anywhere with decoding the beams. The team had discovered three other spies in the outside population who were being rounded up.

One spy tried to get away in his glider, but it hadn't had a full charge in months. After lifting off quite jerkily and flying twenty yards, it thumped to the ground where the spy was intercepted by three of Number Eight's dog-bots. They used shock therapy to keep him secured in their little circle.

One dog disengaged the glider's communication system because the spy was trying to send a message to Tranquility Force and to the World Guild. While he was at it, he sent the incoming and outgoing messages he found to the entire pack's alpha, Rex. It was important to be useful.

～

AFTER ALL FOUR spies had been subjected to the TRFS, their transporters searched thoroughly, and the secret walls of electronics coded for double-agent spying, the TMZ committee agreed to let Rex do a brain swipe just to remove the segment of the mind that dealt with the capture, TRFS, and the interrogations. The men were deposited in their transporters and left to "wake up" from the enforced nap. At that time, they would be "discovered" and escorted to the TMZ border and sent on their way.

All in all, it was a good day. Number Eight's pack was spread out on both sides of the road leading to the TMZ gates. The first group of people was scanned thoroughly and admitted to their new region, house keys in hand. It was a steady procession. Several people needed help to get their transporters charged. One transporter had to be towed through the gate and deposited at their new house.

Everyone was grateful to be a part of the community. Freedom was a new concept. People were so used to being hemmed in, squashed by the global government, that it took a while before they realized no one was going to punish them for crazy infractions and take their money away.

Each new family admitted into TMZ was required to attend a mandatory virtual set of classes to understand how things worked in the free world. The committee required a repeat viewing within two weeks to ensure everyone understood what they had watched and learned.

After two weeks, the skilled people on Pete's list were called to the committee building. They were offered jobs, set up for training, supplied with uniforms, and given a work schedule.

Electricians, electrical engineers, coders, mechanical engineers, and designers were quickly absorbed into the Maxwell company to replace some of the people who stayed behind in WestUS. TMZ would benefit greatly with Bill's innovative company running at full speed. Everything they created would be for the greater good of freedom.

More than three dozen men and women were hired to train as TMZ border patrol officers. The TMZ workforce that built and maintained the patrol gliders took on more employees to keep up with the ever-increasing demand for gliders. Jerry helped with the plans for increasing glider speeds so patrols could apprehend pirates, bandits, and trespassing World Guild or Tranquility Force.

The committee and Bill met many times to discuss updating security, especially since Apollo had discovered the planted spyware.

"I want to open a dialog with you about taking the helm to restore the US, and the world—restoring rights people have lost, getting rid of the Dot, or at least changing the coding to restore it to my original vision for the software," Bill said. "We need to take down the World Guild, plain and simple."

Glacious stared at Bill, thinking about what he had heard. "We can't eliminate the Dot. Our entire communications systems, salary and payment transfers, along with too many things to list, depend on it."

"I know how you feel, Bill," Harold said, "but how would you even go about that?"

"The communicating system that people wear, like old time watches, or buttons, is practically the same thing, without the spyware. I realize that I can't do a global update at this time because people wouldn't get paid out in the world," Bill said.

"But we can start working on it and experiment right here in TMZ to make sure it works properly."

MaryEllen pondered Bill's words. "We could effectively block the World Guild from using the Dot to arrest people for unwarranted purposes."

Pete nodded. "Can you provide a list of what the Dot currently handles and what you propose to change?"

Bailey tapped the table. "I'd like to propose we establish TMZ as a country. Register it with the World Guild. Let them see what's coming. We've been called a region, an outlaw area, and a territory—let's establish our country!"

They all nodded.

"Bill, one of the first things we need to do is to reverse this poppycock that you and Teresa are dead," Harold said. "That will open up a huge door for us by exposing the lying ways of the World Guild. You are one of the most public figures, recognized by everyone everywhere, not just in the US, but around the world. I feel certain people will be outraged. It could be just the push to topple the government."

"That's all fine and good, but how will the World Guild be replaced? There has to be structure, otherwise lawlessness could run rampant," Glacious said.

Pete's eyes widened with an idea. "TMZ could become the new global government!"

Everyone shook their heads.

"No, the global government should be created by delegates from each country. All people should be represented. In the US, many people are unrepresented, like the mountain people who were ripped from their homes to "fit in" with society. Then there are the Native people who had to flee for their lives," Bill said.

Heads nodded.

"There's a lot to think about before we try to storm the gates electronically," Glacious said.

"We should have Rex consider this problem," Harold suggested. "He would be impartial, and he would tackle this as a challenge, looking at all aspects of the current government and the past governing bodies from around the time when people took back the country."

"Good idea," MaryEllen said. "Rex would be unbiased and unemotional in building a report. He would go for facts first."

Again, heads nodded. They stood, stretched, and left the room.

CHAPTER SIXTEEN

A pollo sat in the back of the classroom, while Teresa and Becky taught his unruly pack. Gayle helped when she was available. The puppies were only four-and-a-half months old, and their attention span was as loose as a dandelion puff. One good breeze and the seeds flew through the air. With his progeny, all it took was one of them to go off focus for a split second, and the whole pack was in total chaos, with Teresa blowing her whistle and Becky clapping her hands to get them in line again.

The wolf shook his head, then yawned. He trotted to the front of the class and barked soundly. The puppies sat at attention, eyeing their father warily. They were in trouble, and they knew it.

"You will stop behaving badly! Do you want to be like mindless rabbits and just hop in a circle the rest of your lives, or do you want to be smart like your mother?" Apollo asked. "Your grandmothers are trying to teach you the ways of humans, so you can rise above the wild pack I was born into. The next time one of you acts up, I will take you out to the field and leave you there to survive on your own!"

The pups cowered down on their mats. They remembered the wild. There was no food console, or metal bowl of nice clean water, or bathroom closet where they walked through water, then spongy artificial grass to clean their paws. Nasty bugs bit them and dug into their fur. It was blazing hot—way too hot to sleep on itchy grass. They settled down and all snouts pointed forward, ready to learn.

Apollo shared a glance with Teresa and Becky. "Threats are powerful."

"We appreciate your intervention," Becky said. "They are a handful at this age. I pray they are more like you and Abby than their grandfather, Jimbo."

Teresa led the puppies through counting from one to ten. "Each of your front paws has five toes. That little toe in back of your regular toes is called your dewclaw. Some people call that your thumb."

The pups looked at their paws.

"Don't worry if you don't have dew claws on your paws. Not all dogs have them," Teresa said. "Your back feet typically have four toes. If you have dewclaws on your back paws, those are considered your big toe."

The pups stood and scrunched around to view their back paws.

"Does everyone have dewclaws on their front paws?" Becky asked.

"I do!" Esme exclaimed.

One by one, the puppies confirmed their dewclaws on their front paws.

"How about your back paws?" Becky asked.

"Yup! I've got them," Jim barked out.

"Okay, this next part will be a lot easier. You are going to be able to count all the way up to twenty!" Teresa said. "You'll learn a part of the multiplication table at the same time. If each of your paws has five toes, that means you have a total of twenty toes."

Teresa took a moment to check for attentiveness. Everyone seemed to be on board and interested, even Apollo. "What if someone asked you to put seven apples in a basket? How would you count them accurately? Does anyone know how to do this?"

Wolf exclaimed. "I do! I'd gather one for each toe on my right paw, then two more for two toes on my left paw!"

"How many toes does that leave on your left paw, Wolf?" Teresa asked.

"Three!" Wolf said, excited.

"That's correct! What a smart little pup!" Teresa said. "Does everyone understand what your brother did?"

The puppies were staring at their paws and mulling over what their brother said.

Teresa walked over to Becky. "Wolf certainly got the best of his parents' intelligence. We need to keep an eye on him." She turned back to the class. "Now, we're going to do a fun exercise that will help you to count to twenty. Are you ready?"

"Yes!" they all chorused loudly.

"Okay. This may take some practice, but you'll get it," Teresa said. "Lift up your right front paw. Does everyone remember right from left that we learned yesterday?"

Becky hurried over to Star. "This one, honey." She tapped Star's right front leg. She glanced around at the pups. Everyone had their right paw in the air.

"Okay, when you put your paw down, say FIVE!"

The pups called out Five.

"Now, pick up your front left paw and say, TEN." She

looked around the room before proceeding. "Pick up your rear right paw and say, FIFTEEN."

There were a few wobbly pups, but they all managed the exercise.

"Last, but not least, pick up your rear left paw and say, TWENTY!" Everyone followed the exercise. "Okay, now let's all go a little faster. Five, Ten, Fifteen, Twenty!"

The puppies enjoyed the lesson. When Teresa excused them at the end of the class, she heard a couple of them counting as they left.

THAT NIGHT at the dinner table, Teresa gave a progress report to Bill. "Wolf is displaying elevated intelligence. He's using much bigger words than his siblings, so I think his language skills are more advanced. He also understands math."

Bill thought about that as he chewed steamed green beans. "Sounds as if he's absorbing the information in his Dot quicker than his littermates. Then again, his parents are intelligent. Apollo is just coming into his own, but that wolf is smart. How are the others coming along?"

Teresa pondered the question. "They're average at best. Puppy Rex didn't realize I called on him because I didn't use *Puppy* before his name." She shook her head. "I know it's early, but I hope they all learn how to behave, understand right from wrong, know how to sense danger—get prepared for life on their own, if it ever came to that."

Bill kept his thoughts to himself. It wouldn't do any good to mention that she was being influenced by her motherly instincts. His mind churned about how he would go about getting his wife to take the secret formula he was working on without her knowledge.

"Give it a couple of months, hon," he said. "They're very young right now. Remember, just being capable of thought and speech in human form is an evolutionary miracle. Some are going to grasp the concept quicker than others, and some may not excel. You're going to have to be patient in your expectations and teachings."

Bill stood, crossed to Teresa's side of the table. He bent and kissed her. "I'm going over to the new complex for a couple of hours."

"Okay. We're going over to Becky and Percy's," she said.

"Rex, Apollo, do you want to go to the new Maxwell complex with me?"

Apollo stood. "Yes, I would like to see the new complex."

Rex climbed off his dog bed, which sported his name in red embroidery. "I'm ready."

Bill and the dogs left the house and got into the glider and took off. They flew over the neighborhood to the new business complex two miles away. He settled the glider into the parking area and noted more than a dozen gliders in the lot.

"Looks like Toby and some of the crew are still here," he said.

Bill held the front door open for the dogs. The Communicator swiveled on the built-in stool and acknowledged them with flashing lights.

Apollo stopped in his tracks and emitted a low growl. His hackles rose along his back. He didn't know what he was seeing.

"It's okay, Apollo. This is the Communicator, our mechanical receptionist for the company. She doesn't have any mobility other than swiveling on her platform," Bill said.

The wolf let out a snort of distrust. He hurried along to the elevator where Rex had the door opened through his electronic connection. When Apollo turned and faced front, he curled his lip in a silent snarl as he spied the mechanical abomination before the door zipped closed.

They rode to the eighth floor in silence and stepped out to see several guys moving equipment.

"Hey, Bill," Wynne called out.

"What are you guys doing?" Bill asked.

"Rearranging things. Roland wants to take out a wall or two to make an executive conference room," Wynne said.

"Where's Toby?" Bill asked.

Wynne nodded. "Through that door."

"We'll catch up with you," Bill said. "Come on, Apollo, Rex, let's find Toby."

They walked through the archway Wynne pointed out and found Toby.

"Like your new office, boss?" Toby called out. He had replicated the Maxwell Industries office from WestUS.

Bill's face lit up with a huge smile. "Looks good. Almost like I'm back in the US!"

Rex walked around. He stopped by the transfer surface. "This needs to move 9.2 inches to the left for exact placement to match your old office."

Toby and Bill shared a look that noted their disbelief at the dog-bot's serious concern that something was not spot-on perfect. Bill held up his hand before Toby said anything. He knew how sensitive Rex could get when someone questioned his good intentions.

"It's okay, Rex. Let's make the TMZ office less perfect than the US office, okay? The room looks good, don't you think?" Bill asked.

Rex scanned the room with his eyes. "Yes, everything is in place. It is quite balanced. Should I recalibrate any of the equipment?"

"I hadn't thought about that. It wouldn't hurt to make sure

the lab equipment is up to specs," Bill said. He turned to Toby. "The dog-bots will be able to help with that chore campus-wide. Some recalibrations could take a while to get right. We found that out when I was trying to create a large batch of the formula to make the transporter invisible. We were off by a few grams of something."

"Sodium hydrogen carbonate, or as you call it, baking soda," Rex piped up. "It was off by one microgram because the equipment required an adjustment."

Toby stared at Rex, keeping his mouth shut. After a moment, he finally engaged in the conversation. "I'll send a message to all the teams suggesting they use the dog-bots for that purpose. We need our equipment to function properly."

Apollo wandered around Bill's new office. "Will you work here now instead of the headquarters building?"

"Yes," Bill said. "If they need me for anything, we can either have a virtual meeting, or I'll just fly over there. It's only two miles away." He inspected the cool cabinets that held his industrious bees and the cabinet that held the tiny backup discs. "I'll bring some dog beds over here tomorrow."

Angelica and Roland barged into the office. "Hey, Bill! Do you like the new space?"

Bill looked around and nodded. "Yes, I do. Are you all settled into your office, Angelica?"

"Just about. Maisey is helping me get things organized. I love working with her!" Angelica said.

"Are you in this building? We need to have a new list created so everyone knows the new contact information and office locations," Bill said.

"Should we include home address as well?" she asked.

"That would be helpful since everyone is new to TMZ," Bill said. "Better also include a section to show the people who stayed behind."

Angelica made notes. "Okay, we'll get on this." She walked over to Apollo and patted his head. He wagged his tail. She was about to leave when she thought better of it. She walked over to Rex and patted his head, then left the office.

Bill turned to Roland. "Show me where you want the executive conference room."

They left Bill's new office and walked down a hallway.

"I figured we could tear out the walls between these three small spaces, unless you see a need for them," Roland said.

"Is everything else in place? All offices and spaces set up to accommodate everyone?" Bill asked.

"Building six is actually half empty," Toby said.

"That could come in handy down the line," Bill said. "We could use it as manufacturing space, storage, or something else entirely. If everything is in place, then go ahead and remove those walls."

Bill sat down at his transfer surface and swiveled his chair, looking around his new office space and getting the feel for it. He liked it. The Maxwell CEO had come to terms with abandoning the WestUS complex that he had built from the ground up. Now that all his people were here, or at least most of them, he felt they could carry on.

A loud external alarm sounded.

Rex sent instructions to all dog-bots to push back any beams or anything else the World Guild or Tranquility Force attempted.

Apollo jumped to his feet. He ran over to a window, growling. "What is that loud noise?"

Toby, Roland, Wynne, and Murray thundered into Bill's office.

"What's going on? Is TMZ under attack? What should we do?" Murray belted out.

Wynne and Apollo looked out the window. "See anything?"

"No, but I do not know what to look for," Apollo said.

Bill tackled his transfer surface with Toby, Roland, and Wynne looking over his shoulder. They discovered that the World Guild was attacking TMZ security.

Bill connected to the headquarters and raised Harold. "What's going on? Have you got this covered, or should we hop on board?"

"We've got it. They were trying a new tactic," Harold said. "We figure they're upset because we found their spies and kicked them out, plus we pulled up those devices in the field. Planting that double-agent spyware in those transporters was a good idea. We're collecting data that will help keep us one step ahead of them."

Rex approached Bill. "The dog-bots are collecting data. We will keep TMZ safe."

"Did you get that, Harold? Rex and his pack are collecting data."

"Tell Rex we will compare notes," Harold said.

"I'd better go," Bill told Harold. He disconnected their communication and turned to his employees. "Everything's under control. The World Guild was trying a different trick to try to breach TMZ security, but they discovered that we're too advanced for their child's play. Rex and his pack are helping Harold."

"They just don't give up, do they?" Murray asked.

"I'm looking forward to the day that the whole organization tumbles and falls," Bill said.

"Yeah, and hopefully, we will be behind that process!" Toby said.

CHAPTER SEVENTEEN

I t took a while for Apollo to calm down from the nerve-wracking noise. He finally left the window and curled up on the floor near the transfer surface.

Rex was a different story. He had only ever shown one instance of being freaked out, and that was when he and Jerry had carried out their plan for Rex to defect. Typically, he shouldered on and worked whatever problem cropped up until it was resolved.

"Is Jerry going to come and live with us?" Rex asked.

Bill hadn't thought about where Jerry or Number Eight and that pack would live. "Sure, Jerry can come live with us. We have to find a place where the pack can shelter at nighttime."

"There's enough of them, including Maisey, Timmy and Josh, to have two per building here in the complex, some by the gates, and a couple inside headquarters. Still leaves a couple left over," Murray said.

"Two per building seems a bit much," Bill said. "There's a total of nineteen. We should come up with names for them, too.

Maybe keep Number Eight's pack at headquarters until they are needed somewhere."

"I don't think Angelica's going to give up Maisey," Toby said.

"We'll figure it out," Bill said.

Toby, Wynne, and Murray left to go work on the conference room.

Bill turned to his transfer surface and pulled up the secret file with all the criteria for Teresa's fertility. He contemplated the problem he faced in getting the solution into her without her knowledge.

"Rex, help me with this problem about the secret formula. Would it be effective if it were reduced to something like an essential oil?" Bill asked. "And if so, how many drops would it take for a daily dose?"

The dog-bot churned through the long list of ingredients and went through several possibilities. He determined that they could take one of the small batches Bill had created and reduce it to an essential oil base. Then he went to work calculating the dosage. Within four minutes, he was satisfied with the solution.

"I have determined the ideal dosage would be nine drops," Rex said. "You will not be able to add the drops to any hot drinks or hot foods because the heat would evaporate the formula."

Bill thought about that for a moment. He was stumped. After twirling it around in his head, he thought of a possible solution. "Maybe I could tell her it's an allergy formula that she can't share with anyone else. She has been sniffling lately."

"What if the sniffles don't stop? Then she might not continue to take the formula," Rex said.

"Could I put them on her toothbrush? Would toothpaste destroy the formula?" Bill asked.

"I have watched Mommy T during her morning and

evening rituals," Rex said. "She runs her toothbrush under hot water."

"Let's think about it. I'm sure a solution will come to one of us," Bill said.

BILL, Rex, and Jerry entered the house at the kitchen from the holding area, formerly known as a garage.

"Abby, Jerry's here!" Bill called out.

Abby, Apollo, and the puppies were followed by Teresa.

"Abby dog!" Jerry greeted.

The puppies romped around him, leaving Rex alone (for once). Jerry romped around the kitchen with the puppies as the adults watched.

"Order! Sit! Stay!" Rex belted out.

Teresa rested her hand on Rex's back. "Rex, it's okay. They are playing. Jerry likes to play. He will fit in here perfectly."

Rex glanced up at her for a long moment. He quietly left the room.

"Oh boy, I guess I offended him," Teresa said.

"He still has a lot to learn, and I hope he understands that we are not criticizing him," Bill said.

"I will go talk to him, alpha dog to alpha dog," Apollo said.

Bill and Teresa stared at Apollo.

"That's a good idea," Abby said. "He values your leadership."

Apollo left the kitchen.

"I'll study the coding differences between Rex and Jerry. There must be something I can tweak in Rex's personality codes that will tone down his seriousness," Bill said.

"I don't think that's a good idea," Teresa said. "He's self-evolving and has matured over the past year. Let's see how he responds to Apollo."

~

REX WAS WORKING from his dog bed churning code when the wolf approached. He expected Apollo to continue past him to wherever he was headed, so he was surprised when the wolf stopped at his dog bed.

"Would you be interested in joining me for a walk in the wild?" Apollo asked.

Rex's LEDs lit up as he assessed *walk in the wild*. He had references to what *the wild* meant to the wolf, and he had researched *the wild* when Abby escaped the lab. She had to find food, water, and shelter to sustain herself with no knowledge of how to do those things. She had kept under the shadows to avoid capture from Tranquility Force and the World Guild as she made the long journey to the mountains where she found her cave, then later met her mate.

"Yes, I will join you in the wild," Rex said, as he unfolded his legs and stepped off the bed.

He followed Apollo to the front door, went around him, and released his shoulder claw to open the door. Rex closed and secured the door after Apollo trotted outside. They walked towards headquarters, entered the maze of alleys, the personnel glider parking lots, then the fleet parking lots, outside storage where pallets and whatnot were stacked, finally reaching the back gate.

Rex applied the gate codes, and they exited the TMZ-fenced property. They walked in silence, Apollo steadily sniffing the air, his senses alert for enemies and secret attacks.

The wolf broke the companionable silence. "Are your sensors on the lookout for danger?"

"Yes," Rex said. "My sensors scan the area for enemies from the air and elsewhere."

"Wolves use their noses, eyes, ears, and instincts to make sure they aren't attacked by an enemy," Apollo said. "Sometimes, though, we don't detect an enemy attack. They might be downwind or upwind, and our noses miss the scent. When we are young pups and are looked after and taught by the pack, it is easy to get misguided by someone who is jealous, or has their own agenda."

Rex glanced over to Apollo as they walked. "Wolves get jealous?"

"Oh, sure," the wolf said. "If there are multiple litters, each mother has their hopes and fears for her pups. Sometimes, pups fight among themselves for higher ranking. Abby and I worry about our pups. They romp and play, they learn in the schoolroom; but they don't have any other litters to interact with, so they don't know how different behaviors are viewed by a rival litter."

"I see," Rex said, but he didn't, really. He was running programs to try to understand what the wolf meant.

"Take Jerry, for instance. He is a machine, but he acts like a puppy around my young pack," Apollo said. "He engages in the activities they inspire, if only to join in."

"Was my reaction an overreaction?" Rex asked.

"You are two different dog-bots," Apollo said. "You are the big brother, the alpha of your large pack, and you are used to delivering orders and making sure things get done."

Rex tried to compare himself to Jerry. He internally admitted he was perhaps too stuffy. The dog-bot wondered if he should reconfigure his responses. He didn't feel like he needed to join in all the romping, which he wasn't interested in, but maybe he should not be harshly forthcoming in his statements.

"I will attempt to be more in control of my responses," Rex said.

"Do you want to be more in control, or would you be better off loosening up to have more fun?" Apollo asked.

"Crunching numbers and solving problems is my fun," Rex said.

They stopped walking. Apollo raised his snout in the air. He didn't detect any enemies or danger. "Do you detect any more of those things buried in the ground?" he asked.

Rex scanned the area. "My scans didn't pick up any electronic devices."

"All is well," the wolf said.

They turned back in the direction they came from.

"Sometimes I miss the wild," Apollo said. "The comforts of the house make us lazy, and I worry for my pups. They will never know what it takes to survive out here. Abby and I were both young when we had to discover survival skills."

"They have their Dots which contain the wild wolf and wild dog movies," Rex said.

"That's not the same thing as having those instincts and learning from the pack of elders," Apollo said. "Not even I had that to help me. All the elders were dead. I was scared to leave the cave, but I was scared to stay there where all the heavy death smells surrounded me. I was so happy to find Abby. We learned together."

They arrived at the gate. Rex disengaged the locks. They made their way back to the house where they found the puppies and Jerry playing in the street with the human children. Bill, Teresa and Abby sat on the porch watching the puppies and talking among themselves.

For one short moment, Apollo and Rex were swarmed with six unruly puppies and one goofy dog-bot.

"Go run off your energy," Apollo said, gruff but somewhat pleased.

Bill was surprised that Rex didn't act out. Teresa elbowed him so he wouldn't mention it. Evidently, whatever the wolf said to the dog-bot made an impression.

Apollo and Rex climbed the steps and joined the adults.

"There are no problems in the wild surrounding the TMZ headquarters," Apollo announced.

"No more planted devices?" Bill asked.

"I scanned the area and didn't detect any electronics," Rex said.

"That's good to know," Bill said. "You can bet the World Guild will not give up."

THE ENTIRE COMMITTEE, along with Bill, stood outside the gates and viewed the empty expanse of the old roadway that stopped at the TMZ gates. Now that the tent and transporter city had been admitted into Texmexzona, the land looked naked. They had to hand it to the mob of new citizens. No one left any clutter whatsoever—not even a peanut husk littered the ground.

"Now it will be easy to admit people into the country," Glacious said. "We could not have done this without those dog-bots, Bill. Rex found the housing, and Number Eight's pack did the big work of scanning everyone and every ounce of their possessions."

"We need to name Number Eight and his pack," Harold said. "Maybe make them collars with their number and name? That way we'll be able to tell who's who."

"Good idea," MaryEllen said.

"Has this area been scanned for spyware?" Bill asked.

The committee members looked at each other.

"Not as far as I know," Pete said. He turned to Glacious. "Did you request that any of the dog-bots do an area scan after the last of the people were admitted into TMZ?"

Glacious shook his head. "No, I didn't even think about that. I figured since we found the spies and expelled them from our lands, that was all we needed to do. Perhaps we should do that immediately."

They all looked to Bill.

"I'll have Rex delegate that." Bill worked his communicator.

Within a few minutes, the gate opened and four dog-bots emerged. They approached Bill. Numbers 16, 2, 9 and 12 wagged their manmade tails.

"Father Bill, what would you have us do?" Number 16 asked.

Harold's eyebrows raised as he shared a look with Bill.

Bill shrugged.

"We require you to scan the entire area, back to Blythe, where the people had been living outside the gates, to make sure there are no spyware devices."

The dog-bots spread across the road and walked at a moderate pace.

"Why don't we install a couple of towers on our side of Blythe?" Bailey asked. "That way anything coming down the road is scanned ahead of time, and we'll get a report before they reach the gates."

There were nods among the group.

Bill and Harold shook their heads.

"That gives our enemies more of an opportunity to decipher our coding," Harold said. "We could accomplish that with similar devices that Apollo found buried in the ground. Out of sight devices would provide more opportunity for us to use the device for double duty. Scan all incoming traffic, plus capture any communications from nearby Tranquility Force gliders."

The committee members nodded.

"That's a good plan," Glacious said.

"Now that we have everyone settled in place, we're moving ahead with what Rex and Jonas suggested: expanding patrols. This is going to entail people moving to different outlying locations to live in the areas where they're needed," MaryEllen said.

"We don't want to leave any of our territory exposed to a sneak attack or infiltration of any kind," Pete said. "This is going to require beefing up our patrol gliders like we discussed."

By the time they finished their discussion and were ready to turn back to the gates, the four dog-bots came down the road and stopped in front of the group.

"There are no threats on the TMZ property," Number 16 announced.

"Good job," Bill said. "You may return to your duties."

"That didn't take long at all. I can't imagine how long it would have taken our people to scan the entire area," Bailey said.

Number 16 stopped, turned and supplied the answer. "4.6 hours."

"They sure can be smart-mouthed at times," Glacious noted with a smirk.

CHAPTER EIGHTEEN

Toby and Bill were installing jet boosters on one of the dog-bots from the large pack. They were attempting to circumvent the need for the manufacturing plant to build more gliders for the much-needed patrols.

"Am I okay?" Number 3 asked. "Are my guts sprawled out on the table?"

"Wise guy, huh?" Toby asked. "You know good and well your guts are still inside you."

"Don't you want to fly like a glider, Number 3?" Bill asked.

"Will I be the only flying dog-bot?" Number 3 asked.

"You're the test subject," Toby said. "If everything goes well after we get your boosters adjusted to the right speed, and your maiden voyage does not end in a crash, then all the dog-bots will be enhanced."

"Except for Rex," Bill said. "I don't think he would be onboard with jet boosters. I could be wrong, but knowing Rex like I do, I think he's a ground dog-bot."

"Crash?" Number 3 echoed. "What if I crash into a million pieces?"

"Bless the Earth, but you're a worrywart, on top of being chatty," Toby said, as he rolled his eyes. "Don't worry about it. If you break a leg or something, we'll fix you."

"Just don't throw me on the trash heap," Number 3 said.

"We don't do that," Bill said. "Only the Tranquility Force, and maybe the World Guild, does that."

"They threw Jerry on the trash heap," Number 3 insisted.

"Yes, they did, but Jerry was rescued, wasn't he?" Bill asked. "We know how to fix dog-bots. I'm your creator, after all."

Toby tightened the last screw. "Okay, ready to give this a try?"

"Start with the lowest propulsion, and let's see if we need to make adjustments for placement," Bill said. "Okay, Number 3. Fly slow and easy."

Toby grabbed the dog-bot around its belly and stood it on the floor. "Give it a try, Number 3."

The dog-bot took off like a rocket and spun around the room crazy fast.

"Slow down!" Bill yelled. "Lower your boosters to the lowest level."

The dog crashed into the ceiling and skidded across several feet, wrecking ceiling tiles. He dropped to the floor amid crumbling ceiling material.

Wynne, Roland, and Murray rushed into the room.

"What happened?" Wynne called out.

"You okay?" Murray asked as he spotted the dog-bot in a pile on the floor. A piece of the ceiling whammed down on Number 3.

"Help..."

"I guess we should have conducted this experiment outside," Bill said.

"Live and learn," Roland said.

They walked over to the crash site, pulled Number 3 out of the rubble and set him on the table. Bill retrieved a power blower and sprayed the debris and dust off the dog, then took inventory.

"Nothing appears to be broken," he said. "Want to bring him outdoors?"

"I'm going to adjust the boosters. It didn't seem like he could lower the thrusters," Toby said.

"Might have to code different levels for specific assignments or requirements," Bill said.

The men walked to the elevator with Number 3 between them. They rode down to the ground floor, passed the Communicator and exited the building. The new complex was in a horseshoe configuration. They stopped a good distance away from the main building and judged the distance to be safe for a trial run.

"Okay, Number 3, give it another try, but stay away from buildings and trees," Bill said.

They heard the thrusters kick in, then suddenly Number 3 was airborne. He shot up into the sky as if heading for the moon. Neither Bill, Roland, Toby, Wynne, nor Murray could visually track the dog-bot.

Bill grappled with his communicator and sent a message to the dog-bot. *Number 3, where are you? Return to the test site immediately!*

Roland shielded his eyes as he searched the bright sky.

Murray, Wynne and Toby walked in a circle, staring skyward while shielding their eyes.

"I think we lost him," Roland said.

Suddenly, the dog-bot screeched into view. It looked as if he'd crash.

"Run!" Toby hollered.

The men scattered away from the launch site. When they

were far enough away, they turned to see Number 3 hovering six feet off the ground.

"Well, I'll be darned," Wynne said.

"Land, Number 3," Bill commanded.

The dog landed softly.

"Where exactly did you go?" Bill demanded.

"I had a conversation with a satellite," Number 3 said.

The men shared surprised faces with one another.

"Wait a minute," Toby said. "You flew all the way up into space where the satellites are?"

"Yes, that is correct. Satellite 24BGD39940XQZ asked if I were friend or foe," Number 3 said.

"Wait a minute. Asked you?" Roland croaked out.

"Yes, it was very polite. I told it I was a friend from Earth on a test run," Number 3 said. "I scanned its systems to find its purpose. I determined it was spying on TMZ, so I reconfigured it to spy on the World Guild."

Toby, Roland, Wynne, and Murray barked out belly laughs while Bill simply stared at the dog-bot.

"How is it you didn't burn up leaving and returning through the atmosphere?" Murray asked.

"There may be a little external damage, but the titanium material held through the journey," Number 3 said.

"Could you possibly do a normal test run, say here above the buildings and trees?" Bill asked.

"Of course," the dog-bot said.

THE COMMITTEE, Bill's team, Teresa, Becky, Percy, Gayle and all the dog-bots gathered outside the front gates of TMZ for the demo. Number 3 was ready to show off his new enhancement and was a little egotistical about being the first to get the new boosters to allow dog-bots to take to the skies.

"We have a name scheme picked out," Bill told everyone. "Number 3 will be called Rocky. I'll send everyone the list since there are too many to remember." He checked with his team. "Are we ready for the demo? Rocky knows the rules?"

Roland and Toby nodded.

"He's ready, and we've discussed following orders," Roland said as his eyes grilled into Rocky's LEDs.

"Okay, then. Take off, Rocky!" Bill said.

The boosters engaged, and Rocky lifted off the ground. He gently swooped through the air, then fired up his rockets and zoomed overhead. After going through his demo, the dog-bot did a little showing off and flew upside down, turned right side up and landed safely by Bill's team.

"That's enough of that," Rex said. "Number 3... err... Rocky is a regular comedian."

Everyone clapped. Bill's team noted a lot of nodding from committee members.

"Won't people be surprised to see a flying dog-bot come up alongside them in the air?" MaryEllen asked.

Harold laughed. "Yeah, I'd like to see the expressions on World Guild or Tranquility Force patrols' faces!"

The majority of the dogs could be used throughout TMZ where there were a lot of open spaces vulnerable to air pirates, Tranquility Force, and World Guild patrols. Jonas and Rex brought the air pirates to their attention when they were down in the jungle area of Mexico. There were so many remote places and not enough TMZ patrols to go around.

Even with the new hires, the area was vast. The committee still considered upgrading the fleet of gliders, but everyone felt that the dog-bot upgrades were time and money better spent.

The dog-bots would be harder to take down; whereas a glider could be shot down from the sky easily.

Teresa detected a slight edge of jealousy in Rex, but she didn't comment on his behavior. She checked the list of names for the new dog-bots and decided it might be best to have a physical paper with the list at headquarters, Bill's building, and his home office.

Calling Chart using Palm Spring, CA as TMZ time

	M/F	Breed	Location	Name	Humans	Time
1	F	Pit Bull	Anthony, NM	Chessie	Gonzalez	MDT
2	M	Bull terrier mix	Vinton, TX	Georgie	Jackson	MDT
3	M	Malamute	Alaska/N Slope	Sakari (Sweet)	Meyok	1 hr behind
4	F	Tibetan Terrier	Tibet	Dawa (born Monday)	Chime & Chodak	CA: Tues 7PM Tibet: Wed 10AM
5	M	Tibetan Mastiff	Tibet	Dorjee (Thunderbolt)	Lobsang & Mipam	CA: Tues 7PM Tibet: Wed 10AM
6	M	Chihuahua	Europe	Rolf	Martin	
7	F	Huntaway	New Zealand	Bella	Stewart	
8	M	Labrador Retriever	New Zealand	Charlie	King	CA: Tues 7PM NZ: Wed 2PM
9	F	Cavalier King Charles Spaniel	New Zealand	Poppy	Williams	
10	M	Samoyed	Russia	Boris	Semenov	
11	F	Black Russian Terrier	Russia	Alina	Kuznetsov	CA: Tues 11PM Russia: Wed 9AM
12	M	Caucasian Shepherd	Russia	Alexei	Popov	
13	M	Karelian Bear Dog	Russia	Dimitri	Lebedev	
14	M	Formosan Mountain Dog	China	Gan (brave)	Wang	CA: Tues 6PM China: Wed 9AM
15	M	Chongquing dog	China	Junjie (handsome)	Huang	

"We need to map out the areas where Rex and Jonas discovered problems so we can determine how many dog-bots we'd need for patrols," Glacious said. He swung around and spotted Rex by Teresa. "Rex, think you could lend a hand with this?"

Rex walked over to the committee. "Of course. I have mapped and studied the entire area. If your plan is to have the jet-propelled dog-bots patrol the entire width and breadth of TMZ's 1,265,892 square miles, 250 dog-bots are required. They would each be responsible for 5,064 square miles. If, however, you only require the border areas to be patrolled, those numbers could be reduced. Dog-bots would be an excellent deterrent."

Bill appraised Rex. "Would you like an upgrade?"

"Not at this time."

Jerry charged up to Bill and bounced like a puppy. "I do! I want to fly!"

"Okay, you can get an upgrade, but you aren't going to be assigned somewhere else," Bill said. "Your place is here at headquarters. I'm sure you will have plenty of opportunities to fly though."

Jerry bounded away. "YAY! I'm going to fly!"

Everyone watched Jerry romp away.

Bill shrugged. "He's a puppy at heart."

BILL AND REX entered his new office. Rex lowered his form to a dog bed Teresa had provided, and Bill sat at the transfer surface. He stared into space for a few minutes.

"Rex, I think I'm just going to have to tell Teresa what I'm trying to create. I haven't come up with any surefire way to make sure she would get the formula into her system without making it unviable from heat. What do you think?"

Rex faced Bill. "That would be the easiest way to proceed."

"I'm just worried that she would focus on every body function, malfunction, flinch—anything and everything, and the stress would get to her," Bill said.

"Daddy, you can't outguess her reaction. It's better to be upfront so that you are both aware of any problems," Rex said.

"Okay." Bill stood, walked over to one of the cool cabinets, entered a code and retrieved a tiny vial. He held it up and looked at it. "This could be our little miracle in a bottle, Rex. If this works, think about what it would mean to women worldwide. Let's go to the house."

They left the office building and hopped into Bill's glider. He parked the glider in the holding area three minutes later.

"I hope she isn't busy," Bill said. He didn't see the puppies outside playing, but at this time of day, school was over. They entered the house through the kitchen door, and he went in search of his wife.

"Hon?" he called out.

"In here," Teresa called out. She lifted her head from the sofa where she had been taking a nap in the blissfully quiet house.

"Where're the wild ones?" Bill asked.

"Becky took them. Thank the Earth!"

He picked up one of her hands. "Good. I have something important to talk to you about, and I worried if it would be noisy in here."

Teresa sat up. She scanned Bill's face to determine if there was a serious problem, but she didn't detect high anxiety. He did seem nervous, but he seemed to have it under control.

Bill grabbed both her hands and met her eyes. "I've been working on a formula for several months, and it's ready for pilot testing."

"What kind of formula?" Teresa asked, eyebrows scrunched.

He stared into her eyes. "Fertility."

She stared back at him, mouth open, then she blinked. "Fertility?" her voice squeaked out.

He nodded. "Hon, I don't know if it's going to work or not, but it's ready." He pulled out the tiny brown vial. "Keep this away from direct sunlight, or any heat whatsoever. All you need to do is to count nine drops in your mouth, under your tongue first thing in the morning before you eat or drink anything hot."

Rex piped up from his embroidered dog bed. "At least fifteen minutes before eating or drinking so the formula is in your system."

Teresa turned on the sofa. "Thanks, Rex." She turned back to Bill. "What is this made of?"

"All-natural products." He looked a little guilty. "Starlight helped. She and her family gathered the herbs and other plant matter."

Teresa balked. "You've had secret meetings with Starlight? I've never met her, but you've been traipsing off to the mountains?"

"Don't be angry. This was for a good cause. We discussed every possible scenario for a viable pregnancy. That woman has a lot of knowledge," Bill stated.

"Please, take me to the mountains so I can meet her!" Teresa demanded.

Bill gave her a quick peck on the lips. "You bet. We'll round up the dogs when I find out if she's ready for company."

"Should I begin with this formula now, or wait until morning?" Teresa asked.

"Wait until morning. That way, you'll have a schedule," Bill said.

Teresa flung her arms around his neck. "Oh, Bill. I hope this works. Wouldn't it be wonderful to have a baby?"

CHAPTER NINETEEN

B ill checked out a large loaner glider from the glider pool and landed it at the house. Teresa, Becky, Abby, Apollo, the six puppies, and Rex were waiting for him. Teresa and Becky had their arms full of things they wanted to bring to Starlight, and there were three boxes on the ground.

The puppies could not stand still. They were excitedly jumping and romping in circles. Another glider approached and landed. Harold and Jerry joined them, and Jerry immediately joined in the puppies' glee.

Harold shook his head.

Apollo appeared to be regretting the trip already.

"Don't worry, Apollo," Teresa said. "This trip will do them good."

"That may be so, but what will it do to the adults?" the wolf asked.

Rex took matters into his own paws. "Everyone who wants to board the glider should sit and wait patiently. All those who don't want to visit the mountains, keep playing, and you can stay home!"

That got their attention. Six furry rumps plopped down onto the sidewalk, and one dog-bot joined them.

"You sure you don't want an escort?" Harold asked. He feared the Tranquility Force would arrest them. They were fugitives, after all, even though the news cast them as dead.

"Don't worry," Bill said as he grabbed a box and loaded it into the glider. "If those idiots can get through Rex and Jerry, then we're all done for." He showed two spray tanks. "We're going invisible."

Harold chuckled. "Oh, I forgot about your formula!"

"We'll be back by suppertime," Becky said. "If I'm not at the food console, Percy will starve."

"I understand completely," Teresa said. "It took me a long time to figure out the programming."

"Okay, everyone inside, and I'll spray this glider," Bill said.

The puppies made a mad dash to the glider where they discovered three of them could not fit through the doorway. There was a little scuffle as to who would go first. Jerry took the opportunity to go around them and was the first on board.

"Stop acting like a bunch of squirrels fighting over nuts and get into the glider," Apollo said, as he nipped Esme on the butt. "Move forward, Esme! You're holding up your brothers, sisters, and grandmothers."

Esme squealed, glared at her father, then moved into the glider. Wolf, Jim and Star plowed inside. Puppy Rex complained in dog-talk, and Lulah nudged his butt to either get on board or get out of the way. Abby and Apollo followed their puppies.

Finally, Teresa and Becky climbed inside. They emptied their arms onto the seats on either side of them. Big Rex got into the glider.

Bill began spraying the glider, top to bottom. It vanished before Harold's eyes.

"This is better than the demo you gave when you arrived here," Harold said.

"Stealth is the only way to get there safely, unfortunately. When I get back, we need to step up the committee's thinking about taking down the World Guild and everyone else who hinders humanity."

"I'll plant the seed in Glacious' ear," Harold said. "We've touched on it a couple of times, but I agree with you. It's time to move forward."

The men shook hands. Bill put on his special glasses to see the glider door, then climbed inside.

Bill turned to the cabin.

"Okay, listen up. This will be a long ride. You might want to find a nice comfortable place to take a nap."

"I want to look out the windows!" Star said.

"Me too!" Puppy Rex said.

They all shouted their intentions.

"There will be no jumping or roughhousing in the glider," Becky said. "Do you understand?"

A chorus of *yes's* and innocent faces responded.

The invisible glider lifted off the ground, and they were over the houses and buildings in under a minute. There were a lot of oohs and ahs as the puppies watched the ground recede. They saw birds flying through the air.

"This sure beats our 20-day trip," Abby said. "I'm grateful for Starlight. She made the harness that carried Star and Wolf."

"We had to carry them with our teeth in their scruff to cross deep water," Apollo said. "I learned a lot from Abby on that trip."

"Won't Starlight be surprised you have a Dot?" Teresa said.

After about 45 minutes, puppies were snoozing on their seats or on the floor.

"I detect two Tranquility Force gliders to the northeast," Rex announced.

"What's the best plan of action? Rise up or drop lower?" Bill asked.

"They aren't tracking us," Jerry said. "They won't be able to see us anyway, so they'd just be confused if they picked up any signals."

"I wouldn't want them randomly firing in this direction," Bill said.

Tense adults watched the gliders in silence. They released deep breaths as the Tranquility Force gliders turned to the west and disappeared.

An hour and a half later, Starlight's cabin came into view. Bill swung the glider around and settled the ship a short distance away from the cabin.

"Now listen," Apollo said. "Don't jump on Starlight. She's an elderly human, and you could knock her down and hurt her!"

There was a chorus of *we won't*, but the wolf knew that once the glider doors opened, his progeny would dart outside and go wild.

The glider doors opened, and the puppies shot out like they were fired from a cannon. Starlight appeared in her cabin's open doorway when she heard a squall of barking. She waved when she saw the puppies heading toward her. She was confused about how they got there because she didn't see the glider.

The puppies did restrain themselves somewhat around the Timbisha Shoshone woman.

"Look how you've grown!" Starlight said. "And you're talking!"

"Do you remember me?" Esme squealed.

"I'm bigger than Puppy Rex," Jim said.

"I'm Star. Remember me?"

Lulah wiggled in between her siblings and licked Starlight's outstretched hand.

"Grandma said I was smart," Wolf said.

Jim chomped down on Esme's butt. "Move, Esme! You're hogging Starlight!"

Starlight belly-laughed as she glanced toward where they came from. Bill stepped out of the glider and sprayed part of the glider with the reversing formula that made it visible again so no one crashed into it. She saw the adults get out, along with Abby, Apollo, and the two dog-bots.

Abby ran up to her litter. "That's enough! Go play and let Starlight catch her breath!"

The puppies took off in several directions. Apollo howled in wolf-talk to get their attention. His brood screeched to a halt, turned, and listened to their father.

"You will stay near the cabin, or you will sit in the glider while everyone else visits. Understand?"

His puppies eyed him warily as they returned to the perimeter of the cabin, romped and played.

"I've missed you, Starlight!" Abby's whole body wagged. "Come meet my mother and grandmother!"

Apollo approached. "Hello Starlight. I'm learning the ways of man now that I have my Dot."

"Oh, Apollo! It is so good to hear you talking. We had a hard time communicating, didn't we?"

"Yes, we did, and it was all a misunderstanding back then. I didn't trust humans when I first met you," the wolf said. "You were my very first human contact."

Teresa walked up to Abby, Apollo, and Starlight. Becky held back respectfully. She helped Bill with the gifts they had brought with them.

"Starlight? I'm Teresa, Bill's wife, and Abby's grandmother

—and mother," she said. "I'm so grateful for everything you did for her and her family."

Starlight drew Teresa into a hug. "It is so good to meet you. It was a pleasure taking care of the puppies while Abby and Apollo traveled."

"That saddlebag you created was very ingenious," Teresa said. "I don't know how they would have transported Star and Wolf without it."

Teresa drew Starlight over to Bill and Becky at the glider. "Starlight, this is Becky, Abby's other grandmother."

"It's so nice to meet you," Becky said. "It's so beautiful where you live!"

"This is Rex and Jerry," Teresa said.

"I've met Rex," Starlight said.

"We defected to TMZ," Jerry said.

"That was a smart decision," Starlight said as she looked the dog-bots over. "You are very sturdy machines."

"Hey, Starlight," Bill said. "Good to see you again." He handed her an armful of material. "For your quilting projects."

"Oh! What beautiful material! Thank you so much," Starlight said. "You made the glider invisible?"

"Have to fight fire with fire as far as the Tranquility Force and World Guild are concerned," he winked at her.

"Do you have a pair of pinking shears? I brought some, along with more needles and pins," Teresa said.

"They still make pinking shears? Wow!"

"I found a set of cast iron hearth pots," Becky said. She followed Starlight and Teresa to the cabin and stepped inside and looked around. It was rustic.

Bill carried the heavy box of pots and pans.

"This is like the old-time Christmas!" Starlight exclaimed.

"How's your messaging badge holding up?" Bill asked.

Starlight pulled it out of her pocket. "I like it a lot. This lets me say what I want to say without getting hauled into a jail cell and TRFSed." She leaned in and whispered. "Have you moved forward with your secret plan?"

Bill whispered back. "Yes, Teresa has started taking the formula. I told her about it because there was no way to sneak it into something every day, and it was the right thing to do. No one knows about it except Apollo and Rex."

Starlight nodded. She was a big-time secret-keeper. If Teresa wanted to discuss it with her, they could step outside for a private conversation. She turned to the table and unpacked the hearth pots that Becky had found. She grabbed Becky in a hug.

"Becky, I have secretly been longing for these pots! Thank you so much for your generosity! Now I can cook more than soup and stew."

"Oh, I'm so happy you like them. Abby told me you cooked over an open fire, and I researched what remote people used for cooking. I found a lot of references to before the food console was invented, but it was a challenge to find what people used for cooking over a campfire," Becky said. "Those old stoves sure took up a lot of room in old-time kitchens."

"My grandmother had an old gas stove," Starlight said. "You're right, it did take up this huge square space in the kitchen. So did the big box refrigerator."

"Do you know if anyone has discovered our cave?" Abby asked.

"I don't know. The only time I was there was when you had your puppies," Starlight said.

Abby turned to her father. "Can we show Mommy and Grandma our cave?"

"We sure can." Bill turned to Starlight. "Want to come for a ride and visit the old place?"

"No, I'll let you show everyone. I'm going to look at all this material. I can't wait to scramble eggs in a regular pan!" Starlight exclaimed.

"Oh, that reminds me. I'll return with a friend in a couple of days. We're going to build you a chicken coop and enclose it so no wildlife gets your chickens," Bill said.

Starlight's hand flew to her heart. "Oh! That's so generous of you. Your family has done so much for me already."

"We think of you as part of the family," Teresa said.

BILL FLEW the glider the short distance to Abby and Apollo's cave. He landed the glider on the edge of the forest, turned in his seat and eyed the puppies. "We're going to visit the place where you were born."

Apollo looked his pack over. "There are wild animals that live up the mountain and in the forest. You will stay with the group. Understand?"

Six pairs of eyes looked intrigued.

The glider door opened and everyone piled out.

Abby took the front position. "This way. Stay close behind. There's a nasty badger that lives below our cave, and he will attack you!"

"What's a badger?" Star asked.

"What kind of wild animals?" Puppy Rex asked.

"Will we have to fight off these badgers and wild animals?" Jim asked, as his voice hitched.

"Everyone be quiet," Apollo said. "Follow your mother up the mountain."

Their human family and the dog-bots followed the pack.

"This is where we drank water," Abby explained as they came upon the water bubbling up from the ground.

The puppies all had to sample the cold, fresh water.

"Oh, wow! This water sure is cold," Wolf said.

"Is there a bathroom closet here somewhere?" Esme asked.

Apollo huffed out his disbelief. His puppies still didn't get the whole *wild* concept.

As Abby warned, the badger rushed out of his cave and stopped ten feet from its entrance. It growled a warning.

Lulah squealed in fright and rushed to her father's side. Apollo growled back at the badger, voicing his own warning. After a full minute of a staring contest, the badger retreated into his cave.

They continued to climb until Abby stopped in front of her old cave. "Everyone stay here. I have to make sure an animal didn't move in."

Apollo pushed through his pack and stood by Abby's side. "Stay with the pups and your grandparents. I'll check out the cave."

Rex and Jerry came forward. "No need for anyone to take a chance. We will scan the cave and make sure everyone stays safe."

"Oh, good idea," Abby said.

Rex and Jerry continued to the cave opening. After less than a minute, Rex turned to the group. "The cave is not occupied."

Abby took the lead again. She hopped up onto the wide ledge and waited for everyone. "It will be very dark inside."

Jerry gently bumped her. "Rex and I can light up the cave." The dog-bots entered the cave at the high point and turned their light packs on. Abby went first. Teresa and Becky bent down and made it under the low entrance, then straightened up. Bill followed them, then Apollo and the puppies came inside.

Teresa stared at the wall where Abby had written her name and made her calendar. She noticed that instead of four lines with a fifth scratched across them, Abby had made six lines with the seventh scratched across so she had a full week.

"Oh, Abby. I wasn't sure if you understood the calendar since you were so young, but look what you created!"

Becky stared at the wall. "What a smart young dog you were!"

Abby turned back to the camper's wall. "I saw how the man tracked time, and I remembered Mommy's lessons about seven days in a week." She looked around to her pups. "Do you see how Mommy tracked time in the cave? Do you know about calendars yet?"

"What's a calendar?" Lulah asked.

"It's how to tell how many days are in a week, month, or year," Teresa said. "We have not studied that yet, but we can start on that tomorrow."

Bill left the entrance and went further into the cave, holding a light stick in front of him. Rex caught up with him and provided light. "Rex, there's a skeleton of a man and some possessions further in. I'd like to be able to identify him and find out what his story is. I don't know if he was hiding from the Tranquility Force, or if he was a mountaineer."

"I will see what I can find," Rex said. They were joined by the others.

"This was our leaf bed," Abby said when Teresa and Becky caught up with them. Abby turned to her puppies. "This is where you were born. Right here on this bed of leaves."

"Look at how dirty that blanket is!" Jim said.

"Eeewwww!" Star said.

Apollo huffed. "This cave, leaf pile, and blanket are much more civilized than living in the wild—like in the forest. It is important to have safe shelter."

"I want all of you to go to the front of the cave where the calendar is, and play there or take a nap," Abby said.

Her puppies huffed and made snide comments, but followed orders and headed to the front.

"DO NOT leave this cave," Apollo said, as the six trotted away.

The adults continued deeper into the cave until they came upon the camper and his possessions. Rex and Jerry scanned everything, searching for a clue as to the identity of the skeleton.

"Oh, no. Did this person starve to death, get wounded, or what?" Becky asked when she saw the skeleton.

"We don't know, but I hope Rex and Jerry can discover who this is," Bill said. "There could be a family somewhere wondering what happened to their loved one."

"I believe his name was Ted," Rex said.

Bill hurried to Rex's side. "What did you find?"

"There is an old-fashioned accessory buried under this debris that men used to carry. I believe it was called a wallet," Rex said.

Bill squatted and lifted an ancient piece of cardboard that he thought was probably from a box the man used to transport some of his possessions. Sure enough, underneath the cardboard was an old wallet. He picked it up and carefully opened it. There was an old ID card from before the Dot was invented. He thought it might be from the 2060s.

He gently pulled the card out of the slot and looked it over. The man's name was Ted Daigle. At the issuance of the card in 2062, he had been 34 years old and resided in old Tombstone, Arizona, which no longer existed.

"Good work, Rex. Why don't you and Jerry do a search and see if he was a criminal, or what the story is," Bill said.

Teresa stared at the debris—what was left of this man's life.

"I wonder how old he was when he died. How long had he lived in this cave?"

"You know, people used to hide things under their mattress," Becky said. She turned in the direction of the giant leaf bed.

They all followed her gaze, then started walking that way.

CHAPTER TWENTY

The adults stood in front of the huge leaf bed with the raggedy blanket atop and stared at it wondering whether secrets lay beneath it.

Bill took in the whole area and determined there was enough room across from the leaf bed to relocate it easily. "Let's grab that cardboard and use it like a shovel and move all this over there."

"Abby and I could scratch it over there with our feet," Apollo volunteered.

Bill shook his head. "That would create a dust storm and we'd get dust and dirt in our eyes and ears. It will only take a little while to move it with the cardboard." He, Becky and Teresa returned to where the camper's possessions were and grabbed three pieces of cardboard.

"Why don't we climb around to the back and use our cardboard to push the whole pile?" Becky suggested.

"We could try that," Teresa said.

Bill shook his head. "That sounds good, but we'd end up moving what might be hidden under the pile."

"Oh!" Teresa and Becky said together.

They spread out in front of the pile and scooped up leaves and debris with their cardboard "shovels" and dumped the leaves where Bill pointed. It took about ten minutes to get within three or four inches of the floor. They stood looking down, searching for anything other than leaves and twigs.

"What's this?" Teresa asked as she spotted a zippered pouch on the floor in front of her. She reached down, scooped it up, and dusted it off. There weren't any words on the pouch. She grabbed hold of the zipper tab and pulled, but it was stuck. "I can't get it open." She kept fiddling with the zipper to no avail.

"Let me try," Bill said. "Keep looking. Maybe there's more down there."

Teresa and Becky scooped up little bits of leaves and dumped them on the big pile. Becky spotted something shiny and bent down to retrieve it. She discovered a medallion on a chain and rubbed it against her pants to clear off the dust and debris.

"What's that?" Teresa asked.

Becky studied the medallion. "I'm not sure." She held it out to Teresa.

"Looks like something a spiritual person would wear," Teresa said.

Becky shoved it into her pocket, and they kept sifting through the leaves, twigs, and accumulated dust. She spotted another shiny object and retrieved it. "Looks like a wedding band."

Bill grunted angrily, then triumphantly. He unzipped the pouch , squatted, and turned it upside down. "Got the pouch open."

Becky and Teresa clustered around Bill to see what secrets the pouch held.

A photograph of a happy man and woman, clearly in love, and a sheet of paper dropped out. They studied the photo, then Bill unfolded the paper and read aloud:

Dear Mom,

If you or someone else has found this pouch, then you know I'm most likely dead. I've been hiding out in this cave hoping to prove my innocence. I did not kill Marion. She was my one true love.

A Tranquility Force enforcer had been harassing her and would not leave her alone. We complained formally many times, but nothing ever came of it. We think the enforcer had friends who apprehended our complaint forms.

When I came home and found her dead, strangled, I called TF headquarters to report it. They came, weapons blazing. I barely got out of the house alive, but they lasered me across my stomach. I knew I didn't have long, but managed to make it to this cave in the mountains.

I'm so sorry to have brought this shame upon our family. Know that I love you. I pray for justice for Marion and me, if I'm dead.

Your Loving Son,

Ted

The cave was quiet as Bill, Teresa, and Becky thought about what Bill read.

"Those bastards!" Teresa exploded. "Bill, we have to do something. You need to check this out and find out if that enforcer is still with the Tranquility Force!"

Becky couldn't stop crying. She remembered what had happened to her and Percy. If it weren't for Bill and Harold breaking into the Tranquility Force headquarters and rescuing them, they'd have had their brains swiped. She recovered, wiped the tears off her face with her shirt sleeve, and sniffled. "We need justice for them!"

"Rex, see what you can find out about this Ted Daigle and Marion. I don't know if that was his wife or girlfriend," Bill said.

Rex and Jerry scanned the letter. They quietly went about their business while their systems scanned databases.

"Oh, Bill," Teresa exclaimed sadly. "This poor man died in a lot of pain, all alone. His poor mother!"

Jerry piped up. "Theodore J. Daigle, wanted for murder, disappeared June 20, 2072. There's information about the murder. Marion A. Daigle, wife of ten years. Mother is Helen Daigle in Blythe, California."

"She's close by, if she's still alive," Bill said.

"I do not see a death certificate for her," Jerry said.

"The first enforcer on the scene was Corporal Simon Day," Rex stated.

"SIMON DAY?" Bill exploded. "Are you sure?"

"BLESS THE EARTH," Teresa yelled. "I can't believe it!"

Becky didn't know who that was.

"Becky, that's the name of the enforcer who took Abby away!" Teresa said.

"Oh! I remember him. Rotten to the core. He wasn't going to let me and Percy say goodbye to Abby," Becky said, somewhat growling.

"Affirmative," Rex said. "It is the same Simon Day who was demoted at the tribunal."

Bill sat on the floor of the cave, his eyes darting about as his brain churned. "Oh, we are so going to prove that Simon Day is a murderer. No neckband or brain swipe for him. I want to see him in hard labor in one of the labor camps!"

"Jerry, find where Helen Daigle lives. She may have moved from Blythe after her son was accused of murder," Teresa said.

"Let's gather up everything that belonged to him," Becky said. "We should bury his bones, shouldn't we?"

Bill shook his head. "No, we're going to prove his innocence so his mother can have a proper funeral for him."

Becky and Teresa nodded agreement, then the three of them went about gathering everything scattered throughout the cave.

Bill walked to the front of the cave and took a picture of Ted's calendar scratches. The puppies were snoozing on the cool cave floor. He looked out of the cave opening and saw Abby and Apollo drinking from the bubbling brook. He was trying to cool down his mind from his explosive thoughts. It was difficult. Captain Day was at the forefront of many unpleasant experiences.

EVERYONE PILED BACK into the glider. Bill stored Ted Daigle's meager possessions in the rear storage area, then he manned the glider.

"I'll see if Starlight needs anything, then we'll head home," he said. Five minutes later, he landed the glider near Starlight's cabin. "Everyone stay put. This will only take a minute." He hopped out and went to the cabin. He returned to the glider, and it lifted off. "She's cooking with two of the pans, Becky. She said it was wonderful not to have to make everything in one pot."

"Oh, I'm so glad. I'll keep a lookout for more things she could use. That's rustic living if I ever saw it!"

"Is Starlight our grandma?" Jim asked.

"No, she's a wonderful human, close to the family," Abby said.

"But she COULD be our grandma, couldn't she?" Jim insisted.

Abby, Teresa, and Becky turned to stare at Jim. Teresa and Becky wondered what prompted that question.

"I think she would be honored if you called her Grandma Starlight," Teresa said.

"She took care of four of you while your father and I made the long trip to TMZ with Wolf and Star," Abby said. She turned to Teresa. "I think Grandma is the right title for her."

No other gliders flew in the cloudless, blue sky as they made the journey back to TMZ. Bill landed the glider at their house, and everyone piled out. He, Becky, and Teresa carried Ted Daigle's possessions into Bill's home office. He picked up the pouch that now also included the ring and pendant, and headed out the door.

"I'm going to discuss this situation with Harold, Toby, Roland, Murray, and Wynne," Bill said. "We'll build a case against Captain Day, or whatever his title is these days."

"Okay, I'll see you at dinnertime," Teresa said.

Bill flew the borrowed glider back to the lot and hopped into his personal glider. He stopped at the headquarters building, hunted down Harold, and asked him to ride over to the Maxwell offices for a meeting.

BILL GATHERED EVERYONE, including Angelica, who brought Maisey along, in a small meeting room. He held up the battered pouch. "I'm on a mission, and I need your help."

He explained about the skeleton they identified in Abby's cave. He pulled the letter out of the pouch and read it aloud. Everyone was stone-silent.

"That poor man!" Angelica gasped through tears.

"We need to take that guy down!" Toby said.

"He's on our radar now, so it's only a matter of time—a short period—before he's in chains!" Roland said.

"Tranquility Force will do anything to protect one of their own, even if they are rotten to the core," Wynne said.

"Yeah, but there's some honest enforcers too," Murray said. "You just have to find them."

"Rex and Jerry are on the case," Bill said. "We want to find Helen Daigle, if she's still alive, and give her Ted's things, including this pouch and letter."

Maisey nudged Angelica.

She looked down at her dog-bot. "Did you have something to say, Maisey?"

"My Alpha's second in command has found Helen Daigle. She now resides in the former state of New Mexico in a city called Santa Fe," Maisey said.

"At least we won't have any issues with Tranquility Force. When did she come into TMZ, Maisey?"

"My files show she emigrated in 2074," the dog-bot said.

Harold shook his head sadly. "I'm going to assume she waited to hear from her son, then decided to get out of the US." He shook his head again. "We need to give him a decent burial."

"Tomorrow I'll see if Abby wants to go with us. She could tell Helen about living in the cave, and all that her son did to make Abby's life on the run tolerable," Bill said.

"Let us know when you want to head out," Murray said.

"I'll go in an official TMZ capacity," Harold said. "Maybe Glacious would want in on this."

A DELEGATION that included the TMZ committee, Bill, Abby, Rex, Roland, Toby, Murray, and Wynne left headquarters at nine a.m. in two gliders. They zipped across the sunny blue sky while having small conversations here and there.

Bill couldn't stop thinking about his anger at the Tranquility Force, the World Guild, and his role in everything. He realized he had contributed to the entire mess with his Dot invention. Never did he fathom that his helpful contribution to society, which started out as a way to find lost super-centenarians, dog-children, and human children, would end up enslaving the population.

Bill vowed to take down the rotten government, and if anyone had the smarts to accomplish that goal, Bill Maxwell fit the bill.

"We are approaching Helen Daigle's house," Rex said. "Steer toward that yellow house with the green roof."

The two gliders settled on the ground.

"Let's leave the box in the glider for now," Bill suggested. He held up the pouch. "We'll start with this."

They all exited the gliders and headed to the front door. Glacious approached the door. They could hear the announcement from where they stood. Moments later, the door opened and a wild-haired woman in a caftan with a huge pink heart on the front stared at the people on her stoop.

"Am I under arrest?" Helen asked.

"Mrs. Daigle?" Glacious asked.

She nodded.

"May we come in? We want to talk to you about Ted," he said.

She slammed a hand to her chest and gasped out his name, "Ted?"

"Yes, ma'am."

Helen stood aside, opening the door wide. "Please, come in!"

They all marched into the house, including Abby and Rex. Helen sat on the sofa, afraid her legs would give out.

"Mrs. Daigle, I'm Glacious Ersons, the founder of TMZ. This is Abby, Bill Maxwell, his dog-bot Rex, some of his team, and the TMZ committee members. Do you remember when Abby was announced as the last dog?"

Helen nodded, wide-eyed. "Yes. Yes, I do." She stared at Abby and Rex.

"When Abby escaped the lab, she made it to the Sierra Nevada Mountains where your son had stayed," Glacious said.

"You found Ted?" Helen gasped. She looked among the men in the room.

"I'm sorry to have to tell you, but your son passed on from his wounds. Abby found his remains and his possessions in the cave," Glacious said.

Helen covered her face with her hands and wailed. "He was innocent!"

Bill stepped forward and slipped onto the sofa beside Helen. He put his arm around her shoulders. "We're sorry for your loss, but we have started an investigation against the enforcer responsible for Ted's death and his wife's. We'll bring him down and restore Ted's reputation."

Helen's crying let up. She wiped her face on her sleeve and turned to Bill. "You would do that for us?"

Abby stepped forward. "I owe part of my survival to your son. He had hauled a gigantic mound of leaves up the mountainside into the cave and used it as a bed. That's where I slept, and where my puppies were born. He had scratched a calendar on the wall, and that's how I marked my time in the cave while hiding out from Tranquility Force."

Bill tapped his communication device. "Let me show you the cave." He pulled up the streamed images of climbing the mountain, getting onto the cave ledge, and the cave interior.

Bill showed Ted's wall calendar, the huge leaf bed, and his book. He made sure there were no signs of the skeleton.

He handed her the pouch. "We found this pouch hidden under the leaves a couple of days ago."

With shaky fingers, she pulled the zipper tab and opened the pouch. She pulled out the piece of paper and read her son's last communication, which brought more tears.

"There's more," Bill said. He retrieved the pouch from her and upended it. The ring and pendant dropped into his hand, and he handed them to her.

Helen grasped the ring and pendant. "I can't thank you enough for this. At least now I have closure. I can stop waiting to hear from him."

"We have the rest of his possessions in a box out in the glider," Glacious said.

Toby slid out the front door and returned shortly with the box. He set it on the coffee table in front of her.

"I think I'll wait to look through this," Helen said, in a quivering voice.

"We would like to honor your son and bury his remains," Glacious said. "We will contact you soon with the details."

Helen grabbed Bill's hand. "Thank you so much. I hope you can clear Ted's name. I would like to be able to contact Marion's family, but even now, after all these years, they want nothing to do with me."

"That's such a shame," MaryEllen said.

The group left the house after saying goodbye and headed back to headquarters.

"We need undisputed proof of these allegations," Roland said. "That's the same enforcer who was working on the side for Dr. Roberts, isn't it?"

Bill nodded. "The one and the same. He's most likely been on the take for years."

"Jerry and I are sifting through satellite data back to 2072 and earlier to see what we can find. It would be difficult to dispute the satellites," Rex said. "People don't realize or understand what data is captured, or how it's stored. I feel confident we will uncover enough to clear Ted's name and to see that Simon Day is charged with a double murder."

"Double murder?" Glacious asked. "Who else did he murder?"

"Ted Daigle," the dog-bot said.

"As soon as we get this guy taken down and hauled off to the labor camp, we should have a ceremony for Ted," Pete said.

"We'll take him down, then I'm going to take the World Guild down," Bill said emphatically.

CHAPTER TWENTY-ONE

D og-bots are amazing machines. They don't sleep, get hungry, lonely, or have to go to the bathroom closet at all hours of the day or night. Dog-bots are working machines that can ghost into any network without leaving a trace, thanks to Bill Maxwell's brilliant brain and coding expertise. They are thinking machines with the ability to understand and analyze human beings along with complex governments and organizations.

As Glacious Ersons swiveled in his chair in his TMZ headquarters office; he thought of all those things. He blessed the Earth every single day for having Bill Maxwell in TMZ helping them stave off the World Guild. While the committee had been thrilled when Harold Goanflower and his wife fled WestUS to immigrate to TMZ, Injun Jim was second to his best friend.

Maxwell and Goanflower were a formidable team, along with Bill's tight team that just settled into TMZ. Glacious knew that Bill's determination to take down the World Guild shouldn't be taken lightly. His head was most likely churning out a detailed plan that would take a team of people years to outline. And his planning didn't even have the help of his super-intelligent machines.

Those dog-bots would bury Simon Day with evidence; of that he was certain. Glacious knew that the entire pack was most likely sorting and packeting data. He thought about how Rex and Jonas Biggibottom mapped the entirety of Texmexzona down to the tiniest village or lone house in a remote location. Heck, Rex provided weather data, information on the types of trees and foliage countrywide, soil analysis, animal, insect, and water creatures. What an exhaustive report. Plus, headquarters now had an inventory of available vacant housing, the condition of said housing, and detailed information about the local environment.

Texmexzona was considered a region. Glacious and the committee had tossed around the idea of officially designating TMZ a country. They needed to study how the old countries of Mexico and Canada operated as borders to the United States. Many nations around the world that had changed borders or had been absorbed by larger, stronger countries, so it could be done.

Their government structure would have to change. So many things had to be considered.

NOTHING WAS MORE thought-provoking than seeing a dog-bot standing stock-still in the middle of a room, unless it was a pack of them. Toby, Roland, and Bill stepped off the elevator near their offices. Rex, Jerry, Timmy, Josh, and Rocky faced the elevator, their red LED eyes twinkling to show there was something going on in their noggins.

"Rex. What's going on?" Bill asked. This was new behavior.

"The dog-bot community has analyzed 1,600,426,852 satellite images dating back to 2072. We have pulled significant data showing Simon Day causing harm while performing his duties as an enforcer, on and off-duty."

"Let's go into the conference room and see what you have," Toby said. He led the way to the new conference room.

Jerry projected a list of Simon Day's crimes. As Rex beamed a red dot on each one, Timmy, Josh, and Rocky produced clear images as if the man in question was standing beside them.

They broke the list down by year, then by incident.

"How many pages do you have there?" Roland asked.

"Almost 300," Jerry said.

The men silently studied the incidents through the first dozen pages.

"What're the end results, Rex?" Bill asked, clearly disturbed by what he had read and seen.

"There have been twenty-two murders, six rapes, numerous instances of extortion from both individuals and businesses, and hundreds of beatings. Many so severe that the person was treated by the virtual healing emergency medical team. We have proof via satellite captures that Simon Day used eliminator drones to get rid of bodies. However, in 2070, he buried a body in a wooded area. This must have been before he thought about eliminator drones."

"That's it. He's going so far down he'll never see the light of day," Bill said.

"How can we get this to the high court, then the tribunal, so he doesn't get wind of it and disappear?" Toby asked.

Bill's chair twisted and turned while a smile crossed his face. "I know exactly how this will go down. Leave it to me." He stood and left the room.

CHRISTOVAR SECATSKI SAT in his leather swivel chair smoking a banned cigar, while swigging whisky with his ankles crossed on top of the desk. He listened on his virtual communicator to his egotistical, wealthy client who tried to weasel out of serious charges brought against him after a recent arrest. The Tranquility Force had caught him—not the typical thugs he hired—while he cold-cocked a man during a black-market transaction for a tactile releasing factual stimulator (TRFS, pronounced truffs).

"Listen, Drew," Christovar said, his Russian accent getting stronger as his irritation level rose. "You're going to have to do the time. If it were anything other than TRFS, I could come up with a sob story about your grandmother and get you leniency."

A double beep sounded on his screen. Christovar casually glanced at the message coming in, expecting to read something from a desperate client or another attorney. He did a double take. His feet hit the floor. He sat ramrod-straight. He dropped the cigar into the onyx ashtray as an untold number of things flashed through his head.

"Drew, we will continue this discussion later," he said, disconnecting.

The Russian attorney stared at the screen in disbelief. Someone was either using the identity of a man whose friendship he had valued above all others, or he wasn't dead as the news had reported. If that were the case, he would go after the lying government brutes.

Christovar glared at the screen. If someone had stolen his friend's identity, he would squash them like a bug. He tossed down the whiskey and thought about how to proceed. He sighed in frustration and clicked to open the message.

Which dog do you feed?

He sat as if in a trance. There was only one person on the planet who would use that phrase. He typed an answer. *I starve them both.*

Another message came through with instructions and a long code to enter into his settings for a secure call. He went through the slightly complicated directions and hit the last pound sign. His communication line beeped three times. He placed the call and cautiously waited for the other person to speak first.

"Christovar? Are you there?"

"Bill! How is this possible?" the Russian asked. Then, after thinking it through, "You defected."

"Yes. Everything you heard on the news or read was nothing but lies. Abby found us here in TMZ. She has a wolf mate, and they have six puppies. And Chris, everything you have ever heard about TMZ is false. Every last bit," Bill said.

"How can that be?" the attorney asked. "How could the government hoodwink the entire global population?"

"We have a lot to discuss. You know I called for a reason. Would you be able to meet me at the old log?"

When they were much younger, they had discovered a downed, gigantic redwood tree that was partially hollow. They used to hide out inside the humongous trunk, smoking illegal cigars and discussing Bill's many projects, until, of course, Teresa helped Bill to mend his ways and become smoke-free.

"When?" Christovar asked.

"Four o'clock."

"It's still there? You're sure?" the Russian asked.

"Yes, it's there. See you then." Bill disconnected, then returned to the conference room. "I'm going to meet someone who'll take care of this little problem and will put Simon Day away for life."

"That Russian guy, Secatski?" Toby asked.

"He's the one," Bill said. "Rex, pack up those 300 pages. You're coming with me," Bill turned to Toby and Roland. "Come help me spray a glider with my formula."

The three men and Rex headed for the elevator.

"What about us?" Jerry asked.

"Continue your work while you watch over the puppies and TMZ," Rex said.

BILL CAREFULLY MANEUVERED the invisible glider through heavy WestUS traffic. He changed flying zones frequently to avoid congestion. Since no one could see him, and not everyone was smart enough to turn on their automatic collision avoidance detector, he hopped the glider around to keep safe.

Luckily, the part of Redwood National Forest and park where the fallen tree was located had not broken off into the ocean during the *incident* of 2076. It was strange to see what was now called Redwood Island out in the Pacific Ocean. The government forbade anyone from moving to the island because it was still considered a state park. It was a well-known fact, however, that squatters had set up shacks that were almost impossible to identify. They were like the forest people Abby had come across in the Sierra Nevada mountains but could never find again.

Bill made his glider circle the area. "Rex, do you detect any problems in the area? Any beams directed to our meeting place?"

"The area is safe. If I discover any beams, I will nudge them out of the way," the dog-bot said.

"Okay. Keep an eye out for Christovar's glider so he doesn't accidentally try to land on top of our glider," Bill said.

"I'll handle it, Daddy," Rex said.

Bill wondered if there was a little attitude in Rex's answer, but kept his thoughts to himself. After exiting the glider, the door closed with a soft whoosh. They headed to the gigantic downed tree. Neither Bill nor Chris had ever discovered what had hollowed out the part of the tree they used as their secret meeting place all those years. It was as if someone used a spoon to scoop out tree guts, much like one would do to a kiwi fruit or avocado.

They climbed into the tree and turned to the right. The benches Bill had built decades ago still stood opposite each other. He approached *his* bench and tested it with his hands. It felt sturdy. He sat on it, keeping the majority of his weight on his legs and feet to make sure it would not collapse. When he was sure it was sturdy, he settled his weight onto it and sat comfortably.

Bill and Rex waited another ten minutes before Christovar's glider circled the area. They went outside to greet him. Bill waved his arms to direct Chris to fly to the right before landing. The Russian landed the vehicle and disembarked. He loped over to Bill and grabbed him in a fierce bear hug.

"You're alive! You're really alive!" the attorney all but shouted. When they parted, Chris glanced down at Rex. "And who is this?"

"My name is Rex Maxwell," the dog-bot said.

Christovar stared at Rex. "And do you know who I am?"

"You are my father's best friend," Rex said.

The Russian harrumphed, looking from Rex to Bill. "Your father, eh? I see his programming skills are not disappointing. You may call me Uncle Chris." He looked around. "Where's your glider?"

Bill smirked, outstretched his arm in the general direction.

"Right there. Had to make it invisible to get through WestUS." He handed Chris a pair of eye-shields.

Christovar slipped the shields on. His face lit up. "I may need these!"

They went inside the tree and sat on their benches with Rex standing at Bill's side.

"I want you to take someone down... legally," Bill said.

"You don't want them taken behind the woodshed and beaten with a 2x4?" Christovar asked.

Anyone else would assume he was joking. Bill knew his Russian friend meant business, a point of reference for punishment for some heinous crime that someone had committed.

"No, the legal system will suffice, as you will understand momentarily," Bill said. "Remember the enforcer who took Abby?"

"Simon Day?" Christovar asked.

"That's the one. When Abby escaped the lab, she ended up in the Sierra Nevada mountains and hid in a cave. There was a skeleton in the cave that we've identified as Theodore Daigle. He was mortally wounded by Simon Day in 2072 as he fled his wife's murder scene. We found a letter Ted wrote to his mother that outlined what happened that day. I put Rex and his pack of dog-bots on satellite duty, and you're not going to believe what they found."

"Satellite duty? What do you mean?" the attorney asked.

"They got into the files and downloaded 300 pages of events involving Simon Day," Bill said. "Let Rex show you a sample."

Rex transferred a bulleted list to Christovar's communicator. He then brought up his holographic communicator and presented incident after incident of Simon Day's criminal behavior.

"You sure you don't want the woodshed for this scum?"

"I think it would be better to have him in a maximum-security labor camp doing hard labor for the rest of his life," Bill said.

Christovar nodded. "Yes. The woodshed would be too lenient. I will personally take this to Judge Growarth. He will have a field day with this in the High Court! I'll urge the judge not to suggest a brain swipe. This criminal needs to suffer every day for the rest of his life."

"We found Ted's mother in TMZ and brought everything he possessed in the cave to her. Once Simon Day is taken care of, we'll have a burial service for her son. It's imperative his name is cleared. It has left a bad stain on his mother, which is the reason she fled WestUS in the first place."

The Russian observed his friend. "I know there's more. Get it off your chest."

Bill gave a tiny smile. Christovar knew him well. "I'm going to take down the World Guild."

"What can I do to help?" No questions asked. The Russian knew that once his smart friend made a decision, he might as well consider it done.

"Think about who should run things. Do you want a part in a new government? You are ruthless, but I know you to be spot on with right and wrong, and you don't take bribes for heinous crimes against humanity."

"I would consider being an advisor. World government is too complicated, and there's a lot of infighting. Even the best people lose track of why they wanted to turn things around," Chris said. "Where are you with this?"

Bill tapped the side of his head. "I'm in the planning phase."

They talked for another forty minutes, catching up. Bill was always entertained by his friend. The lawyer was ruthless in the courtroom, and his clients paid dearly without batting an eye, because they knew they would walk away from whatever scourge brought them to the Russian.

"Come to TMZ for a visit. Teresa would welcome a visit outside of any legal issues," Bill said.

"Let me see how Judge Growarth wants to handle this Simon Day, then I'll come visit," Christovar said.

They climbed out of their meeting place, man-hugged, then walked to their gliders. Rex took his place in the glider cabin, and Bill joined him. They waited until Christovar's glider took off, then journeyed back home.

CHAPTER TWENTY-TWO

Bill returned home to TMZ without any problems. He sprayed the glider after he settled it in the Maxwell Industries parking area and watched as it became visible once more.

"Let's go upstairs and report in," he said to Rex. They entered the building, hopped into the elevator and breezed to the top floor. "We're back," he called out.

Roland, Toby, Wynne, and Murray piled into Bill's office.

"Well?" Roland asked. "What did your Russian pal have to say?"

"He's taking the case to Judge Growarth," Bill said.

"Bet he wanted to take Simon Day to the woodshed," Murray said, with a knowing smirk. He was familiar with how Bill's friend thought about certain criminals. If they touched close to home, the Russian could easily revert to his dark roots.

"It won't be long," Bill said. "Then we can move on to bigger and better things."

"Planning how to infiltrate the World Guild," Toby stated.

∾

ALL THE WAY back to his office, Christovar scrutinized Rex's files while silently cussing to himself. This Simon Day was rotten through and through. He also considered the enforcer's supervisors. They had to be just as bad. He could not find any write-ups in a separate search of attorney databases. That meant they looked the other way, or Day somehow doctored his employment files.

He tapped his GPS and changed the destination. Thirty minutes later he landed the glider at an oppressive building that housed the High Court. He was pretty sure the judge would be on-site, gossiping with his cronies.

He entered the building with his authorization code and took the elevator to the 13th floor. This was one of only a handful of buildings in the entire US that actually named the bad luck floor. Considering it included the High Court, luck could swing either way.

The elevator doors slid open, and Christovar stepped out and headed toward the judge's office. He entered the empty outer office and continued to the partially open door of the private office. He tapped on the door.

Judge Growarth looked and waved Chris into his office. "Odd time to make a visit. Is this business or social?"

"Business—dirty business," the attorney said as he settled into one of the plush leather chairs in front of the desk. "Do you recall Simon Day?"

The judge crinkled his brow. "That's the Maxwell case?"

Christovar nodded. He thought about how to proceed, then just jumped in. He knew the judge well enough to know that he would listen and believe what he told him.

"First, let me inform you that Bill Maxwell and his wife are alive and well, having defected to TMZ."

The judge sat straight up in his chair. "NO! Why..."

"Because the World Guild is a bunch of liars," Christovar said. "Not only that, but Abby, the puppy who was taken and then escaped, she's alive and well in TMZ, along with her wolf mate and their puppies!"

"So, where does Simon Day fit into this? We know he was the one who confiscated Abby," the Judge said.

The Russian filled the judge in about the cave, skeleton, and everything else. Then he transferred the files Rex had gathered to the judge and waited while he speed-read them.

"How many pages are here?" the judge asked.

"About 300," Christovar told the judge what Bill suggested for sentencing.

"A brain swipe would be the easy way out. I agree with Maxwell, though. We want this guy to suffer, and to suffer greatly for his remaining days. I'll have him picked up immediately." The judge worked his communicator.

"I don't think there's any way this unlawful enforcer would not have been written up over the years, yet I could not find one instance in his files," Christovar said.

The judge nodded. "Let me have my team begin a thorough investigation on that end. We may have to clean that house." He shook his head, sat back, and folded his arms. "So, do you have any more of that whisky?"

The Russian grinned. "I'll send a case tomorrow."

TWO AND A HALF WEEKS LATER, Bill and Teresa snuggled on the sofa after dinner, while the puppies played with Jerry. Abby and Apollo kept a close eye on their offspring from their dog beds, and Rex appeared to focus on keeping his mouth shut about the noise level.

Bill's communicator announced an incoming call from Christovar. "Hey," Bill said.

"What's that racket?" the attorney asked.

Bill and Teresa laughed. They were becoming immune to the six loud voices—seven counting Jerry, who joined in with his playmates.

"That's Abby and Apollo's pups, and Jerry, one of my dog-bots who thinks he's a puppy."

"I'm coming for a visit," Christovar said.

"You can't just fly here... "

"I will fly with immunity. They can't stop me," the Russian said.

"When?" Bill asked.

"What's for breakfast?" Christovar asked. "Do you still serve that café mocha?"

"You can have anything you want for breakfast," Teresa said. "And yes, you can have all the café mocha you want. I've taken lessons on the food console. We eat like kings in this household."

"As long as we don't have to eat like paupers, I'll be very happy. Do you want me to bring you anything from here?" Christovar asked.

Bill and Teresa silently conferred. "We took everything with us from the house, and my team stripped the offices," Bill said. "We can't think of anything we need right now, but thanks for checking."

"See you in the morning," Christovar said, signing off.

"He must have important news to be delivering it in person," Bill said. "I'll contact the gate to let them know he's coming. He can be a tad antagonistic when he's questioned."

"No kidding?" Teresa said. She was well aware of the Russian's short-fused temper. How anyone could think to go up against him in any situation, not just in the legal system, was beyond her thought process. She had seen him in action. He always over-prepared for every situation. Christovar Secatski may not have coined the phrase *leave no stone unturned*, but that was the way he operated.

She sat up and clapped her hands to get the rowdy playmates' attention. "Calm down right now. You too, Jerry." When the puppies were quieter, she continued. "Tomorrow morning we are having company from far away. A man named Christovar..."

"Our Uncle Chris is coming to visit?" Jerry asked, excited.

"How did you know about him?" Bill asked.

"My alpha told me and our pack that he was a trusted individual," Jerry said.

"Yes, then, your Uncle Chris will be here for breakfast. I want every puppy, and you, Jerry, on your best behavior," Teresa said. "Don't yell at each other. Keep your voices soft, do you understand?"

Jim perked up. "We shouldn't talk loudly in the house, right?"

"Very good, Jim. You understand," Teresa said. "How about the rest of you? Will you try to be nice?"

"We'll go outside to play loudly," Esme said.

THE NEXT MORNING typical chaos broke out at the Maxwell house, while Teresa lined up food bowls on the counter by the food console. Bill scrubbed the large stainless steel water bowl in the sink, refilled it, and settled it into the raised stand.

The front door announced visitors.

"Rex, answer the door. It's most likely your Uncle Chris," Bill said.

The dog-bot went to the front door. "Who's there?"

"It's Harold, Rex, with your guest," Harold said.

Rex extended his shoulder claw and opened the door. "Welcome, Harold, and Uncle Chris. Please come in."

Bill called out from the kitchen. "We're back here. Come in and join the morning party!"

Harold led Chris to the kitchen. The puppies forgot their hunger pangs and swarmed the company.

"Hi, Uncle Chris!" Wolf said. He was shoved out of the way by Lulah.

"Move your butt!" Lulah said. "Hi, Uncle Chris!"

The others competed for attention.

Apollo stood. "SILENCE! You will all go to your beds until you are called to eat!"

Six tails lowered, and the puppies skulked off to their beds.

"I apologize for my unruly pups," Apollo said, facing the stranger called Uncle Chris.

The Russian stared at the magnificent wolf. "I'm surprised all adults aren't deaf by now."

Abby approached the guests. "Hi, I'm Abby, and this is my mate, Apollo."

"I'm happy that you were reunited with your parents," Christovar said. "It was a sad day for everyone when you escaped the lab and no one could find you."

"Hi Abby, Apollo," Harold said.

Teresa and Bill settled all the dog food bowls in their stands.

"Please sit down!" Teresa said. "We're serving breakfast. It's best to stay out of the way when I call the puppies to eat."

Christovar and Harold scurried over to the table and sat.

"Come to breakfast," Teresa called out.

Twenty-four legs galloped into the kitchen, skidding on the

wood floor. After a little pushing and shoving, they lined up at their bowls.

"Slow down! No gulping your food down!" Teresa warned. "It's not like you're starving."

Bill brought two larger bowls to two stands away from the puppy's food station. "Here you go, Abby, Apollo."

The adult dogs ate their food with nice table manners.

"Okay," Bill said. "Who wants a café mocha?"

The front door announced more visitors, and Rex took the job of finding out who was there and let them in.

Toby, Roland, Murray, and Wynne came inside and walked back to the kitchen.

"Sorry we're late," Toby said. "Figured we'd let you get the dogs fed first."

"Chris, this is my team. I'll let them introduce themselves. Figured I'd gather everyone for your news so we know what direction we need to take with our plans," Bill said.

The Food Console prepared eight individual cups of café mocha, then seven breakfast plates of scrambled eggs, bacon, sausage links, pancakes, sliced kiwi fruit, and toast. The last plate was queued up with much smaller portions.

The Maxwells served the drinks and the plates. Everyone settled down to eat, and Christovar explained recent events.

"Judge Growarth brought Simon Day before the high court. He presided over the case, presented the truth seekers with all the evidence that Rex put together—but don't worry— no one knows he was involved, and made his suggestion for punishment," Chris said between slurps of his café mocha. "Teresa, this is wonderful. I need to know how to make this when I go home."

"I'm glad you like it," Teresa said. "It's easy. I'll send you the food console settings. It comes out perfect every time."

"After Tranquility Force officials were investigated for the lack of write-ups over so many years, it was determined that Conan Zerlich and Hemrey Branch were guilty of expunging Simon Day's HR file, and even taking part in some of his rampages," the attorney said. He stabbed eggs with his fork, munched a piece of toast, picked up a piece of bacon with his fingers and took a big bite.

"There were several times when the judge had to ring the gong to get order in the court. It was so out of control. The media literalists swarmed all over the place. You should have been there. I thought one of the truth seekers was going to jump out of the box and beat Simon," Chris said.

"Where did it go from there?" Bill asked.

"Well, Simon Day will spend the rest of the year in solitary confinement at the maximum-security labor camp to contemplate his deeds, while his thoughts and actions are monitored and assessed. Then he'll be collared and sent to work duty on the road deconstruction project," Chris said.

"What's that include?" Roland asked. "I thought that was accomplished with eliminator drones."

"They don't use the drones on road or building deconstruction. Everything that's left over from what the equipment broke down that's hauled off for reissue and reuse, has to be manually smashed," Harold said. "He'll use a sledgehammer to break down pieces of concrete into smaller rubble that can be hauled away. That means he will be out in the sun every day for 10 to 12 hours. The region makes sure it gets its money's worth out of the hardened convicts they have to feed and shelter for the rest of their lives."

"That sounds like the right place for that man," Teresa said. "What about when he's put in with the general population of the labor camp? That might be dangerous for him."

Chris leaned forward. "That's his problem. He caused it, and he has to face the consequences. I'm sure he'll discover there's no love for him there among so many of his former captives."

"I just hope he lives long enough to experience that hard labor," Roland said.

"Can we plan a burial and ceremony for Ted now that his killer has been sentenced?" Toby asked.

"Yes," Bill said.

"I hope that Ted's in-laws find it in their hearts to apologize for their harsh treatment of Helen," Teresa said. "That poor woman suffered alone all these years."

"We need to get Ted's remains from the cave, provide a casket, a marker, and prepare the ceremony speech," Murray said.

"First, we should provide the Literalists with the story about the celebration, so that Ted's in-laws can attend," Wynne said.

"We can't have US Literalists come into TMZ," Harold said. "It's strictly forbidden."

"Then we'll get with Helen and plan the celebration, record it and send it to the Literalists," Bill said. "Before we do that, though, I would like to do a full global media blitz informing the world that the Maxwells are alive and well, and reunited with their dog-daughter."

Everyone nodded.

"The judge practically fell out of his chair when I told him you and Teresa had defected," Christovar said. "He was furious about the lie the World Guild churned out about you dying while trying to find Abby."

"Good," Teresa said. "We have a solid plan. Helen will be relieved. She'll be free to choose where she lives. She gave up a lot to come here, and I truly hope people are ashamed for turning their backs on her."

CHAPTER TWENTY-THREE

Bill, his top team and Harold's team scrambled the World Guild's outlets to all media channels. Every personal communication device, Advanced Multimedia Device (formerly known as a TV, and now known as an AMD), and Literalist were captured and held hostage for a special presentation.

The Maxwells, including Bill, Teresa, Abby, Apollo, their puppies, Rex, and Jerry, along with Becky and Percy Smythe, stood on the street in front of Bill and Teresa's house in TMZ. Bill spoke to the TMZ media Literalist that hovered in front of him. A crowd behind the Literalist watched the event that included many people the Maxwells didn't know, plus the Maxwell employees, and the TMZ committee members. Another Literalist captured the throng of people.

"My name is Bill Maxwell. You may be familiar with me through my many inventions, including The Dot, but you are most likely more familiar with my late dog daughter, Lilith. My wife and I defected to TMZ. We did not die in an accident climbing a mountain searching for Abby, the last known dog, as the World Guild would have liked you to believe.

"As you can see, Abby found us. We were surprised that she found a mate, and they had a litter of puppies. Apollo, Abby's mate, is a gray wolf, most likely the last of his kind. We are all well, as you can see, and we love our life in TMZ that is free of the World Guild. Don't believe a word they say about me, my family, or TMZ. They are nothing but liars who twist the facts.

"The World Guild also spewed lies about Abby's grandparents, Percy and Becky Smythe. They were only guilty of questioning the Tranquility Force about our empty house. Unfortunately, the Smythes were picked up in the middle of the night and found guilty of ridiculous charges. They were scheduled to have brain swipes when we rescued them.

"We wanted you to know that we are all living a peaceful, joyful, loving life here in Texmexzona. It's a lot warmer than what we were used to in WestUS, but we like it. I urge you to pay attention to the news bulletins. The news is sponsored by the World Guild, so they really spin the facts the way they want you to hear them. Most of the stories are fabricated or embellished. Unless you were involved in a particular news story, you have no idea if what is reported is true or not. Be cautious. Don't make a lot of noise with questions, or you will be dragged into custody.

"The world is changing. We'll leave you now to whatever you were watching or listening to before we captured the communication airwaves, but know that you will be hearing more from me in the near future. Be well. May the Earth bless you."

The media blitz ended. The TMZ crowd roared approval. Literalists went back to their duties searching for other news bits in the community.

Many people came forward welcoming the Maxwell clan to TMZ.

"Glad you set them straight."

"That was a very good infomercial!"

"I hope the world listens to what you said!"

Bill and Teresa thanked people. The puppies ran wild through the crowd. For once, Jerry stayed by Rex.

Glacious approached Bill. "Hopefully, that will set people straight."

Harold joined them. "Now we can get started on Ted's service."

"Yeah, let's get on with that so we can tackle the World Guild," Toby said.

Bill watched Rex for a moment. He figured his dog-bot was busy with something. It was difficult to know what was going on in all those circuits at any given time. Rex seemed to have his own agenda, which typically ended up being a time-saver for everyone involved.

"What do you think they're doing?" Roland asked. He jerked his chin in Rex's and Jerry's direction.

"No telling," Bill said. "But whatever it is, we'll most likely like it, or find it useful."

Rex chose that moment to approach his creator. "We have been gathering statistics from around the globe. Your special broadcast has an 88% approval rating, but I suspect that will rise as we continue fact-gathering."

Glacious, Harold, and the committee members nodded their approval.

"That will help tremendously when we begin the campaign to eliminate the World Guild," Pete said.

"We've discussed changing TMZ's status from a region to a country," MaryEllen said. "I suggest we send out a blitz to the world's Literalists stating that change. We don't need anyone's approval. The World Guild unknowingly helped us when they passed that law stating that anyone who moved here renounced their US citizenship."

Everyone nodded approval.

"Why don't you work something up, and Rex will be able to blast that out to the Literalists Worldwide Network. Won't that just steam the government!" Bill said.

BILL, Harold, and the committee members spent the next several days in meetings that lasted 10-12 hours each day. They put together a list of topics for each of the captured media blasts. Since Bill was recognized worldwide, he was the chosen spokesperson. He would address changes to the Dot—removing government claws. The Dot would remain the personal information bank for health, DNA, family ancestry, and income/payment devices. It would also remain active in all animal implants.

The vocal transmitter was a blessing for the deaf community, as well as for the dogs that communicated like humans. Cats, while candidates for the Dot, chose to be persnickety—if they wanted to talk to someone they would, but don't hold your breath.

For the deaf community, the Dot worked the same way as the animal transmitter worked allowing a deaf person to focus their thoughts into words that were spoken through a chosen voice app.

The committee agreed they should show historical footage of the 2030 era when everyday people took back their country from deceiving, criminal (in many cases), greedy and power-hungry bureaucrats whose only interest was wealth building (theirs) and power over their constituents.

The group felt certain people would become enraged watching something they most likely hadn't thought about in fifty years. Complacency was a dangerous thing. When citizens sit back and never question their government, enslavement happens quietly, painlessly. Punishment was easy to enforce in this day and age when anyone in any government office could simply click on a button and withhold your income until you complied with whatever they wanted.

Young people in their 20s and 30s weren't around when the population of the USA revolted, then every country around the world jumped at the opportunity and took back their governments. These twenty- and thirty-year-old's most likely never spared a thought to study that conflict or the way it had changed the lives of every human being on the planet.

Rex and Jerry were sorting through the Dot programming, separating the original purpose from the changes and upgrades over the years, so Bill could see what programs to block. Freedom was the top priority, but the basic application that made it easy to find a lost super-centenarian, animal, or human child was also a top priority.

A BLAST OUT to the world took place ten days later. They announced that Texmexzona (TMZ) had designated itself a country and would require a passport or visa to enter the area. Rex provided details on how to apply for a passport to visit the country.

Current TMZ inhabitants would be provided with their permanent resident ID cards, which would automatically show up in their Dot. Infant and toddler IDs would show up in their parents' Dots.

Committee members worried they would be overrun by

people wanting to visit. The dog-bots put together a list of hotel accommodations, maps of different areas, historical sites, and fun things to do. Teresa heavily edited the fun things list because the dog-bots' ideas of fun were not on par with human fun things—the dog-bots were too young to understand what fun was. The exception being Jerry, who seemed to be a puppy at heart and recognized anything fun. Rex's idea of fun was stodgy things that not even senior citizens would like, such as data gathering, statistics, and chart building. Rex had no idea what was considered fun.

The governor of Louisiana inquired if his state could become a part of TMZ. The committee members told him that they would consider his request. There were a lot of great things to do in Louisiana, and they could see the benefits of letting them join their new country. The great flood of 2060 had swept the city of New Orleans back into the ocean. Baton Rouge became beachfront property, including a new French Quarter and a new Bourbon Street. The Garden District had also been reinvented.

The entire area before the great flood had been 79.1 square miles (204.9 km), of which 76.8 square miles (198.9 km) were land and 2.2 square miles (5.7 km) (2.81%) were covered by water. After two years of resettlement from absorbing New Orleans people and businesses, the greater area of Baton Rouge was approximately 252 square miles (405.5 km) of land. The area covered by water that was considered part of the city limits was 5.8 miles (9.3 km).

"It would be nice to visit Baton Rouge," Bailey said.

The other committee members nodded. They would have to think about how to absorb the state into their new country.

～

THE AIRING of the 2030s footage caused considerable unrest throughout the world. Rex had created a downloadable *Declaration of Life* document, which the majority of people had most likely forgotten about. The vast changes that occurred during that time hadn't been revisited by anyone to consider what exactly HAD changed.

When Bill and Harold finagled a way to provide TMZ with Literalists reports from across the USA and the world, they discovered civil disobedience running rampant. When Simon Day's crimes were exposed on air, along with Conan Zerlich, and Hemrey Branch's participation, people overpowered Tranquility Force enforcers and World Guild enforcers. Both of those groups had some rotten eggs in their baskets, and the population was sick of constantly looking over its shoulders.

"Looks like people are waking up," Glacious said as he watched the Global News Network in the command center. "GNN can't hide everything, so it looks like they chose to be impartial this time."

"It would be stupid to attempt to censor what's happening across the globe," MaryEllen said. "Especially when you have these large crowds swarming into open areas to protest the World Guild."

Helen Daigle watched the high court sentencing proceedings. She felt vindicated when her son's in-laws were interviewed by Literalists and cried about how awful they had treated their son-in-law and his mother.

Rex captured the TMZ ceremony honoring Ted, and it was released to Literalists worldwide.

"Another chapter closed," Teresa said. "At least now Helen can be at peace with her son being exonerated."

CYBER-ATTACKS STARTED in the middle of the night. Rex called out to all dog-bots, and they flicked off the beams that tried to break through the tight coding created by Harold, fortified by Bill and further strengthened by Rex. It seemed to Rex that the World Guild and the Tranquility Force must have forgotten that Bill Maxwell was the coder who designed their systems and maintained everything up until the day he defected.

Rex made sure none of his pack would take any action against the invasions other than flicking them away from TMZ headquarters. His father would have to determine what to do about the attacks, but that could wait until daybreak when humans and dogs woke up.

Apollo wandered into the room where Rex was working on his dog bed.

"Did I wake you?" Rex asked.

"No, but I sensed activity," the wolf said. "Is there anything I can do to help?"

Rex's LEDs twinkled in the dark. "No, my father will take control of the current problem, but it isn't worth waking him."

"What's happening? Are there invaders?" Apollo asked. He sucked in a breath to taste the air, then listened with his sensitive ears for any unusual noise. He was ready to become wild to protect his home and family.

"TMZ is ready to take down the World Guild government. They are evil on so many levels," Rex said.

Apollo shook his fur. "I have watched and listened to the broadcasts, and I'm trying to understand what has happened."

Rex stood up, stepped off his bed, then sat beside the wolf. "The current year is 2087. A long time ago, back in 2030, the people of the entire United States of America revolted against the government. No one was killed in the protests, but everyday people... like Becky and Percy, threw government people out into the streets. They installed new people to run the country.

"Now, here we are fifty-seven years later, and it looks like history is repeating itself. Our father—I consider him your father since you don't have a wolf father—who is a very smart human, is leading the world into more social reform."

"This is a good thing for the people?" Apollo asked. He realized there was so much he needed to learn.

"Yes. The World Guild has become too big and its governance has become diabolical. People are deeply afraid of them and the Tranquility Force because they use so much unnecessary force," Rex explained.

Apollo went inside the dictionary in his head to look up the word he didn't understand. He broke the word down into little parts, like Abby taught him when he didn't know how to spell something. di-a-bol-i-cal. "I do not understand the meaning of this diabolical. What is devilish?"

Rex focused on the wolf. "What I should have said so you could understand more is that the World Guild government has effectively stolen people's freedom. People feel that they are caged in. If they do anything that the government doesn't like, they could be arrested.

"Remember when we rescued Abby's grandparents? That's a good example. Becky and Percy questioned the Tranquility Force about Bill and Teresa's empty house in WestUS. Then they were arrested in the middle of the night and thrown into jail. There wasn't even a trial, but they were going to have their brains swiped."

Apollo thought about what Rex had just told him. "What happens to the brain when they do that?"

"All memories are erased. You won't know who you used to be. If you had a brain swipe, you would not remember Abby, your puppies, your family and life here, your wild wolf family, the cave—nothing at all. You would most likely have to learn how to walk, talk, eat, hunt—all that would be gone. But I'm not sure about some of this because a wolf has never had its brain swiped, and some of that would be pure instinct from your heritage," Rex said.

"That is a very bad thing! That government is bad for the people!" Apollo said.

"That's why Daddy is trying to fix what he helped build," Rex said. "His good intentions were swept under the rug— that's an expression that means hiding something. He was duped into changing his programs that were intended for good but made bad for the people."

CHAPTER TWENTY-FOUR

pollo ate his breakfast with a frown on his face. For a wolf, that meant his forehead was creased, and his eyes squinted. Abby noticed.

What's wrong, Apollo?

Rex and I had a long talk last night while he was working. You will most likely hear this subject from Daddy or Rex today.

Abby stared at her mate. It was not common for him to refer to her father as *daddy*. She didn't have to wait long for an answer.

As Bill and Teresa sat down to eat, Bill checked his communications.

"Rex, why didn't you wake me when these attacks began?"

The dog-bot walked up to Bill and sat. "I did not see the point. My pack and I subverted the attack."

The front door sounded an alert that visitors were outside.

Romping could be heard as Jerry, followed by the puppies, swarmed the door.

"Who's there?" Jerry asked through the closed door.

"It's Harold, Jerry."

Jerry used his shoulder claw and opened the door. "Hello. Won't you come in?"

The puppies encircled Harold, each vying for his attention. He could never tell one from the other—he just couldn't remember their names.

"Hello, puppies," Harold said, as he patted foreheads and butts.

"Everyone go outside and leave Harold alone," Abby called out as she walked to the door. "Good morning, Harold. Mommy and Daddy are in the kitchen. Please go help yourself to coffee and breakfast."

"Hi, Abby. Thanks, I'll head back."

Harold headed to the kitchen. "Morning, Teresa... Bill. We had a cyberattack last night, but no one was alerted to it!"

"We were just talking about it. Rex and his pack took care of it without telling anyone about it," Bill said.

Harold swung his eyes over to the dog-bot. "Next time, please alert us, Rex. We might want to take different action."

"Why don't I lock them out of the systems I developed?" Bill said. "I would make sure that the Dot was not affected by any controls we removed."

"I think that's a good place to start," Harold said. "They'll be quaking in their shoes."

JUST BEFORE LUNCH, World Guild military flyers invaded TMZ airspace. Dozens of TMZ patrol gliders sped to each area along their borders, along with airborne dog-bots that fired warning lasers at the invaders.

People grabbed their children and ran into their houses, ducking their heads while screaming.

Rex was on the ground, turning in different directions

while monitoring his pack. "Disable their ability to take scans of TMZ. Do not provoke a firefight." He received acknowledgment from the entire pack.

All the puppies were outside, necks stretched to the sky while they watched the massive gliders with the World Guild logos plastered on their sides. Teresa opened the front door.

"Everyone inside, right now!" she yelled over the racket of zooming gliders overhead. She was freaked out. There hadn't been a war in her lifetime, and she didn't know what to do if bombs suddenly dropped from the air.

"I want to fly!" Jim shouted as he jumped in the air.

"Jim, come into the house right now before you get hurt!" Teresa's nerves were on edge.

The reluctant puppy joined his siblings and parents in the house. "Can we get upgrades so we can fly?"

Apollo looked at his puppy. "You aren't a machine, Jim. There isn't anything to upgrade. You're made of fur, teeth, bones and a tail."

Wolf came to his brother's side. "We could wear jetpacks."

Apollo and Abby looked at their smart son.

"Dogs and puppies belong on the ground, not up in the sky flying around unless they are inside a glider," Abby said.

"But..." Jim said.

"No buts," Apollo said firmly.

"Fine. I'll discuss this with Rex," Wolf said. He walked away in a huff.

Teresa kept quiet as she watched the interactions between parents and puppies. Wolf reminded her of Lilith. She had been so much smarter than any other dog, adapting to technology with zest. Her dog daughter had loved the pawboard and her Dot. Teresa shook off her sentiments and returned to the situation at hand.

"Why don't we have a snack?" Teresa suggested. "We'll let

headquarters, Rex and his pack take care of what's going on outside."

There were multiple cheers for a snack. Teresa worked the food console and produced eight dog snacks. Two large-size snacks for Abby and Apollo, and six smaller snacks, much to the disappointment of the puppies.

A galloping noise sounded on the roof. Everyone ducked down in fear.

Teresa sent an inquiry to Rex. "What's happening? Is someone on the roof?"

A tense moment passed, then Rex's voice boomed out. "It's just Jerry."

"That Jerry," Teresa muttered to herself. Her communicator dinged a call in from Bill.

"Everyone okay? We've run them off," he said.

"We're okay. Jerry scared us just now. He's up on the roof running around," Teresa said.

She heard Bill huff.

"No casualties?" she asked.

"No, we fired warning shots. It was tense, but when they discovered they were being attacked by flying dog-bots, they turned tail and left," Bill said.

"Are all the dog-bots accounted for?" Teresa asked.

"Rex, has your pack checked in?" Bill asked.

"Yes, all safe and accounted for. Ruff, Number 5, said he has a screw loose," Rex said.

Bill and Teresa each held back chuckles. A clueless Rex stared at them.

"Have Ruff check in with Toby or Roland," Bill said. "Hon, I'll see you in a little while."

"Okay. We're heading to the schoolroom," Teresa said.

When the puppies heard *schoolroom*, they whined in dog-talk.

Teresa clapped her hands. "Okay, enough excitement for one day. Everyone head for the schoolroom. We have work to do."

ROLAND HAD RUFF ON A TABLE. He examined the jet pack on the right side of Number 5, while Rex and Benji (Number 8) stood by and watched. "Have all the bots come in so I can check their jet packs. Seems like vibrations loosened this screw. See how this jet pack has dropped down and isn't facing the right direction to fire? Ruff could have blasted his rear foot off."

Benji sent out a silent call for the dog-bots to come to the building. Rex called Jerry to have his jet pack checked out.

One by one, the dog-bots trotted through the door. They watched as their compadre was repaired on the table with a high-powered screwdriver.

Roland set Ruff on the floor. "You're good to go. Everyone line up, and I'll check your jet packs."

Ruff joined Rex and Benji.

"Return to your duties," Rex said.

Benji was about to leave with Ruff.

"Not you, Benji. Your jet pack has to be checked," Rex said.

Roland was checking the fifteen remaining dog-bots when Jerry came into the room. "Over here, Jerry."

"Were you on the roof?" Rex asked his pal.

"Yes, it's a good place to check the skies," Jerry said.

"It's not good for the people in the house when they hear you galloping on the roof," Rex admonished.

"Oops!" Jerry said. "I'm sorry."

"Don't tell me you're sorry. You have to tell our family you're sorry," Rex said.

Roland scooped Jerry off the floor. "Sorry to interrupt your little challenge, boys, but let's keep focused." He examined Jerry's jet pack and tightened the screws. "All set, Jerry. Rex, how about an upgrade? Want me to install a jet pack?"

"I'll think about it." The dog-bot turned, walked out the door and headed home. He let himself inside and silently checked the emotional atmosphere. Rex felt the tension among the dogs and Teresa. He walked to the schoolroom.

"Everything is under control. There is no reason to worry," he said.

Wolf piped up. "Some of us want jetpacks."

Rex's LED eyes seemed to squint. "What would you do with a jetpack?"

Jim pranced in place with excitement. "I want to fly! I want to shoot at the bad people!"

"Puppies and dogs are not candidates for jetpacks. You can fly in a glider or run on the ground," Rex said. "If you learn how to fly a glider, perhaps this subject will be revisited."

Wolf stared down Rex. "I can learn how to fly a glider."

Rex knew he was in trouble with this conversation since Wolf was one smart puppy. "The decision would be up to Daddy Bill." He turned and left the room, his head churning over the problem. He was convinced Wolf could learn to fly a glider using mental controls.

AFTER SCHOOL LET OUT, Teresa, Abby, Apollo, Rex, and all six puppies were outside. The adults and Rex were on the porch while the puppies ran wild with the human children and Jerry. Bill's glider approached and came in for a landing in the holding area. He joined everyone on the porch, but Teresa gave him big eyes and nodded toward the door. Bill, Teresa and Rex went inside.

"I'm going to join them inside and talk to Daddy about Wolf and Jim," Apollo said as he got to his feet.

"Good," Abby said, her eyes wide just thinking about puppies jetting around overhead.

Apollo stood at the door and realized he could not get inside. He bonked the doorbell with his snout and waited. Within a few minutes, Bill came to the door. He studied Apollo.

"I have to give you, Abby, and the pups a way to get into the house if no one is available to open the door," he said. While the dogs could go into the controls to unlock the door, it didn't pop open for them to use their paws or snouts to open the door. "Come in. I'll solve this problem later."

Apollo preceded Bill into the house and joined Teresa and Rex in the living room. He shook himself to release the uneasiness he felt.

"What's going on?" Bill asked. He noticed the tension on Teresa.

"We have a situation," she said. "Jim wants a jetpack so he can fly. I told him that wasn't possible, then Wolf jumped in and said he'd discuss this with Rex."

"Wolf said he could learn how to fly a glider, and I believe him," Rex said.

"Wait... wait... wait," Bill said, his hand raised out in front of him. "Let me get this straight. Jim and Wolf want to fly? A glider is one thing, but jetpacks? No, to both of those. Think how dangerous that would be for everyone!"

"Puppies and dogs belong on the ground," Apollo said. "They don't need to be zooming around. Jim wanted an upgrade so he could fly. I had to explain that puppies were flesh and bone and fur and teeth. They couldn't be upgraded. Then our smart boy had to get involved." He shook himself again.

"I don't see that there's much to discuss. The answer to all questions regarding flight and dogs is a resounding NO," Bill said. "I realize we are technologically advancing rapidly, but common sense can't fly out the window either. Think of the havoc with a bunch of numbskulls flying around overhead, and I don't mean just dogs. People would want to have jetpacks. I can envision people slamming into each other hundreds of feet in the air and dropping to their deaths." He shook his head at the thought.

"Daddy, I think it all started with Jerry flying. He's their playmate," Abby said.

"And running across the roof didn't help," Rex said.

"They're still too young to have a lot of common sense," Bill said. "This should pass if they don't see any dog-bots flying."

Apollo did not look convinced. "I don't know about that."

"Let's tackle a problem I can solve," Bill said. "I need to install a keypad on the exterior of the house at the front porch so Apollo, Abby and the puppies can get inside if no one is home."

"Can't they use the program..." Teresa asked.

"The door won't pop open. I'm going to use a special code they can key in outside," Bill said.

"Do you mean key in mentally?" Teresa asked.

"No, physically, like with a stick on a string," Bill said. "Let me go see what I have in my office." He headed to his home office with Rex and Apollo at his heels.

Teresa shrugged at Abby. "I don't know why a code on the current system wouldn't work."

"I think Daddy needs something to do to calm his mind," Abby said.

Several minutes later, Bill, Rex, and Apollo returned to the living room. Bill held up a keypad in one hand and a short, thin dowel with string tied around it in the other hand. "This will do. Everyone knows their numbers, right?"

Abby and Teresa both said, "Yes."

They all marched to the front door and went outside onto the porch. Bill pulled his electronic tape measure out of his pocket, along with his small, high-powered drill and four screws that he placed on the floor.

"Abby, let me measure how tall you are, then I'll measure Apollo," Bill said. Once he had those measurements, he measured from the porch floor up and drew a line to mark the height. "Teresa, would you hold the keypad in place so I can insert the screws?"

"Sure." She aligned the top with the line Bill drew.

He inserted one screw in the hole and drilled it partially down. He slipped the loop of the string through the other top screw and drilled that into place. Once all four screws were in place, he tightened them down.

"Okay, I came up with a seven-number code: 2417359. The 24 was our house designation in WestUS; 17539 is the new Maxwell Industries locator. Want to give it a try, Apollo?"

"2-4-1-7-3-5-9," the wolf repeated as he walked up to the keypad.

"No, you have the 3 and the 5 switched. It's 1-7-5-3-9," Teresa said.

"Oh!" Apollo studied the keypad, the dowel, and the string. He gently snagged the dowel with his teeth, making it stick out in front of him. The wolf poked the number 2, then 4, then the rest of the numbers. He heard a click, and the door popped open. He dropped the dowel, went to the door and nudged it open with his paw.

"How do I get back outside if I'm in the house?" he asked.

"I'll have to install another keypad inside," Bill said as he turned to Rex. "Is there any way you can trigger the house code to make the door pop open?"

"I will look at the code," Rex said.

"Okay, Abby, you give it a try, then we'll have each of your pups to experiment."

Apollo seemed to be thinking about something.

"What's on your mind?" Teresa said.

"Currently, my pups can't go outside unless someone opens the door. I'm concerned about someone going outside without supervision," Apollo said.

Bill pondered what could easily be chaos in the making. "I hadn't thought about that. On the other hand, I don't want anyone trapped in a house in case of a fire or some other disaster."

Abby grabbed the dowel in her teeth and applied the code. The door popped open, and she pushed it inward. "This works, Daddy. Do we teach my pups, or not?"

"I think it's better to teach them," Teresa said. "We will just have to instill in their minds that there will be bad repercussions if someone leaves the house without explicit permission."

Abby left the porch and headed over to where everyone was playing in the street. She called out the names of her litter and told them to go to the porch where their father and grandparents waited.

"Aw, I want to play," Esme whined.

"Are we in trouble for something?" Lulah asked.

"I didn't do anything!" Puppy Rex said.

"You pushed that boy," Star said.

"Did not!" Puppy Rex yelled.

"Did so! I saw you!" Star yelled back.

Wolf and Jim seemed to know when to shut up.

"You'd better play nice with the children," Abby said. "If

you don't, their parents might not want you playing with them at all."

Puppy Rex became wide-eyed. He didn't want to jeopardize playtime with the human children!

They all climbed the steps to the porch. Bill looked them over. "I have installed a keypad so you can open the door if you are outside and need to go into the house. Does everyone remember their numbers?"

"Yes!" they shouted.

"Memorize this number," Bill said. He said the numbers slowly, then repeated them. "Never share the number with anyone. That would leave us vulnerable. Do you know what vulnerable means?"

"Defenseless!" Wolf blurted.

"Yes, that's right," Bill said. "We'll start with you, Wolf. You need to grab this wooden dowel with your teeth and hit the numbers in the correct order. Then the door will pop open."

Wolf approached the keypad. He sniffed it all over, then the dowel and string. He finally grabbed the dowel with his teeth and bashed the 2, then the 4, but accidentally bashed the 5.

"Okay, when that happens—when you accidentally hit the wrong number, hit the pound sign to clear your mistake so you can start over. This is the pound sign (he pointed to the #). Give it a try," Bill said.

Wolf hit the pound sign, then hit all the correct numbers. The door popped open.

Teresa clapped. "Very good, Wolf. Who's next? Why don't you give it a try, Lulah."

The rest of the puppies tried out the keypad with only a few blunders. Apollo looked over his brood.

"If anyone is caught sneaking outside without permission,

they will be punished," he said, with a stern expression that creased his forehead.

"Can we go play now?" Esme asked.

"Yes, go play," Abby said.

Rex moved closer to the group from where he was mentally zinging through code and options. "I have a solution for the possibility of leaving without permission. When the door code is used, all adults will be notified. If Abby or Apollo use the code, there's nothing to worry about. If one of the pups uses the code when they aren't supposed to be outside, they can be rounded up."

Everyone thought about it and then nodded.

CHAPTER TWENTY-FIVE

L ulah arrived first to the front door after supper. She grabbed the dowel in her teeth a little too aggressively, and the string broke.

"Uh oh!" Esme said. "Look what you did!"

"Grandpa!" Jim hollered.

"You little tattletale!" Lulah sneered at Jim.

Bill walked to the front door. "What's the problem?"

"Lulah broke the string!" Star said.

Bill entered the code and opened the door. "Go outside and play. Just be careful that you don't yank the string when you want to come inside."

After the last puppy went outside, he walked back to his home office and searched through cabinets and drawers until he found a sturdier twine. He grabbed his power driver and returned to the front door and solved the problem. He went outside and replaced the string with the twine to avoid any problems. Then he went back inside.

Abby and Apollo came out of the house to watch their brood. Apollo flopped down on the top step and watched the running, jumping, and playing in the street. There were only a couple of human kids outside, so the puppies played more roughly with their littermates.

Someone's grandfather came outside and plunked a chair down on his lawn to watch playtime. He called out to his granddaughter, encouraging her to run and jump, and have a good time. He clapped and laughed at the goings-on in the street. Two of the dogs raced up and down the street, then slowed to a stop, panting.

Suddenly, the grandfather clutched his chest and fell forward out of his chair onto the lawn. Apollo jumped to his feet. He ran over to the elderly man, Abby pulling up behind him.

"Are you hurt?" Apollo asked. He and Abby sniffed the man from his head down to his shoes.

When the man didn't respond, the wolf blinked on his directory in his head and clicked on Bill and Teresa's pictures. "An old man has fallen out of his chair. He's not talking!"

The front door opened. Bill and Teresa rushed out and ran over to the dogs and the old man.

Teresa kneeled on the ground and felt for a pulse. "He's still breathing. Erratic pulse."

Bill used his communicator to call for assistance.

All playtime in the street stopped. The little girl ran up to her grandfather. "Grandpa!" She ran up to her house, panicky, and returned with her mother.

"Dad! Dad! What happened?" the woman asked Bill and Teresa.

Apollo spoke up. "He was encouraging the child at play when he fell out of his chair."

A medical emergency glider raced through the air and landed on the street. Two medics hurried out of the glider; one slid the panel door open and exposed the portable Virtual

Healing frame. A large, brilliantly lit caduceus symbol was mounted above the large, blue, human-shaped mold. One medic grabbed the frame and rearranged it from vertical to horizontal, then slid the frame out of the glider on its sturdy steel structure. Both medics manipulated the frame, so it was now lying flat with the human shape easier to access.

With the equipment settled, the medics grabbed a portable gurney and rushed over to the ailing old man on the lawn.

"Status?" One medic asked the group of people.

"Heart attack, I think," Teresa said.

The medics wasted no time lifting the man onto the gurney and racing back to the medical glider. They lifted him into the mold and settled his limbs into the shapes of his body. A medic engaged the machine, then stood watch. The mold lit up around the man with a bright red light. Then it changed to white, then peach, and finally black. After twenty seconds, the black light shut off.

"Temporary healing is complete. Please make an appointment within fourteen days for a thorough physical and diagnostic evidence of your condition. Please scan your Dot at the credit panel," the virtual healing device said.

The elderly man held out his shaky wrist to the credit panel. A green LED appeared on the screen. "Credit accepted. You owe zero balance. Thank you for your business," the automated voice said.

The medics maneuvered the frame back to the vertical position and helped the man step out of the mold and onto firm ground. His daughter and granddaughter rushed up to him. Bill and Teresa joined them.

"Here, let me help get him back to your house," Bill said. He put one arm around the elderly man's waist, supporting him, then scrunched down until the man's arm crossed his shoulder, then straightened up again. The daughter took the other side and between them, they guided the man to the front door.

"Wendy, open the door so we can get grandpa inside safely," the woman called out.

The little girl rushed around them and opened the door.

Teresa, Apollo, Abby, and everyone else stayed on the lawn. The medical glider took off on another emergency call. A few minutes later, Bill emerged from the house.

"That was fast thinking, Apollo. I'm glad you called for help," Bill said. "If something like this happens again, first click on Emergency, then call us. That way the emergency medics will arrive quicker."

"I didn't understand what happened to him at first," the wolf said. "Will he be okay, or is his time here about to stop?"

Teresa patted the wolf's back. "His daughter will take him to the VHO where he will be examined more thoroughly."

"What's a VHO?" one of the puppies asked.

"Virtual Healing Office," Abby said. "They have a dog and cat, VHO."

Bill smirked. "You've had experience with that, haven't you?"

Abby glared at Bill. "It's not funny, Daddy."

"Never said it was," Bill said. "Goes to show you how important it is to pay attention to what your parents tell you. Guess you're learning that right now."

"What happened, Mommy?" Esme asked.

"When I was very little, younger than what you are right now, your grandfather brought me to work with him. We were outside walking down a pathway when a lizard ran out in front of me. I chased after it, then the security globes told me to stop and to return to the path, and I didn't." Abby huffed out an exasperated sound. "They zapped my nose because I was a silly puppy who would not listen to her father. It was very painful."

Abby glared at her father and returned to their porch, leaving everyone to follow or return to playtime.

THE FOLLOWING MORNING, Teresa was in a foul mood. It started when she practically went flying in the kitchen after slipping on sloshed water by the large water bowl.

"Who spilled this water and didn't say anything?" she fumed.

The adult dogs and their litter recognized the tone of voice that clearly indicated they were in for trouble, so they chose the *Silence is Golden* stance and hunkered down on the floor, trying to make themselves invisible.

Bill walked into the kitchen dressed for work in his laid-back style of a buttoned-up shirt, linen slacks, and his ever-present Birkenstock sandals. He was ready for breakfast.

Teresa was on her hands and knees with a dish towel wiping the floor dry.

"Did someone spill water?" Bill asked.

"These dogs are fully capable of grabbing a towel and wiping up their spills," she raged.

Bill blinked. This was so unlike Teresa; he hardly recognized her. He carefully worded his response. "This sounds like today's school lesson. They need to understand what it means to be responsible for their actions."

"It's not easy trying to educate these puppies," Teresa said as she scooted around on the floor. "Even Becky has her hands full with them in the classroom."

"Why don't you and Becky make a list of all these annoyances? They should be able to do simple chores like wiping up water," Bill said, treading lightly. He honestly didn't know what they were capable of doing. Lilith had ordered her food and shopped on the PawBoard. Bill knew that Abby used the PawBoard at home and when she was hostage at the lab, but he didn't know what else she did on the device.

"Have they learned how to use the PawBoard yet? They should be ordering their own food, or at least Abby should be doing that," he said.

Rex stood in the doorway. He sent a silent message to Bill via his communicator. "Retreat!"

Bill glanced his way.

Teresa grumbled to herself when she stood, wet towel in hand. "The PawBoard is on the list of things to do. Maybe we should drag it out of my office and put it in the living room."

"I can do that now if you show me where you want it," Bill said.

She turned to face him, hands on hips. "Find a blank wall where they can see the AMD and put it in front of it!" Teresa glared at him as if he were an idiot for not thinking of that.

Rex blasted a message to Bill: RETREAT. FALL BACK. LEAVE NOW, BE QUIET!

Bill froze, then turned around and exited the room, biting his tongue to keep his retort to himself. Abby darted after him, followed by Apollo.

"Daddy!" Abby whispered. "What's wrong with Mommy?"

The dogs followed him into the schoolroom, along with Rex.

"Sometimes people get annoyed by little things, and they sort of blow up after they've kept the feelings hidden for too long," Bill said. "It's like a hidden resentment. It's best to let her temper cool down for a while."

"Should we go hunt for our food?" Apollo asked. "Are we a burden?"

Bill stopped what he was doing, turned to the wolf, and ruffled the fur on his back. "No, Apollo. None of you are a burden at all. There's no need to hunt for your food. Everyone has a bad day every once in a while."

Bill grabbed one end of the rather large PawBoard and dragged it out of the schoolroom to the living room.

Rex beamed a red dot on the wall where the PawBoard would be accessible to all, and where it would have a clear view of the AMD where the user's choices would appear.

"Where's Jerry?" Bill asked. He hadn't seen the dog-bot in the kitchen with the puppies, and he wasn't in the schoolroom or the living room. If left to his own devices, Bill felt that Jerry's curiosity might get him into trouble. After he moved the PawBoard into place against the wall where Rex indicated, he searched the rooms where the dogs slept on their dog beds. Jerry was on his monogrammed bed, feet up in the air with a grin on his mechanical face.

Bill took a picture of the clown and hoped it would bring a smile to his wife's face. "What are you up to, Jerry?"

"I thought it would be a good idea to show the dogs where food comes from," Jerry said. "They most likely have never seen a farm structure unless they caught a glimpse of one on the AMD."

Bill was stumped. He had never thought to bring Lilith to one of the facilities when she was alive, and as far as he knew, Abby had never seen one either.

"That's a good idea, Jerry."

"I bet no one knows how food gets in the food console either," the smart dog-bot said.

"Well, as a matter of fact, Becky knows all about that. She develops recipes and teaches instructions on how to use..."

"But does she know how it works so that what you order is delivered to your food console?" Jerry persisted.

Bill stared at the dog-bot. "I don't really know. We'll have to ask her." After a moment, he shook his head. "That subject is too advanced for the dogs. They can't use the food console to begin with. All they can do is place an order from the pictures they see on the AMD and then wait for someone to deliver it to their food stand."

"Okay, we'll scrap that one," Jerry said.

"I think it's a good idea to visit one of the farming structures," Bill said. "Let's go back to the kitchen."

"Do you think that's a good idea?" Abby asked.

"It's breakfast time," Bill said. "If your mother is still in a bad mood, I can get everyone's breakfast."

Rex stared at Bill.

"What?" Bill asked.

"I've never seen you operate the food console," Rex said.

"It's been a while, but how difficult is it to order food?" Bill asked.

They walked down the hall and entered the kitchen. The puppies stood at their food bowls, eating. Teresa was sitting at the table drinking her café mocha. She looked up as Bill, Abby, Apollo, and Rex entered the room.

Bill bent, kissed her on the cheek, then straightened up. He went over to the food console on the counter.

"Abby, did you place the food order for you and Apollo?" he asked.

"No, we haven't been using the PawBoard, but we will now," Abby said as she cast a quick look at her mother.

Bill stared at the appliance. "Okay, what would you want this morning?"

"Choose A-3 for me, and AP-3 for Apollo," she said.

He studied the menu and couldn't make any sense of it.

Teresa sighed, stood up and approached the counter. "Honestly, Bill. You'd starve if I were incapacitated." She eased in front of the machine. "Press this button to start the order. Then press this menu button. See the list of names? For Abby, you press her name, then scroll down to the third option and press that. Then go back to the list of names...."

"Oh, okay. Let me order Apollo's food," he said. He followed her directions and placed the order. Next, he found his name. "How do I know what my choices are?"

"B is for breakfast. L is for lunch, S is for snack, and D is for dinner. Click on the numbers to see the choices. Everything you typically choose for breakfast is listed there," Teresa said in a normal voice.

A soft ding announced the arrival of Abby and Apollo's food bowls. Bill lifted the first bowl out of the console, then the second appeared. He placed their bowls in their elevated dish stands. Then he returned to the food console and ordered his breakfast and coffee, while Teresa watched over his shoulder.

He brought his plate and coffee cup to the table and sat.

"What are you going to do today?" Teresa asked.

"I'm meeting with the TMZ committee to discuss our next plan of action against the World Guild," he said.

"I think you should send a media blast to that list I put together. Get people thinking about the government, and list the services that are in the process of changing, and things that should take place," she said.

"My team is already in the process of shutting out governmental controls on the Dot. That will bring a lot of things to a screeching halt without hurting payments or communications for emergencies and all the rest," Bill said. "No one will be able to hold anyone hostage by messing with their Dot."

"You might want to send out a notification to employers that they will no longer be able to interfere with wages and payments," Teresa said. "I recall that in the past, some employers were quite nasty to an employee or a team that was tasked with some hair-brained idea when they didn't like the outcome. They had the power to withhold money from the wages of those who were just following orders, or following the employer's plan."

"That's a good idea, but we need to make sure that this does not interfere with raises or bonuses," Bill said. "Rex, can you add those things to the list? I don't want to forget something. There's too much at stake."

"Got it," Rex said.

"There's going to be mass chaos when things come to light," Teresa said. "Especially if we experience something similar to the 2030 takeover again. TMZ better make sure all of its borders are protected. The World Guild is going to be pretty pissed off."

"Yeah, we've discussed that. Now, with Louisiana wanting to join TMZ, that's extending the borders even more, but I think it's a good plan to accept them into the fold."

"Maybe Oklahoma will want to join," Teresa said.

Bill shook his head. "I don't think they'd ever consider it. There are two major World Guild bigwigs in Oklahoma."

"Oh, you're right. Razden and Comherst. They'd cut off their left foot before giving up their nice cushy income from what I consider bribes," Teresa said. "They haven't done one thing for the needy in their state, and if I recall correctly, Razden even tried to push a bill through to limit the rights of people who fell below the minimum earnings level. As if they weren't suffering enough!"

CHAPTER TWENTY-SIX

Bill's face appeared on every AMD and communicator across the planet as the spokesman for TMZ. A large bulleted list was superimposed on the screen beside him. It read like a laundry list of grievances against the World Guild. He talked about how the newly formed global government had been established in 2030, and the *Declaration of Life* had been established. Then, in 2045, the Unified World Pact was formed, and peace and prosperity took center stage.

It was shortly after the *incident of 2076*—the earthquake that changed the world—that people started to notice the changes in the World Guild. There was no more *peace and bliss*. In the current climate, people looked over their shoulders and were careful who they spouted off to for fear of being turned in to the Tranquility Force, henchmen for the World Guild.

"I created the Dot for a specific purpose—so elderly people, or all children—human or animal who became lost, could be found again. Over time, the Dot was updated to hold all those long ID numbers, and it eliminated having to carry money in your pocket, and made it easy for your banking and payments," Bill explained. "Then the government got involved, and all sorts of bad things were added, including spying. As the developer and patent holder of the Dot, I am happy to announce that the World Guild has effectively been permanently blocked from your Dots.

"If you discover an important feature that has been removed from your Dot, please fill out the form in your communication device. My team will compile a list, and we will contact you when the problem has been researched and resolved, if it's for the common good."

On the sidelines, Harold held up his index fingers to make a T, alerting Bill he needed to end the announcement.

Bill inclined his head ever so slightly to Harold, then concluded with, "Take the time to think about the life changes I mentioned today. Only you can bring about government reform."

The bulleted list disappeared as the connection was severed. Bill joined Harold, Glacious, and the committee members.

"What do you think?" he asked. "Will people take action?"

Rex came forward. "My pack is surveying random people. I will report when data is available."

"Oh, great work, Rex," Harold said. The others nodded in agreement. The dog-bot was one step ahead of everyone else, as usual.

One man who worked in Harold's area tapped on the door-frame. "Excuse me, Harold, but we're receiving alerts from around the stateside borders of TMZ about Tranquility Force and World Guild gliders being sighted. What are your orders?"

"Send all interior guards to the perimeters to control this situation," Harold said as he rushed out of the meeting room and headed to his domain.

Bill, Rex, and the committee members followed Harold and his staff into the command center. They studied the monitors that showed hostile gliders hovering at the border. They didn't spot any threats around the Gulf of Mexico or the southern-most parts of Mexico.

"Rex ..." Harold started.

"I've sent my pack to assist along those borders," Rex said, one step ahead of the request.

"Good. Thanks for taking action," Glacious said, as he acknowledged the dog-bot.

"The World Guild feels its power unraveling," Bill said.

"It may get dangerous," MaryEllen noted. "Send an alert to the citizens in those areas in case fighting breaks out. We don't want any civilian casualties."

"We're on it," Harold said, as he watched his staff members jump onto the task and send the alert.

Suddenly, images appeared on the screen from Blythe. A dozen Tranquility Force gliders hovered over the area.

"Who's broadcasting these images?" Glacious asked.

"Looks like Jerry is sending them," Bill said, as he checked the status of Rex's pack.

"That is correct," Rex stated. "Jerry is there on the ground. He will take flight if those Tranquility Force gliders enter TMZ by even an inch."

In the next instant, Jerry hovered in the sky in front of the invading gliders, facing the enemy. He was joined by TMZ gliders and two other dog-bots. The Tranquility Force started taking potshots at the defenders. Without hesitating, Jerry disintegrated one of the invading gliders. The others turned tail and zoomed away, fearful for their lives. Jerry must have received a call for help from one of the pack because his jet boosters kicked in and off he flew to the east.

"What's going on, Rex?" Harold asked as his people tracked Jerry via satellite pictures.

"Shiprock, New Mexico is under attack! Tranquility Force and World Guild gliders have breached the border and are 3.4 miles into the interior. Citizens are defending their community from the ground. We have lost Mary, dog-bot Number 13," Rex reported.

"What can we do?" Pete asked.

"We're doing everything possible," Harold said.

"Don't be distracted by this attack," Bill said. "This gives the enemy a chance to sneak into another area. Rex, make sure all dog-bots are aware of this tactic."

Harold's team expanded the view on the screens so that all the TMZ borders were visible on multiple screens. They could see a raging battle in the Gulf of California between the strip of land that contained Baja, and the town of Hermosillo in Sonora, Mexico. A squadron of Tranquility Force gliders shot at ground forces.

Suddenly, the tables were turned. Someone on the ground at the edge of the water aimed an old-timey rocket launcher into the sky. The explosion would have been deafening.

Everyone in the room watched as gliders exploded in the sky, then fell to the water. Whoever was on land must have had experience with the rocket launcher. The way the explosives hit the three gliders flipped the odds. They watched as the Mexican man on the ground handed off the rocket launcher to another man, and was handed another fully loaded weapon. He took aim, but waited for the right moment. When he fired at the enemy, he only managed to take out one glider, but damaged another one with the shrapnel that exploded outward.

The damaged glider limped to the ground at the edge of the water.

"Make sure they take everyone in that glider as hostages—we don't want to kill them," Glacious said.

The team at the controls swiftly sent messages in both Spanish and English to the people who were defending the territory. The return acknowledgment was received. No remaining threats from the sky were visible. After the last rocket launcher attack, the enemy gliders turned and zoomed back to the US.

They viewed other border areas and saw some skirmishes. The TMZ border patrols, along with the dog-bots, made for quick and efficient handling of the attacks. Along the far southern borders of Mexico, where only lush wild lands remained, they saw gliders hovering around what used to be Belize and Guatemala, which had been absorbed by Mexico thirty-five years earlier. The gliders were identified as World Guild and were passing through Chiapas moving westward.

Rex received a message ding. He allowed the call to be broadcast over his speaker so everyone could hear.

This is Manny Torres and Chief Yaotl. There are ships in the air. Are they friends or enemies?

"Manny, this is Rex, the dog-bot you met with Jonas. Those are World Guild ships. They are the enemy. We will send help immediately. Keep the tribe safe!"

"Why would they want to mess with natives?" Bailey asked. He had been quietly observing the entire fiasco.

"It's the World Guild. They think they can do whatever they want," MaryEllen retorted.

"I have contacted Jonas. He is familiar with the area. Lottie, dog-bot Number 6, and Cole, Number 16, will be there within minutes. I have shared my experiences with them, so they know all about the Nahua and the local natives," Rex said.

"Let's hope this doesn't burn down the forest!" Glacious said.

The two dog-bots zoomed over the land and crept up behind the gliders. Lottie opened her communication system and blasted out a fair warning to the World Guild gliders.

You will leave this area of TMZ at once, or we will destroy you!

Three TMZ gliders led by Jonas Biggibottom arrived at the scene. They appeared to be outnumbered 8 to 5, but it was a well-known fact among the TMZ guard that the dog-bots were armed and dangerous and should never be underestimated.

The World Guild was having none of it. They opened fire.

The dog-bot jet boosters let them shoot up into the air so fast that the human eye could barely track them. Jonas and his crew retaliated while defensively zipping their gliders through the sky.

World Guild glider number WG8643297 was blasted out of the sky. Flaming parts crashed onto the jungle floor. Tiny dots were seen on the control room screens scurrying around. They assumed it was the natives Rex had spoken with.

Cole chased three World Guild gliders back to the Gulf of Mexico. He opened fire and blasted one into the ocean. The other two crossed the GOM on a trajectory toward Mississippi.

The remaining enemy gliders fled when they figured their chances of advancing were not worth the losses. Cole returned to the muster point that Jonas had set up. They landed on the forest floor and helped the natives contain the fire.

Harold, Bill, the committee, and Rex studied the screens. Everything appeared to be under control. The invaders retreated.

"Would it be wise for me to keep my meeting with the governor of Louisiana?" Glacious asked.

"Take Timmy with you," Bill suggested. "It's important to get Governor Chaline onboard as soon as possible."

"I would suggest creating an army like they had in the old

days," Rex said. "It's okay to hire more patrol officers, but it may get to a point where we need a mass of citizens trained with weapons and war skills."

Everyone in the room stared dumbly at the dog-bot. There hadn't been an army in decades, since the New World Order was established with the new global government.

"I have studied the history of these things, and the current situation with the World Guild and the Tranquility Force has an 85.435% chance of military escalation," Rex continued. "It is critical that we accelerate preparations."

After everyone digested Rex's words, there were nods around the room. They realized they couldn't be unprepared.

"We should draft a message to the entire population of TMZ," Pete said. "This should include a voluntary signup for the new army, including a call for craftspeople to manufacture more gliders, weapons, dog-bots, and those boosters."

MaryEllen shuddered. "Just the thought makes my skin crawl. I remember seeing those old war broadcasts when I was young. All the death, destruction and decades it took to rebuild and restore vast areas."

"It's better to be prepared to defend our borders than to be caught off-guard," Bill said. "People need to learn how to fight— including all of us." He turned to Rex. "Are there any old generals or military people here in TMZ? We need expert guidance."

Rex studied his database. "I have located retired four-star General Charlie Thunderhorse near the Grand Canyon in Arizona, retired Major General Richard P. Stonedanice, right here near headquarters, and retired Naval Commander Cicely Wynnecats on the beach in Austin, Texas."

"I remember Commander Wynnecats," Bailey said. "She headed up the Gulf of Mexico rescue during the flood of 2076 when Galveston, Houston and all those coastal towns submerged under 18 feet of water. She's probably in her 70s now."

"We need to contact them and get them here to provide assistance," Glacious said.

"Are we reinstating them into service?" Bill asked.

Everyone pondered that.

"TMZ doesn't have any military branches, and even if we did, we couldn't reinstate them because they served in the USA, not TMZ. We can hire them as consultants," Glacious said. "We require their experience."

"Does this mean we should create an army?" MaryEllen asked.

GLACIOUS AND TIMMY flew to Baton Rouge to meet with Louisiana Governor Clarence Chaline. They discussed the state's seceding from the US and joining TMZ. Timmy helped with the historical information and how to proceed.

The current warlike situation was brought up. Glacious wanted Clarence to understand what they were getting into prior to their giving up their US statehood.

"Listen, we can greatly help with this situation," Governor Chaline said. "We have the Cajun Army. We can send military strategists to Blythe."

Glacious' face screwed up in a questioning expression. "Louisiana has an army?"

Governor Chaline grinned. "Cajuns are always prepared."

IT TOOK a couple of weeks to coordinate an in-person meeting at headquarters. General Thunderhorse, Major

General Stonedanice, Commander Wynnecats, and four rough-looking Cajuns sat in the large conference room with Glacious and the committee members, including Bill and Rex.

General Thunderhorse was discussing the draft when Zephirin Boudreaux piped up.

"Don't draft anybody younger than twenty-two. They'se don't have brains yet," Zephirin said. "Want 'em to be able to follow di-rections. Younger 'n that, they'd be useless. Git themselves killed."

"Good point," Major General Stonedanice said.

"Are we going to initiate a military draft, or put out a call for volunteers?" Commander Wynnecats asked.

"If they want to live in TMZ, then they should want to fight for TMZ freedom," Edmee Richard said. She and her male counterparts of the Cajun group nodded in almost synchronized rhythm.

"I agree, Captain Richard," MaryEllen said.

"It's Ra-Chard, ma'am," Edmee corrected.

"Oh, the French pronunciation! I'm so sorry," MaryEllen said.

"Understandable, being as you're not a Cajun," Captain Richard said, then winked.

CHAPTER TWENTY-SEVEN

The war committee added more names to its list of craftspeople. Recruits would have to be trained in hand-to-hand combat, weapons, glider tactics and choreographed flight patterns, glider weapon use, chain of command, and so much more.

"We have all that open space outside the fenced area," Bailey said. "We could set up tents for registration and physicals back there. The dog-bots can scope out existing possible locations for training camps already within TMZ."

"When do we want to begin?" Glacious asked.

"Time's a-wasting. Takes a good while to get troops organized and up to speed," Zephirin Boudreaux said.

"They need to register first so we know how many people to plan for," Harold said. "Why don't we start the day after tomorrow when we have a better idea of how many sessions to schedule."

"We should have alternating schedules so people can learn the basics of all the proposed training. That way, in case of an attack, we could have a larger base of people to protect the country," MaryEllen suggested. "Basics, then more advanced, all the way to fully trained."

Everyone, even the Cajuns, nodded at MaryEllen's logic.

"Who wants to handle the message and registration?" Pete asked.

"Gayle's really good at that," Bill said. "Harold, see if she wants to sign up for this position."

"THIS ISN'T AN INVITATION, OR AN ORDER," Gayle said. "It's more of a take-action piece." She typed away on the communication device. She outlined the critical problem, listed the training and responsibilities, created a registration form that included a place to list their trade, if any, and presented it to the committee for approval prior to hitting the send button.

They noticed she had a section for volunteers to help with food prep for the trainers and trainees. There would be an awful lot of people to feed and house. Everyone discussed whether they should have multiple training centers across the country.

General Thunderhorse would prepare the training center in Arizona at the TMZ headquarters, and Commander Wynnecats could take over Texas, but that left New Mexico and the vast area of Mexico without leadership or a training center. They didn't have to worry about Louisiana, which had its own Cajun army.

"There must be some veterans out there," Major General Stonedanice said.

Gayle added veteran status to the form with a blank for rank and special abilities. "I feel that we'll have inquiries about things we didn't think about."

"Go ahead and send it out," Glacious suggested. "As Zephirin stated, *time's a-wasting.*"

∾

FIRST OF ALL, they underestimated the patriotism displayed in the sheer volume of responses they received, and realized how unprepared they were to handle all the inquiries. The first order of business was to bring in the volunteers to help handle details, sorting through the hundreds, then thousands of people who responded just in the first few hours.

Pete's wife Mimi stepped up to lead the volunteers. She was like a drill sergeant barking out orders and ironing out the wrinkles.

Craftspeople were taken aside to begin the process of what the country needed regarding building gliders, weapons, and everything that the war committee required.

Registrations poured in from veterans. They were called in to meet with the top retired military who were already on board. These veterans would be assessed to determine how they could help train the new army.

People in Blythe and the surrounding headquarters area opened their homes to the influx of people scheduled for short-term training. Spare bedrooms and living room sofas filled up.

Rob Williams, the former Tranquility Force enforcer, joined the TMZ patrollers. He was happy to be back at work again, and for a good and just employer. Since Harold was the default head of the perimeter guards, he teamed Rob up with Jacob Terry, who had taken on the position of a guard when he joined Glacious at the conception of TMZ way back when. Harold made a mental note to make Jacob the head of the guard so he could step down to run the security end of TMZ along with Bill's help. He didn't want to be stretched too thin. That's when mistakes became liabilities.

TOBY, Roland, Wynne, and Murray were studying the dog-bot designs when the door opened and Rex entered. The men looked up, surprised.

"Hey, Rex, what's up?" Roland asked.

Rex approached the engineers. "I have decided its time that I put my foolishness aside and had an upgrade."

"Did you figure Jerry was having too much fun?" Murray asked.

"I determined that my pack requires a leader who would be in the trenches with them. If I don't have the ability to fly off with boosters of my own, how can I lead them appropriately?" Rex said.

Toby nodded. "Good point. I'm glad you've reconsidered, Rex."

"Do you want to do this now?" Murray asked.

"Might as well, so I don't change my mind," Rex said.

Roland reached down and scooped up the dog-bot. He settled him on the table. "How about we tweak a few things?"

"What would you upgrade?" Rex asked.

"More flexibility," Roland said.

"Do you have to shut me down, or can I watch?" the dog-bot asked.

"There's a system upgrade, but we'll wait and do that last, okay?" Toby said. He knew how touchy Rex was about going offline.

Wynne opened a cabinet and gathered supplies. He returned to the table and handed things off to Roland, the mechanical engineer. "Two boosters and four flex joints."

"Okay, Rex, I'll start with the flex joints, one leg at a time," Roland explained. "You'll be able to crouch, jump, and twist around a lot better than the joints you currently have installed."

Roland got to work on Rex's left rear leg, then moved to the front left leg, then tackled the right legs. "Okay, now for your boosters and your system upgrade with all the booster controls."

Once the boosters were installed, Roland went to the transfer surface and pulled up the programming. Wynne grabbed Rex and carried him to the transfer surface.

"Ready, Rex?" Wynne asked. "You'll only be down for a short spell. Check your time."

"It's 2:12 p.m.," Rex said. "I'm ready."

Wynne reached underneath Rex and pressed his belly button. The dog-bot's head crashed to his chest. Roland drew a line from the program to the circle where Rex stood, and the upgrade started.

"Uh oh. He's going to freak out when he comes to. This upgrade will take 12 minutes," Wynne said.

"Nothing we can do about it now. He'll be okay once he gets all the programming updates, but we could have a little fun with this," Roland said, grinning. "He's such a stickler for control."

Twelve minutes later, Wynne pressed Rex's belly button to bring him back online. The dog-bot raised his head, LEDs flashed, and system noises sounded as he came back online.

"Hello, Cinnamon, you're back online," Roland said, keeping a straight face.

"Cinnamon? My name is Rex!"

"Rex? No, my records show your name is Cinnamon," Roland said, with a dead serious expression.

Whirring sounds alerted them to a full system scan.

"You are mistaken; my name is Rex. How could your records differ from mine?" Rex asked.

"No, man, you're a girl dog-bot named Cinnamon," Roland said with a little smirk.

Rex studied the mechanical engineer. "Oh, I understand. You are playing a joke on me."

Roland grabbed Rex and settled him onto the floor. "Let's go outside and do a test of your boosters and joints."

"This system upgrade took a full 12 minutes. I see other areas have been upgraded as well," Rex said, as he walked out of the office with the men.

They entered the elevator and rode to the ground floor, then went outside to the front of the office building.

"We upgraded your system to match the newer dog-bots. I'm pretty sure you'll appreciate the differences," Murray said.

"First, try out the new joints," Roland said.

Rex crouched, then jumped a full six feet on the sidewalk from where he started.

"Try twisting around as if you wanted to see your tail," Roland suggested.

"This is very handy," Rex said as he twisted first to the right, then the left.

"Okay, now you can try out the boosters. You might want to read up on the different settings..." Roland said.

Rex's boosters engaged. He shot up into the sky like a rocket ship.

"...or not," Roland said. "Where'd he go?"

All faces stared at the cloudless blue sky, hands shielding eyes. They turned and looked in all directions, then got worried.

"Bill's going to kill me," Roland said.

Murray pointed to a speck in the sky. "Is that him?"

The speck grew larger, very fast. Before they knew it, Rex screeched to a halt, hovering right in front of them.

"The Earth looks beautiful from space," Rex said as he settled on the ground.

"Does everything work the way it should?" Murray asked. "Anything I need to tweak?"

"I'll inform you of any changes I make so you can keep the code pure," Rex said.

Murray nodded. "Good. If everything's okay, then I'm going back inside." He looked to his team members. Everyone nodded.

"See ya, Rex," Wynne said.

Rex lifted off and headed to the house. He flew right up to the porch and settled gently as everyone looked on, amazed.

"I thought you didn't want boosters?" Teresa asked.

"I changed my mind," Rex said.

Jerry pranced around him. "We're going to have so much fun!"

"Our boosters are for work. Dog-bots do not have fun," Rex said.

Jerry stared at Rex. "I have fun every day. Why don't you have fun?"

"I was the first dog-bot. My purpose is to serve our creator, and to make sure we are all safe from harm," Rex stated.

"Maybe your programming needs to be updated," Jerry said.

Teresa kept her lips buttoned. She was sure Jerry would get an earful pretty soon, but she was surprised when Rex stayed quiet and faced the street. Abby stared at her mother with expressive eyes. Teresa was sure her dog-daughter had wanted to make a comment, but knew better.

"My programming was updated. I also have upgraded leg joints," Rex boasted. "I bet I can jump further than you, Jerry."

Not one to be bested in challenges of this type, Jerry rushed down the steps and over to the sidewalk. "Does anyone have chalk? We need to mark our starting point."

Teresa stood. "Yes, I have some in the schoolroom." She went into the house and returned with a piece of blue chalk. Rex followed her and joined Jerry for the competition.

"Are you going to jump together, or one at a time?" she asked.

"Let's jump together," Jerry said.

Rex stared down the sidewalk for a bit. "Fine. We'll jump together."

Teresa stood several feet down the sidewalk. "Ready, set, GO!"

The dog-bots took three or four straight running starts, then leaped through the air. It was a clear win for Rex. His front feet landed a good six-inches ahead of Jerry's. Teresa took a video with her communicator, then marked the sidewalk with the chalk. She made a straight line across the cement for each dog-bot with their initial by the line.

"Well, looks like your new joints are winners, Rex," Abby said.

CHAPTER TWENTY-EIGHT

Mimi Clearhanger wanted to set things up for her volunteers so that most of them were not running all over the place. There was no point wearing out her team right out the door. Not put off by committee rules, or anything for that matter, Mimi waltzed right into headquarters and spoke to Glacious, her husband and the others.

"Joey's doing reconnaissance to find a space large enough for a cafeteria setting to feed all the troops," she told them.

"Who's Joey?" Pete asked, with a hint of a jealous undertone in his question.

"Dog-bot #14," Mimi said, giving her husband a snide look. "You've got a problem with that?" She harrumphed. "After thinking about it, I asked Joey to look for abandoned buildings that could be used for barracks. That would ease the burden of TMZ people having strangers in their spare rooms and on their sofas."

Everyone nodded.

"Good idea," Glacious said.

"There's several vacant warehouses about five miles from

here," MaryEllen said. "I don't know what shape they're in, but Joey could check them out. Tell him they're over on the lower part of Tucson Street."

Mimi sent Joey a message, then engaged the committee again. "This will require commercial cooking, refrigeration, and freezing equipment. Think we can procure those when we find the space? We'll also need bunks for the troops. Men's and women's barracks."

"When Joey finds the appropriate places for both the cafeteria and the barracks, let us know and we'll take a look," Glacious said.

APOLLO SNOOZED on his dog bed; his legs twitched as he chased a rabbit in his dreams. He was a millisecond away from snarling at the pesky rabbit when a shrill noise jerked him out of his dream.

Teresa and Becky both blew their whistles in the schoolroom.

Apollo snorted, sat, scratched his head, and woke fully. When the whistles blasted again, he stood, shook himself awake, and trotted to the classroom to witness complete chaos. His pack of youngsters was in a pile, squabbling about something.

"What's going on here?" Apollo asked.

"Oh, Apollo!" Becky said. "They're not too good with differences of opinions."

Apollo delved into the pile of pups. He grabbed Star by the scruff and flung her out of the heap. He continued flinging his sons and daughters until the bottom of the pile—Wolf—was free to stand.

"There'd better be a good reason for this insubordination," he growled.

"They're a bunch of idiots," Wolf stated, his spine hair bristling. "All I did was tell them they could use the calendar in their communication menu. They didn't have to learn how to make a bunch of scratches."

Apollo looked to Teresa for help.

"Wolf, you have to understand something important," Teresa said. "There may be a time when your communication system is offline. Say, for instance, if the entire power grid went down during wartime or a hurricane. You would have to know how to do things without your communication system."

"But we could bounce things off the satellites," Wolf insisted.

"Sometimes during a war there would not be any communication systems at all," Becky said. She figured she'd better jump in. She could tell her smart grand-pup was getting aggravated. "Gliders wouldn't work. The food console would not work. Understand?"

"Son, it is important to learn how to do things the old-fashioned way, like your grandmothers are trying to teach you," Apollo said. "Over here in grandma T's house, you have not seen the preparations that Uncle Harold, Grandpa Bill, and the TMZ Committee are putting together because we are on the brink of war with the United States, which is all around us."

The puppies looked at each other, worried.

"Will we have to live in the wild?" Jim asked.

"What will we do if the food console doesn't work?" Esme asked.

Lulah's eyes opened wide with fear. "What's a war?"

Puppy Rex's tongue hung out as he contemplated everything.

Teresa held up her hand. "I've got this, Apollo." She made

eye contact with the puppies. "War is a terrible thing. When the leaders of different countries don't get along, and they declare war, they send armies to the country they consider an enemy. The army men and women are told what to do by generals. Many people die, and houses, cities, and buildings are destroyed. It's a very dangerous time for everyone."

Abby wandered into the room. She saw that everyone seemed stressed. "What's wrong?"

"Your mother was explaining war," Becky said.

"Can we help with the war, Daddy?" Star asked.

"War?" Abby asked. "Who are we going to war with?" She remembered watching video footage of wars when she was held captive in the lab. Wars were scary. She remembered seeing those big planes flying through the sky, dropping bombs, and everything exploding.

"The United States and the World Guild," Teresa said.

Abby plunked her butt on the floor and shivered in fear.

The puppies picked up on their mother's fear and started whining in dog-talk. Apollo was beside himself. He didn't know what to think.

"Let's all settle down," Teresa said. "Why don't we continue to learn about the calendar today? Remember our counting by fives? One paw, two paws, three paws, four paws? That'll help you with the calendar."

"Everyone back to their mats," Becky said.

JOEY MESSAGED MIMI. *I have discovered a warehouse district that would suit your purposes for both the cafeteria and the barracks.*

Send me your GPS location, and I'll come take a look, Mimi sent back. Her communication system dinged. She walked over to her glider and hopped onboard, and took off. In less than five minutes, she spotted the warehouse district ahead. As she got closer, she noticed that the warehouses were two stories, which would house a lot of bunks.

Mimi landed her glider on the ground close to where Joey stood waiting.

"These look pretty good. Have you been inside yet?" she asked the dog-bot.

"Yes. These buildings appear structurally sound. They contain old equipment and clutter, so they would have to be cleaned out. The central building would be good for the cafeteria," Joey said.

He led Mimi inside the building they were in front of.

"Better leave that door open so we have some light," Mimi said.

"Not to worry," Joey said. He activated his lights, which changed his red LED eyes to bright white light. A wide path lit up.

They wandered around equipment, tables, and all manner of refuse that had been moldering for decades.

"Look, there's an elevator," Mimi said. "That could be handy." They climbed the stairs to the second floor, where they discovered stacks of boxes and massive cobwebs. "I wonder why no one is using these buildings?"

"There are newer warehouses that are being utilized by the population," Joey said.

They explored several buildings, then returned to the glider.

"This is excellent for the war effort, Joey. Let's go back and tell the committee," Mimi said.

~

THE HEADQUARTERS MEETING room was empty. Mimi stopped at Lynette's desk and asked the admin where everyone was.

"You can find them outside the gates in the troops training areas," Lynette said.

Mimi and Joey left and got into the glider. Joey used his electronics to open the back gate, then they flew out to the large field where tents had been set up. The committee members, the generals, and the Cajuns were there. Mimi landed her glider, and she and Joey trudged across the grass.

She addressed the committee, but made eye contact with the other groups. "Joey found a warehouse complex that would be excellent for the cafeteria and barracks."

"Mess hall. We're not talking about a restaurant," General Thunderhorse huffed out.

She glared at him. "Potato patotto. Would anyone like to take a look before I call in volunteers to start clearing the old equipment and debris out of them?"

The majority of the group flew over to the warehouse complex. Before long, all the doors were open, and the group stomped through each warehouse.

Major Stonedanice was particularly interested in the equipment. "When your team begins to clear out the warehouses, have them put all the equipment in one area so we can see what's there. All those cartons should go in another area so we can see what was stored. Could be historical material there."

"Better store the cartons inside a building in case of rain," Edmee said.

Mimi pointed out which building could be used as the mess hall. Everyone agreed. They went back to their business, and Mimi and Joey flew back to the place she had set up as her volunteer headquarters. She gathered her chosen five people.

"Okay, I need you to assemble the volunteers so we can get these warehouses cleared out, then built out. We can utilize the second floor in the mess hall building for our operations offices," she said. She further explained where to store any cartons and where to offload all equipment.

The next day, close to a hundred people swarmed all over the warehouses. Electricians tackled the elevators, lighting, and all electrical sources. Cleaners wielded large poles wrapped with cloth to bat down cobwebs.

Two architects stood at a table outside, designing new troop barracks on their tablets.

Each room in the barracks would contain a twin bed, a desk, a chest of drawers, a bedside table, and a lamp. There would be a shared bathroom with an adjoining roommate's room, and a shared eating space that contained a basic food console, a cool chamber (formerly called a refrigerator, but a quarter of the size), and a small counter with two chairs.

Each warehouse contained 150,000 square feet. Once they had the barracks for the two floors of each building laid out (with lists of needed furniture, plumbing fittings, and all the rest), they would start on the mess hall. They handed off the list for barracks equipment and furnishings to a volunteer to give to Mimi.

The mess hall would deviate from food console food prep to actual cooks preparing large hot and cold bins of food in a cafeteria style that hadn't been seen or used by people in the West for at least forty years. The Cajuns provided visuals from their army base for the architects. Zephirin Boudreaux flew a small group back to Louisiana for closeup details.

Troops were trained.

Carpenters were put to work.

Dog-bots were created.

Gliders were manufactured.

TMZ citizens were schooled on what to do in case bombs were dropped.

Months of preparation went into the war effort. There were skirmishes along the borders of TMZ, and enemy gliders were spotted and dealt with inside the country's boundaries.

Barracks housed men and women. A six-weeks on and two weeks off rotation allowed people to serve their country and to keep their households back home thriving.

The new dog-bots were dispersed throughout the country. It was up to the new jurisdictions to name them. Rex silently bellowed orders to make sure all the new dogs followed his rules.

Cajun and TMZ military trainers were rough on the recruits. Every man and woman who signed up to protect their country was fully prepared in all aspects of hand-to-hand combat, weapons training, and glider military use. Once training was complete, the recruits practiced daily to hone their skills for the war that was heading their way.

Able-bodied Maxwell employees were required to sign up for war training and learn everything the recruits did. Bill realized just how out of shape he was, even though there wasn't an ounce of fat on his body. The extensive exercises the Cajuns dished out were hard on him and his people, but the training was necessary. No one realized just how unprepared they were until they started basic training.

BILL and his team sat at the conference table. Status reports were shared. Everything was on schedule. Angelica reported she was discovering suppliers in TMZ who could replace old WestUS suppliers.

"Has anyone else noticed how quiet it's been today?" Toby asked. "I haven't seen anything on GNN about this war."

Roland glanced at his communicator and did a double take. "Holy smokes! Turn the AMD on! Something's going down!"

Murray grabbed the remote and clicked. The enormous screen came alive with yelling, screaming crowds of angry people.

"Where is that?" Angelica asked.

"Looks like Tranquility Force headquarters," Bill said.

They watched as the crowd turned vigilante. People dragged enforcers out of the building, stripped them of their uniforms, and shoved them through the gate. Another news Literalist showed a similar scene at World Guild headquarters in Washington, DC.

"History repeating itself!" Wynne said.

A Literalist interviewed a well-dressed man. "We are taking back our country from these thieving bastards. They pushed Bill Maxwell to the point where he left the country. What does that tell you? Thank the Earth Bill is the one who developed the Dot. Now he can right some wrongs!"

"Who's that?" Murray asked.

"That, my friends, is the next leader of the World Guild. Josef G. Feduccian," Bill said. He immediately brought up Christovar's name on his communications device and connected with him. "Chris, did you put the bug in Josef's ear?" Bill listened. "I thought so. Good choice. Let me know if he needs anything."

Bill cleared the communication and nodded to his team. "Doesn't look like there will be a war."

They heard the elevator ding.

"Where's everyone?" Harold called out.

Toby stuck his head out the door. "Back here."

Harold and the committee marched back and entered the conference room.

"Did you hear the news?" Glacious asked.

Everyone talked at once as they gawked at the AMD screen.

Bill held his hand up. "We should not stop training the troops. I suggest everything stay the course. We need to be like the Cajuns. Always be prepared."

CHAPTER TWENTY-NINE

F or the next several days everyone was riveted to the AMD. Any politician who had a whiff of rotten behavior was dragged from their government office. Some were thrown into a cell to await a long overdue appointment with justice.

Several someone's apparently got together and thoroughly studied what happened on September 9, 2030 and took action. The new reform party gathered followers in every state and district in the USA, including the new islands that had fallen into the ocean off the West Coast. Then the rest of the world jumped on the same train.

Italian-American Josef G. Feduccian was declared the new world leader by an overwhelming vote. The people approved his agenda: Restore rights and freedoms that had been reduced to isolation and enslavement.

Bill had many conversations with Josef about the Dot. The new government party agreed with Bill's policy of preventing the government from punishing workers through their paychecks.

TMZ thought Louisiana would change its mind about seceding from the USA, but Governor Chaline was adamant that the citizens of Louisiana wanted to join the new country.

REX RECEIVED a ding on a subject he had actively been pursuing for several months. His quest to find mates for Abby-dog's and Apollo's pups was high on his list. After a long search that would have exhausted a human, he discovered two dogs in TMZ. He wasn't surprised that they didn't show up before he and Jonas Biggibottom scanned the entirety of TMZ. According to his map, the two dogs were in obscure, tiny towns.

A female pit bull was discovered in Anthony, New Mexico, and a male bull terrier mix lived in Vinton, Texas. Since only four miles separated the two places, Rex wondered if the dogs were related.

A male Malamute was discovered in a remote Alaskan North Slope village. A female Tibetan Terrier and a male Tibetan Mastiff were located in Tibet. A Chihuahua was found in Europe. But Rex dismissed the small dog due to the size difference between the breeds.

He was tracking down three dogs in New Zealand, two in China, and four in Russia. Rex thought about the language barriers but knew his daddy could tweak their Dots so that the foreign dogs could understand and speak English. He just hoped there were three compatible males and three compatible females.

Rex thought about where the paired dogs would live. He didn't know how Abby and Apollo would feel about their pups living in other countries. They would only see them via their communicators, or when Bill or Teresa used the AMD, and possibly once or twice a year in person.

Another ding announced more news. The New Zealand dogs were a female Huntaway, a male Labrador Retriever, and a female Cavalier King Charles Spaniel. The Russian dogs included a white male Samoyed, a Black Russian Terrier female, a male Caucasian Shepherd, and a male Karelian Bear Dog. The two Chinese dogs were both males, and Rex had never heard of them before: a Formosan Mountain Dog and a Chongquing dog.

He gathered the pictures and information about all fourteen dogs, but didn't send the information yet. The dog-bot thought it would be better to sit down with the entire family and present what he had found.

THAT NIGHT AFTER SUPPER, Bill and Teresa sat on the sofa watching the latest GNN broadcast. The dogs and puppies sprawled across the floor with Rex and Jerry nearby.

A GNN Literalist hovered in front of a camera. "Now a word from our new leader, Josef G. Feduccian."

Josef stood in front of the White House of the World Guild amid Literalists from across the world. "After many decades of being considered a rebel region, the World Guild has recognized Texmexzona as a sovereign country. There will no longer be restrictions on anyone passing through or visiting TMZ."

Literalists went wild with questions.

"Has TMZ opened its borders?"

"Can people move back to their old homes in the USA and other places?"

Josef held up a hand. "We are discussing these and many other things with TMZ."

Bill and Teresa shared surprised expressions.

"Did you know this was going on?" Teresa asked.

"No one mentioned this to me," Bill said. "But Glacious has been very busy lately."

"Looks like we should step up tourism," Teresa said. "Are there sufficient hotels in TMZ? You know, Bill, we really haven't explored this new country of ours."

Bill faced Teresa. He took hold of her hands. "Why don't we plan a second honeymoon?"

Teresa pulled her hands out of his, cupped his face, and kissed him gently. "That's a great idea."

Rex did his impression of clearing his throat. It didn't really sound right, but it got their attention.

"You have something to share?" Bill asked, with a hint of sarcasm.

"Mommy, Daddy, Abby-dog, Apollo... I have news to share," Rex said. "My network has discovered ten male dogs and five female dogs from around the world, two of those right here in TMZ."

Abby was on her feet in a second, and Teresa threw herself at Abby and grabbed her in a hug. She rocked her dog-daughter for a long moment, then released her.

"Oh, Rex... that's wonderful news!" Teresa said, as she slid back on the sofa.

Apollo, ever the fierce wolf, scrunched his brow. "Where are these dogs located? When will we meet them?"

"I have dismissed one of the males. A chihuahua is not the right size for a mate," Rex said.

The dog-bot noticed the confusion on both Abby's and Apollo's faces. He brought up a picture of a chihuahua on his communicator. The small dog hovered in the air, standing beside a beagle.

"The chihuahua is the smaller of the two dogs shown here for reference," Rex explained.

"That tiny dog could not protect any of my daughters, or their litter," Apollo said. "You were right in casting it away."

"Thirteen dogs are in other parts of the world," Rex explained. "I don't know how you would feel if your pups were scattered—you would not have a chance to be with them and see their litters grow up."

Abby and Apollo engaged in a private discussion via silent dog talk. They creased their brows. After a lengthy debate, they faced Rex, Bill and Teresa.

"We don't want our pups to live far, far away," Apollo said. "It is important for us as potential grandparents to help our children's children understand the pack. I have a responsibility to my wolf heritage to train the mates of my pups so they can pass along what they learn to their litters."

Abby shoulder-butted her mate gently. "Plus, we don't know if these mates are educated or illiterate. Not everyone teaches their dog children. I remember what you told me about my grandfather, Jimbo. Grandma Becky didn't know how to teach him."

"It seems to me that your mother and I should have conversations with the human parents of these dogs," Bill said. "But you do realize when your pups have pups, there may not be mates for them other than the dogs you currently don't choose."

Teresa nodded to Abby. "If you and Apollo have more pups, they won't have mates."

"If Rex found these dogs, maybe there are others hidden somewhere," Apollo said.

"Let's just focus on these six puppies, shall we?" Bill said. "There's no point in getting all worked up about future litters. We'll set up a time to contact everyone and see about getting the dogs here for a meet and greet."

"Daddy, you'd better make sure all these dogs have a Dot," Abby said.

"That's a good point," Bill said. "If they don't have a Dot, I'll have to arrange for someone to install one. It took Apollo a while to get acclimated, so we wouldn't want to bring someone here too soon."

"Apollo and I could talk to them in dog talk, but that is very limited," Abby said.

Apollo shook himself. "I never realized how limiting dog talk was until I received my Dot. It would be better to have fully functioning Dots in these dogs with them understanding the ways of man and our language so we can communicate."

"When we contact them, I will find out what language they speak, and if they don't speak English, I can walk them through the translator in their Dots," Bill said.

"Rex, would you send me the list of dogs so I can set up a spreadsheet?" Teresa asked.

"I have shared the list with all of you," Rex said.

AFTER BREAKFAST TERESA created a series of tables in her word processing program for each of the possible guest dogs and their humans. She had a list of questions, and she knew Rex and Bill would be investigating everyone before they set foot in TMZ, or even the USA.

It was important to know the environment these dogs and people lived in. They certainly didn't want any undesirables. Bad humans affected the dogs they raised, and neither Teresa, Bill, Abby, nor Apollo would tolerate cruelty, lowlifes, criminals, or the extremely ignorant. Poor people were not considered undesirable. Their station in life didn't matter as long as they were loving, respectable people who had enough to take care of their families.

∽

BILL AND TERESA sat on the sofa with Abby and Apollo in front of them, and all the puppies lined up in front of their dog parents. Rex and Jerry sat beside the sofa, ready to take any action that was required for the interviews.

Teresa held up a clipboard with a chart of all the dogs and their families to be interviewed

Calling Chart using Palm Spring, CA as TMZ time

	M/F	Breed	Location	Name	Humans	Time
1	F	Pit Bull	Anthony, NM	Chessie	Gonzalez	MDT
2	M	Bull terrier mix	Vinton, TX	Georgie	Jackson	MDT
3	M	Malamute	Alaska/N Slope	Sakari (Sweet)	Meyok	1 hr behind
4	F	Tibetan Terrier	Tibet	Dawa (born Monday)	Chime & Chodak	CA: Tues 7PM Tibet: Wed 10AM
5	M	Tibetan Mastiff	Tibet	Dorjee (Thunderbolt)	Lobsang & Mipam	CA: Tues 7PM Tibet: Wed 10AM
6	M	Chihuahua	Europe	Rolf	Martin	
7	F	Huntaway	New Zealand	Bella	Stewart	
8	M	Labrador Retriever	New Zealand	Charlie	King	CA: Tues 7PM NZ: Wed 2PM
9	F	Cavalier King Charles Spaniel	New Zealand	Poppy	Williams	
10	M	Samoyed	Russia	Boris	Semenov	
11	F	Black Russian Terrier	Russia	Alina	Kuznetsov	CA: Tues 11PM Russia: Wed 9AM
12	M	Caucasian Shepherd	Russia	Alexei	Popov	
13	M	Karelian Bear Dog	Russia	Dimitri	Lebedev	
14	M	Formosan Mountain Dog	China	Gan (brave)	Wang	CA: Tues 6PM China: Wed 9AM
15	M	Chongquing dog	China	Junjie (handsome)	Huang	

Everyone decided to begin the interviews with the local people from Texas and New Mexico, then they would continue down the list as time zones and times were appropriate. Teresa scolded Bill about calling someone in what would be the middle of the night for their part of the world.

The Gonzalez family sat on a battered sofa with Chessie on the floor leaning into their knees. Their AMD system had too much static, so Bill made adjustments on his end. New Mexico was one hour ahead of TMZ, so there weren't any problems scheduling a call.

"Hello Mr. and Mrs. Gonzalez," Teresa said. "Hello Chessie. How are you doing today?"

"Hello Mr. and Mrs. Maxwell," Mrs. Gonzalez said. "Chessie is a little shy until she gets to know you."

Abby took matters into her own paws. "Hi Chessie. I'm Abby, and this is my mate, Apollo, and our six pups." Abby nudged Esme, who was sitting in front of her. "Everyone say hello to Chessie."

There was a chorus of hellos. Chessie sat up and looked directly at the AMD. "Hello. It's very nice to meet all of you."

"Do you know Georgie Jackson in Vinton, Texas?" Abby asked.

"Yes! Georgie's my cousin. We're the only ones who survived in our canine families," Chessie said, somewhat sadly. She studied Apollo. "Are you a wolf?"

"Yes. As far as we know, I'm the last of my kind," Apollo said.

"I bet there are other wolves around the world," Chessie said. "Especially in cold or mountainous environments where there are caves. From what I've seen and read through the AMD, some remote places did not have the die-off like the more populated areas."

Teresa's finger tapped Bill's arm. She determined that Chessie was educated and would make a good choice for one of the boys. The friendly conversation continued between the Gonzalez's and the Maxwells for thirty minutes, with a promise from Teresa to get back in touch with them.

The next call was made to the Jacksons in Texas. That part of Texas was one hour ahead of TMZ. They discovered that Georgie didn't have a shy bone in his body. He was an assertive and confident bull terrier mix. Apollo liked him immediately.

He would be good for Esme, Apollo sent to Abby.

We can't make choices for them, but we can make suggestions for them to think about, Abby responded.

Apollo licked his mate on her cheek.

After they finished their call with the Jacksons in Texas, Teresa studied her chart.

"We can call China now. It will be nine tomorrow morning for them," Teresa said.

"How come its tomorrow there?" Jim asked.

"Because they are way on the other side of the planet," Bill explained.

"But how can it be tomorrow? We are on today," Puppy Rex said.

"The world is divided into time zones," big Rex said.

Teresa could see Rex was going to go down a road that brought more confusion to the puppies.

Bill held up a hand. "We can discuss this later. Right now, we need to make two calls to China."

Both the Wangs and the Huangs seemed like very nice people. Both families found someone locally who helped them set up the translation app in their Dots.

Gan, the Formosan Mountain Dog, was mostly used as a guard dog. They were known to be protective and territorial. Apollo liked those traits, but Abby nixed that idea, telling her mate that Gan might not be a good choice for a family structure.

The Chongquing dog was a little better, but still not the family type everyone was looking for. Apollo muttered to himself about the Chinese dogs, but he did not win the tick marks for being chosen.

The next evening they contacted the New Zealand dog families. It was seven PM in TMZ and the next day in New Zealand at two in the afternoon. Bill connected with the Stewarts, Bella's family. Everyone liked the Huntaway dog. She was gregarious and looked like a very strong breed.

Charlie, a Labrador Retriever, was a happy-go-lucky boy. The Kings mentioned that Charlie was fond of word games and liked to look up the definitions. Abby, Teresa, Bill, and Rex noted that intelligence. Apollo huffed out exasperation when he realized he should be doing that as well.

The last call was to Poppy's family. The Cavalier King Charles Spaniel was the apple of the Williams family's eye. Poppy was a beautiful, long-haired dog with nice manners. She received a check mark beside her name on the chart.

Bill ended the communication calls. "We have to stay up late tonight to call Russia."

"Why don't we plan on one late call a night?" Teresa suggested. "That way, we can have all the calls finished this week."

"Okay. Tomorrow we can call Alaska after supper, then stay up late to call one of the Russians," Bill said. "We'll call the Tibetan families the following two nights, then the Russians, and end the last night with a late call to the last Russian family."

"Good. We have a plan," Abby said.

CHAPTER THIRTY

S akari the Malamute was a handsome boy. His humans, the Meyoks, were rather shy people, but the conversation was stimulating with their tales of life on Alaska's North Slope.

The call to the Semenovs was an eye opener. Mr. Semenov got right to the point, asking how much Bill would pay for Boris, their Samoyed. The beautiful dog sat hunched over, not making eye contact with the screen. His fear of being reprimanded, or worse, was palpable. Bill terminated the call.

He and Teresa were aghast, but it was Apollo voicing his opinion that started a conversation.

"Those people have hurt that dog!" Apollo said, anger radiating in his voice. "We should rescue him whether he is going to be a mate or not!"

"We could have Boris here in TMZ by this time tomorrow if we act now," Rex chimed in. "Jerry can go along to deal with any unpleasantries."

Teresa glanced from one to the other, following the conversation. "Should we pay them? We don't want to be accused of kidnapping."

"I have a feeling we could prove both physical and psychological abuse," Bill said. "No, I will not pay the Semenovs a dime." He turned to Rex and Jerry. "Have Jonas fly you there, Jerry. You'll have to fly partway so Jonas can get some rest. It's a long flight round trip."

The dog-bots left the house, the puppies were dismissed to their beds, and the adults stayed in the living room a little longer.

"Is that the way of life in Russia?" Abby asked, a little shook up from the vicious personality they encountered.

"I don't believe all Russians are like that," Bill said. "They do live a harsh life in certain parts of that country, but as humans go, remember that there are good and bad in every species, humans at the top of that list. Look at what Christovar had to do to just get through a week before he moved to the USA."

"We will take care of Boris and restore his confidence," Teresa said. "Remember, I once had a thriving business as a dog psychological service provider. I have the tools to help him, and all of you will be instrumental in his recovery through your friendship."

"Let's go to bed," Bill said. "Jerry and Jonas will bring Boris home here to TMZ, and we'll take it from there."

JONAS CHOSE AN UPGRADED glider to cut the trip across the world in half. As soon as they crossed into Russian airspace six hours later, they were swarmed by Russian Confederation Army gliders that tried to force them to land.

Jerry took control of the matter with a warning. When the

Russians would not stand down, the dog-bot opened his door and flew out of the glider. He positioned himself in front of Jonas' glider.

"You will stand down before I am forced to take defensive action," Jerry broadcast in Russian.

Jonas and Jerry both heard the conversations among the six Russian gliders as they discussed options. Some of the Russians recognized the dog-bot for what it was and knew it was a weapon. In the end, they withdrew.

The Russian gliders took off and disappeared into the snowy distance. Jerry took his place inside the glider with Jonas, and they arrived at the Semenov's house a half hour later.

"I will use force to secure Boris, if necessary," Jerry stated.

Jonas nodded, grim-faced. "Let me activate my translator."

They exited the glider and trudged to the front door of the house through the pathway, which was covered with at least ten inches of snow. Jonas glanced at Jerry. "Ready?"

"Ready," the dog-bot said.

Jonas rapped on the worn door that was almost devoid of the original blue paint.

The door was yanked open by a barrel-chested, bearded man in warm clothing and scraggly hair that hadn't seen shears in a while. "What do you want?" The man stared at Jerry. "You are one of those dog robots?"

A woman wrapped in a tattered shawl huddled with Boris, the white Samoyed dog, several feet back. A look of terror masked the woman's face.

"I am Jerry, and this is Jonas. We are here for Boris," Jerry said.

Mr. Semenov laughed a full belly roar. He snapped his fingers. Four hefty, rough-looking men appeared from the inner room. "You think you can get through my men?"

"Step outside then," Jonas said.

Semenov and his thugs lumbered through the door. Mrs. Semenov and Boris quivered in the corner.

In under a minute, all the thugs were on the ground, out cold, thanks to Jerry's ability to stun without killing.

Jonas and Jerry hurried into the house.

"We will have to take Mrs. Semenov with us, or she will pay a heavy price for Boris' escape," Jonas said.

They approached the traumatized dog and the woman.

"Mrs. Semenov, we will take you to America where you can have a good life,'" Jonas said.

The woman wailed. "He will kill me!"

"No, you will be protected," Jerry said.

"Hurry. Gather what you want to take with you," Jonas said.

The woman snapped out of her terror, understanding her gift of liberty. She spoke softly to Boris, slipped into her raggedy coat, pulled on heavy boots, grabbed her purse and looked around the room. She snatched up a framed photo from a side table, then faced Jonas and Jerry.

"We are ready," Boris said, using his translator.

They all hurried to the glider. Jonas didn't waste any time putting distance between the knocked-out thugs and Boris and Mrs. Semenov's freedom.

"Report in to Bill," Jonas told Jerry.

"I have alerted Rex," Jerry said.

LESS THAN SIX HOURS LATER, Jonas landed the glider in front of Bill and Teresa's house. "Mrs. Semenov, you should remove your coat. It's 97 degrees... ah 36.111 Celsius outside.

Boris and his mother whispered quietly. "I have turned my mother's translator on."

"Oh, it is so hot!" Mrs. Semenov said, as she slipped out of her coat.

The front door opened and the entire Maxwell household poured outside, along with Harold and Glacious. The adults lined up, including Abby and Apollo.

The pups clumped together on the sidewalk, each vying for a good spot to see and be seen by the guests.

The glider doors opened. Jonas stepped out, then helped Mrs. Semenov out with Boris following. Jerry slipped out the other side of the glider.

Bill and Teresa stepped forward.

"Welcome to our home, Mrs. Semenov, Boris," Teresa said, her hand held out as she approached the woman.

"Irina," Mrs. Semenov said. "This is Boris. We are very happy to be here."

Boris romped over to the pups and started a bark-fest. He was surrounded by puppies happy to greet him.

"I'm Jim."

"My name's Star."

"Do you speak English?" Lulah asked.

"Of course he does," Wolf said. "He has a translator in his Dot."

"Do you want to play?" Little Rex asked.

"Are you hungry?" Esme asked.

"Don't devour our company," Apollo boomed out.

Abby stepped forward. "Everyone go into the street. You're very noisy, and our families can't hear over this racket!"

The puppies, Jerry and Boris, didn't need to be told twice. They charged into the street with Lulah in the lead.

Glacious stepped forward. "Mrs. Semenov, we are happy to

grant you immunity to live here. We understand your situation in Russia."

Irina became teary. "It was not good. My husband treat Boris bad. Treat me bad."

"You don't have to worry about him anymore," Harold said. "We will protect you."

Teresa reached out and put her arm around Irina's shoulders. "Come into the house. You are not used to this heat." She turned to Abby. "Boris isn't used to this heat either, so bring him inside in a few minutes."

After the humans went into the house, Apollo nudged Abby. "It isn't hot where Boris lives?"

"No, Russia is cold. Go into your communicator and look up on the TMZ GNN. You'll see information and pictures," Abby told her mate.

Apollo became quiet as he muddled through all the mental clicking. He turned his head this way and that as he explored Russia through his Dot. "That's a lot of snow! We should have Boris go into the house now. He could get overheated."

Abby barked to get everyone's attention. "Into the house. We'll ask Grandma T if you can have a snack."

All they needed to hear was *snack*. The puppies raced to the door. Wolf manned the keypad with the thick dowel, and the door popped open. Seven rambunctious young dogs galloped into the house, followed by Abby, Apollo, and Jerry.

Abby trotted up to Teresa. "Mommy, I promised I would ask you for a snack."

"That's okay, honey." Teresa went into the kitchen and took over the food console. She chose seven mid-sized snacks for the pups and Boris, then two large-sized snacks for Apollo and Abby.

Everyone lined up with Boris catching on. Teresa handed

out the treats. When everyone was through eating, she saw that her grand-pups were getting ready to charge through the house.

"Boris isn't used to this weather. It's very cold where he comes from. Go to your room and talk quietly," Teresa instructed. She thought she would get some snide remarks from the peanut gallery, but they surprised her as they filed out of the kitchen and down the hallway to their bedroom.

Teresa, Abby, and Apollo returned to the living room where Jerry had already settled. The dogs sat quietly, taking in the emotions of the room. Teresa sat by Bill on the loveseat.

Irina dabbed her eyes with a wilted tissue as she sat on the very edge of the wingback chair as if she were going to spring up and out of the chair and make a run for it.

"You don't know him... he will find us," Irina wailed between sobs and sniffles.

Bill got up and squatted in front of the distressed woman. He took hold of and patted her hand. "Did you see how the dog-bot knocked out your husband and his thugs? We have an army, and dozens of dog-bots. Believe me when I tell you that the entire Russian army could come, but they would be defeated. You and Boris are safe here."

Irina blew her nose, nodded and presented a tiny smile. "Okay."

Teresa stood. "Let me show you to a guest room so you can rest." She held out her hand, and Irina stood. She grasped Teresa's hand as if it were a lifeline to safety. They walked out of the room.

"That poor woman," Glacious said, with a shake of his head.

"You should have seen her huddled in the corner when her husband answered the door," Jonas said. "She and Boris were terrified."

"Teresa will be able to help Boris adjust, but we should offer Irina counseling at an appropriate time," Harold said.

The kitchen door opened, and Becky and Percy came in. "Anybody home?" They walked through to the living room.

"Oh, are we interrupting a private meeting?" Percy asked.

"No, come in!" Bill said.

They brought the visitors up to date on the Russians.

Teresa returned to the living room. "That poor woman is shaking with fear."

Becky nodded. She knew all about terror from when she and Percy were arrested and Truffed. "Maybe she and Boris would consider staying with us. I could teach her about living in TMZ, and our super-modern conveniences."

"That's a good idea," Teresa said. "She's going to need clothes. All she has is her purse, coat, boots, and the clothes on her back."

Becky nodded. "I'll take her to one of the distribution centers."

"It will be nice to have a dog in the house again," Percy said. Losing Jimbo, his dog-son, had hit him hard. Abby's munchkins were a lively bunch. There was never a dull moment, especially since they started talking.

"Next week my virtual food console classes will debut," Becky said. "I hope people will sign up. Irina can attend. She'll be able to create some of her native foods, while I introduce her to some American dishes she would most likely enjoy."

"Did she have a food console?" Teresa asked.

"No," Jerry said. "The kitchen was more convenient than what Starlight has in her cabin, but it was outdated pre-2000s." He projected his picture of the entire visible part of the Russian house.

Threadbare overstuffed furniture with handmade throws across the backs, tattered braided rugs on the floor, and a wooden rocker made up the living room. A couple of old end tables with dated lamps completed the room. The kitchen contained a table that looked to be made from old planks of wood nailed together, and four wooden chairs that didn't look very sturdy. The kitchen itself looked as if it were from pioneer days. A pump-type water fixture adorned the sink. What looked like a gas stove with a pair of pliers lying on the scarred counter to turn the missing knobs, and an old, short refrigerator were the only appliances.

Teresa and Becky weren't the only ones gawking at the projection.

"No wonder she looked amazed when I showed her to the bathroom," Teresa said. "Do you think they had one in that house?"

"They'd have to," Bill said. He started to say more, but shut up when he realized he didn't know what would have been in the rest of the living quarters. "I'll ask Christovar when we talk next."

"How can we be so comfortable, and they seem to be destitute?" Harold asked, somewhat dazed.

"We live privileged lives compared to many parts of the world," Glacious said. "We should strive to bring changes to places like where Irina comes from. It seems that the global government has only provided for large cities, expecting everyone to relocate from remote areas."

CHAPTER THIRTY-ONE

The remaining calls to the other dog-children families were made. Bill and Teresa discovered that the other Russians were city-dwellers and quite lovely people. It had been unfortunate that their first experience was with the likes of Mr. Semenov.

"Why don't we plan to bring everyone together within the next couple of weeks? We can check their schedules and coordinate for when everyone is here at the same time," Teresa asked. "I can book rooms in the TMZ Excelsior hotel, and we can plan some events so everyone can get to know each other."

"Good idea. Those dogs that aren't matched up to Abby and Apollo's brood may find their own matches," Bill said.

"Do you think we should invite the chihuahua? I feel bad to exclude the Martins from this gathering," Teresa said.

Bill hemmed and hawed and finally gave in. "You're right. Let's invite them, and the Chinese dogs."

"I don't think they would be good family dogs," she argued.

"Look, let's not be judgmental. Invite all of them, and we'll see how things sort out," Bill said.

Teresa made all the arrangements for the hotel, a meeting place, and even set up tours of TMZ two and a half weeks later.

Becky had her hands full with Irina. Boris was comfortable in his new environment, but Irina considered Becky and Percy's house opulent and was afraid of breaking anything she touched.

Becky dragged two barstools over to the food console. She patted the stool beside hers and coaxed Irina to sit. She pushed a pad of paper and a pen over to Irina.

"Write down the steps so you can create your Russian foods," Becky said. "First, press T to translate, and click on your language." She nudged Irina and nodded to the paper and pen.

The Russian picked up the pen and wrote the instructions.

"Press R for recipe. This is where you can create and store a recipe so you can make it anytime you want that food," Becky explained. "M is for measures, Irina. You can choose the way you measure ingredients. Make enough of something for just yourself, or for several people."

Becky noticed that the Russian woman understood. Every time her face lit up, she understood the process.

"When you make something, the machine delivers it through this door. When you taste it and determine it needs something else, place the dish in the area where it came from and pull down the door. Then press A to adjust. The recipe will appear here on the screen. Use the arrows to scroll up or down to the ingredient you need to adjust. When you're finished, press S to save the changes. Pull the dish out of the door and see if it's what you wanted."

"Oh, this very good," Irina said. "I make beef stroganoff for supper tonight! You and Mr. Percy..." she thought about the words. "Love eat it!"

❧

THEY INVITED Bill and Teresa for dinner. Becky prayed to the Earth that Irina could create a delicious meal.

"I make spicy Russian tea, yeah?" Irina asked as everyone sat at the Smythes kitchen table. She passed around teacups of the hot beverage, then served the stroganoff.

"Smells wonderful," Percy said.

After Irina joined them at the table, everyone sampled the stroganoff. Becky's eyes widened.

"Oh, Irina! This is delicious!" Becky said between bites.

Bill slurped a mouthful of tea. "Oh, this tea is so different from what we are used to. You're going to have to teach Teresa how to make this."

Teresa raised her eyebrows, set her fork aside and sipped the tea. "Cinnamon and cloves." She looked across the table at Becky.

"I think lemon juice and maybe something else," Becky said as she sipped.

"Lemon and orange juice," Irina said with a big smile.

"Looks like the food console cheered you up," Teresa said.

"No food console in Siberia," Irina said sadly. "Only very old stove. I like food console!"

"This stroganoff is very good," Percy said. "I bet a lot of people would like this recipe."

"I can share this with the people who take my class," Becky said.

When they finished the meal, they turned the conversation to the dogs and all the arrangements Teresa had made for the upcoming visitors.

"First, I'd like all the dogs to get to know each other. Abby and Apollo said they would try not to influence their puppies, but I can see Apollo making some decisions," Teresa said. "After everyone gets settled into the hotel and rests up after their travel, we will have a getting-to-know-you event in one of the big meeting rooms.

"Abby suggested we have a meal. She wants to see if any of the dogs are overly aggressive about their eating habits."

"Will that be in the meeting room?" Becky asked.

"Yes. I've arranged for a dozen food consoles, dog food and water bowls, and people plates," Teresa said.

"I suggested we have Rex and Jerry on hand," Bill said. "Apollo didn't think that would be necessary, but if any fights break out, especially with some of the more aggressive dogs who are bigger and bulkier than the puppies, I worry about Apollo's wolf instincts kicking in."

"Even though he's a big wolf..." Percy started.

"This is why Rex and Jerry will be on hand. No one will get hurt," Teresa said.

TUESDAY AFTERNOON AT 2:00, the meeting room was filled with barking dogs. Abby and Apollo walked among the dogs, supervising in both dog-talk and verbal human language. The wolf kept a critical eye on the visiting dogs as he and his mate watched out for their pups. As typical, Jerry romped around with some of the new dogs, while Rex, stoic down to his circuits, stayed on the sidelines with his people.

At the last minute, Teresa added to the number of food consoles so no one had to wait. She didn't want anyone to be irritated by being last in a long line. Bill showed everyone how to turn their translators to identify languages so that everyone could easily communicate.

Irina perked up when she was introduced to the other Russians. The human parents mingled, getting to know each other, all the while looking for a good match for their dog-child.

Either the parents had warned their dog-children to share food and drinks with strangers in the room, or all the dogs felt comfortable in the crowd and wanted to fit in. None of them had ever met any other dogs before, not even the New Zealanders or the Russians, but that was understandable considering the vast territories of those countries.

Abby changed her mind about the Chinese dogs. While their breed was considered guard dogs—protective and territorial—both Gan and Junjie romped with the other dogs and got along with everyone. Apollo liked both dogs for his girls. They would always be protected. The tricky part was to find out if any of his daughters were interested in them.

All the humans and canines were rounded up and ushered out of the meeting room. Bill and Teresa led the group outside where several large gliders waited to take them on a sightseeing expedition.

The adults wanted to see Maxwell Industries, where their Dots came from and where the dog-bots had been created. Everyone loved playful Jerry. Teresa wondered how that was affecting Rex. While he didn't show any outward signs of being jealous or having his feelings hurt, she was sure there was something just under the surface.

Bill had arranged the standard tour with Mayvena at TMZ headquarters. The woman who guided everyone through the storyboards on the ground floor here and back at the WestUS headquarters related the story about all the marvelous inventions Bill had created to make their lives easier.

As the group piled into Maxwell Industries, the majority of the young dogs hunkered down in fear when they saw the Communicator whirling around on her permanent post on the other side of the counter. Her tentacle-like arms swayed, and her colors changed according to how she was directing calls and inquiries.

Gan let out a ferocious growl in her direction, but walked with the crowd, looking over his shoulder at what he most likely thought was an abomination.

Abby spoke up for all the dogs. "That's the Communicator. She's a machine and can't leave where she sits because she doesn't have a body. Do you want to see what she really looks like?"

There was nervous twitching among the group, but everyone decided to return to the front with Abby to see the monstrosity. Abby led them around the side of the console where they all crowded and saw that the Communicator was mounted on the base of a rolling chair.

"See, she's not human. She's a machine and can't do anything other than what the engineers programmed her to do," Abby said.

A lot of sniffs, snorts, and eventually tails wagged when they returned to the group of humans where Mayvena patiently waited to start the tour.

Abby shivered as she whispered to Apollo about how she was scared of the Communicator when she was a little pup, especially when she was brought to the secret lab where Dr. Roberts had her held in captivity. She would never forget Captain Day setting her cage on the countertop right in front of the monster.

Apollo licked her face to help release the awful memory. They joined the group and went through the tour, which was new to them.

Becky and Percy joined Bill and Teresa on the sidelines.

"I hope Jim and Chessie end up together," Percy said. "She's a smart little girl, and I would hope that Jimbo's gene pool could be diluted a bit."

"Don't forget how that gene pool helped Abby escape from the lab. If it hadn't been for Jimbo's fence-climbing skills that

Abby had watched over and over in her Dot, she would not have made it over that fence," Bill said.

Percy squirmed on hearing that. "You're right. I just hope little Jim has more common sense than his canine grandfather did."

"I'll never forget how excited Jimbo was when he learned how to color," Becky said wistfully. "He experienced a lot of firsts when he visited at your house in WestUS."

Teresa had a moment. "I still miss Lilith and the puppies." Her eyes became watery, but she snapped out of her nostalgic pain and blinked back the tears. Bill slid his arm across her shoulders and pulled her into a hug.

THE NEXT SEVERAL days were a whirlwind of activities for the dogs and the visitors. On the second day, Bill and Teresa noticed the pups spending more time with particular visiting pups. A few days later, the dynamics changed a bit with different dogs partnering up.

By the end of day six, it was apparent that choices had been made all around. Percy got his wish. Jim and Chessie paired up. Wolf chose Dawa, the Tibetan Terrier. Star and Charlie, the New Zealand lab, were an item. Esme didn't leave Boris' side. Rex and Alina were a nice-looking pair. Lulah stuck to Gan's side and warned off all other females.

Bella, the New Zealand Huntaway, and Sakari, the Alaskan Malamute, paired off. Poppy, the Cavalier King Charles spaniel from New Zealand, and Georgie, the bull terrier mix from Texas, romped together.

That left four males, and Rolf, the tiny chihuahua without mates.

Bill did his best to convince the parents of the unmated

dogs that they were still searching the world, and there were most likely more dogs in hiding. He and Teresa felt bad for the families that felt left out, but there was nothing they could do. Choices had been made.

Now, however, was the time to begin discussions in regard to where everyone would live. While Chessie lived in Anthony, New Mexico, it was 561 miles from TMZ headquarters, where the Maxwell dogs lived. Apollo would not budge an inch. He didn't want his children to live far away while they were growing up. He wanted to teach his kids and their mates how to fend for themselves and to be more wolf-like than domesticated dogs tied to air conditioning and a food console.

The humans jumped at the chance to relocate. Meetings with the TMZ committee about arranging moving permits, visas, passports, and every possible problem that could crop up for people pulling up roots and moving across the planet.

Irina and Boris were already in TMZ, but Glacious and Harold brought up the consequences of them being there illegally. They would backtrack and get the paperwork to the World Guild, then to the Russian Confederation.

Gan's family, the Wangs, had an herbal business that they would reestablish in TMZ. They had relatives who would continue to run the business in China. Everyone else were workers in various industries and would find work when they settled in America in TMZ.

The Maxwells and Smythes would be on the lookout for six houses close by to help with the transitions. Once everyone was established and used to their new environment, they could then plan trips back to their origins with Abby and Apollo's pups to see where their mates had come from.

The wolf made it clear that he would accompany the families each time so he could see where and how they had lived.

He didn't quite trust that his pups would return to the USA without his presence.

"Apollo, don't worry. We would assign a dog-bot to accompany you on these trips," Bill said. "I understand your concern, but we have to trust that these people—our new family members—would not try to pull something so sinister."

The wolf shook himself. "I guess you're right, but as a wolf, I'm instinctively suspicious and untrusting."

Abby licked his face. "Everything will be okay."

CHAPTER THIRTY-TWO

"Bill, I don't feel so good," Teresa said shortly after she woke.

"What's wrong?" he asked. "Head, stomach, back...?"

"I think I ate too much yesterday, or I had something that didn't agree with me," she said.

"Want me to make you some tea and toast?"

"That sounds good. I'm going to take a shower," she said.

Bill got up, grabbed his robe and slipped his feet into his house shoes, then left the bedroom.

Teresa made it to the bathroom, turned the water on in the shower and stepped under the water. She felt instantly revived. She finished her morning ritual, dressed, and grabbed the doorknob. Suddenly, she rushed over to the toilet and spewed her guts. She dropped to her knees and rested her head in her hands, trying to determine if that was it.

She finally made it to her feet and left the room to join Bill in the kitchen.

He took one look at her and rushed to her side. "You don't look so good. Do you want to go back to bed?"

Teresa shook her head. "No, tea and toast sound good." She sat at the table, and Bill served breakfast.

The rest of the day was a repeat of the morning.

"I wonder if one of the visitors brought a bug from their country?" Bill said, thinking out loud.

"Has anyone else mentioned being sick?" Teresa asked.

"I haven't asked, basically because I just thought about that as a possibility," Bill said.

Teresa was sick for the next three days.

"We'd better go see the VHO," Bill said. "I don't dare go to the office if I might be a carrier. Sure don't want to spread this around."

"I don't think you have to worry about that since you aren't sick," Teresa said. "I'll go get changed and we can go to the VHO."

Ten minutes later, they stood in front of the Virtual Healing Office. Teresa stepped into the shell of a human.

"Welcome, Teresa Maxwell," the virtual doctor said. "Please state the reason for this visit."

"I'm experiencing nausea and vomiting," she said.

The VHO scanned her. Lights of multiple colors went through two rounds, then the machine quieted and the lights dimmed to off.

"The diagnostics are complete," the virtual doctor said. "Congratulations, new mother-to-be. You are in your first trimester of your pregnancy. The sickness you are experiencing should dissipate within thirty to sixty days. Be sure to take prenatal vitamins."

"I'M PREGNANT?" Teresa shrieked as she practically leaped out of the machine into Bill's waiting arms.

"Oh, Teresa," Bill said, choked up as his arms surrounded her. He buried his face in the crook of her neck.

"Please scan your Dot at the credit panel," the VHO announced.

The credit panel read the Dot on Bill's wrist. A green LED appeared on the screen. "Credit accepted. You owe zero balance. Thank you for your business."

The End

ABOUT THE AUTHOR

D.E. Greenfield, aka Dawn Greenfield Ireland, is a powerhouse storyteller and the award-winning author of 22 novels across five distinct genres, alongside 7 acclaimed nonfiction books. A prolific creator of worlds, Dawn frequently adapts her own high-concept screenplays into books and develops her novels into structured TV series formats.

On the film side, Dawn is an alum of the UCLA Professional Program in Screenwriting and ScreenwritingU. Her scripts have been optioned twice, and she has worked as a screenwriter-for-hire. Known for her relentless work ethic and zero tolerance for writer's block, Dawn's background as an award-winning technical writer makes her a meticulous, detail-oriented professional—the self-described "organizational queen of the known universe" who never misses a deadline. Through her company, Artistic Origins (est.1995), she also works as a high-level writing coach, editor, and independent publisher.

How about leaving a review? Reviews help authors so much.

Sign up for the newsletter and get the inside scoop ahead of everyone else: http://degreenfield.com